MW01094644

F

2022

THE SECOND WIFE

MIRANDA RIJKS

INKUBATOR
BOOKS

Published by Inkubator Books
www.inkubatorbooks.com

ISBN (eBook): 978-1-915275-54-7
ISBN (Paperback): 978-1-915275-55-4
ISBN (Hardback): 978-1-915275-56-1

PROLOGUE

I know what it's like to feel ill. Very ill. How your body becomes separate from your mind, overcome with terrifying sensations that, however hard you try, you can't control. How your limbs become uncoordinated, like useless appendages on a rag doll, and your head feels so stuffed full of cotton wool, all your senses are muffled, and the only thing you can hear is the irregular beating of your heart trying so very desperately to keep you alive.

I know what it feels like because I felt it then, and I'm feeling it again now.

'Who's there?' I think I'm shouting, but my voice sounds distant, as if it's been muffled and distorted. The footsteps fade ... or are they footsteps? Perhaps the sound is in my head, the regular beat, getting fainter and fainter. I need to get up; I fumble with the light switch, trying to flick it on. Why aren't my fingers working properly? I wonder if this is it, the blood leaving my fingers and toes, making them utterly useless.

I hear it again. A thump. And this time, I'm sure I'm not imagining it. The noise is definitely outside my body.

Someone is there. But they've all gone out. This place should be empty. I begin to panic, but then my fingers find the light switch. I blink a few times, and I can see. Relief pours through me. I'm lying on top of the bed, which is surprising because I'm not even cold. In fact, I'm too hot, perspiration running down my face. I need to get up, get out of here, before they do anything else to me. I sit up, and the room spins, so I take it very slowly, gripping the side of my bed as I lever myself to my feet. This dreadful feeling of impending doom is gripping me from the inside out. It's as if my body is expecting something terrible to happen, but my brain isn't keeping up, can't decipher what's happening.

I remember that feeling. I had it all those years ago, and I think perhaps it has left an imprint on my DNA, so that fear is compounded by guilt and guilt is compounded by fear. I know I can never make it truly better, but I'm doing the best I can. Is that good enough? Perhaps this is my penance. Perhaps this is my time.

The trouble is, we're not designed to give in to death. It's programmed into us that we need to fight, so I force one foot in front of the other, holding onto the bed, the wall, the door. My heart, which I thought was failing, is pumping hard, louder than my metronome at full volume. I need to get out of here.

Now.

I shuffle along, consciously placing one socked foot in front of the other.

The first time, I heard it. A horrible, muffled thud. Death. Yet it wasn't mine. And then it became so distant that I could pretend it never actually happened.

The second time, I saw it and I felt it. My life disintegrating in front of my eyes, kind people all around me, looking, prodding, stroking, needling. The bright hospital lights, the horrible, discordant beeps of the machines, the loud, thoughtless voices. But it turned out, that was the practice run.

The third time, I smelled it. Right here, in my bedroom, the place that is meant to be my sanctuary.

This time, I can taste it. There's an acidity on my tongue, something metallic on the back of my throat. I try to swallow, but my mouth is too dry. It's not normal, yet I know it's only fear. One foot in front of the other. Just one more step. The corridor is spinning, and I know now that I have used up all of the five senses.

I need to find help, now.

If I drink a gallon of water, perhaps my brain will start processing again, and the solid sensation in my gut will dissipate.

'Are you alright?'

The voice is familiar, but I can't work out where it's coming from. I shrink backwards to the wall. They're coming to get me.

'Leave me alone,' I say, but the sounds are muffled, and then I realise why. It's because I'm flying through the air, speeding past the paintings on the wall. As I tear by my favourite picture, the young girl playing the violin, the momentum stops, and I crash downwards, headfirst. And now I know for sure that it is happening.

I have avoided this for so long, but no more.

Blackness.

Death.

1

MIA

TWO MONTHS EARLIER

I'm doing exactly what I shouldn't be doing. Lurking in the corridor by Robin's studio, listening to him put the finishing touches to his latest composition. It's a haunting melody, the tune played by an oboe over a bed of shimmering strings – very English classical, but he's combined it with repetitive drum rolls and offbeat hi-hats normally found in House Music. A synthesised riff comes to a sudden stop. I hurry away, a bright yellow duster in one hand and a dustpan and brush in the other.

I have been working for the renowned composer Robin Featherstone for the past nine months. It would have been my dream job if it weren't for the fact that I'm a cleaner. Don't get me wrong, there's nothing demeaning about cleaning; Dad's done it as a job for years. It's just I've spent most of my life training to be a musician. When I was accepted as a student at the Royal College of Music in London, I dreamed of a glittering future as a professional violinist, making music across the globe, bowing to adoring audiences inspired by my crossover style merging classical and rock, being hailed as the next great thing. If you can't dream in your early twenties, when can you? Of course, it hasn't panned out like that. Despite putting my everything into my studies and completing my many more than ten thousand hours of practice, here I am, making ends meet by dusting and scrubbing. The only upside is that I'm working in Robin Featherstone's house. You might not have heard of Robin Featherstone, but I guarantee you'll recognise his music. His creative genius is behind some of the catchiest theme tunes on popular television series, and those annoying television adverts with songs that leave you humming them for hours.

As I'm scuttling past the kitchen, along the limestone floor corridor towards the back door, Pavla appears, wearing a thickly padded white anorak and a black beanie pulled low over her forehead. She's clutching a stack of empty carrier bags. 'I'm nipping out now. I've left your money on the kitchen table.' She speaks with a strong Czech accent, and I can count on one hand how many times she's smiled at me.

'Thanks,' I say, relieved that she no longer feels the need to remind me that I mustn't leave a minute before 3 pm. As if.

Pavla Whittaker is the Featherstones' housekeeper. I can't work out exactly how long she's been working here, but it's very clear that she considers herself part of the furniture. I'm guessing she's in her late forties, although she looks older, with deep wrinkles around her lips and heavily stencilled eyebrows. I'm sure if she made the effort to wear makeup and dress in something other than elasticated trousers and baggy jumpers, she would be an attractive woman, with her high cheekbones and piercing blue eyes. I gaze out of the window in the utility room and watch Pavla walk across the gravel drive and down towards the little driveway that branches off to her cottage. When she glances back at the house, I hurry away. I need to clean Mr and Mrs Featherstone's bedroom and bathroom.

When I started cleaning here at Stave House, there was no official Mrs Featherstone. Claudia, Robin's first wife, would pop in from time to time, and I always knew when she'd visited, because Robin would spend the next couple of hours bashing out discordant chords at high volume. So when a woman, probably in her early thirties, appeared just over a month ago and introduced herself as Tamsin Featherstone, Robin's new wife, it was quite the shock. For starters, she's twenty-five years younger than him, extremely beautiful in a perfectly groomed way, with caramel wavy hair and big dark brown eyes with eyelash extensions and a model's body.

I assumed she might be a singer or a dancer perhaps, but according to Pavla, she used to work in PR. Of course, her marriage to Robin means she doesn't have to work anymore. I wondered whether Tamsin might fire me and do her own cleaning, or employ her preferred cleaner so she can put her mark on the house, but so far, I've barely spoken a word with her and rarely see her. According to Pavla, she's either out shopping or having beauty treatments or inside the brand-new greenhouse Robin has had built for her, and she's shown no desire to make any changes around the house.

From what I can gather, Tamsin is the strangest mixture: She's a socialite who wears designer clothes (we now have a constant flow of deliveries from designer boutiques) and clearly spends a great deal of time on her looks, but at the same time, she's obsessed with her cacti collection. I wondered why Robin installed a fancy greenhouse, the size of a small bungalow, shortly before Christmas. It's her wedding present, apparently. Despite the designer clothes, Tamsin has eschewed any fancy cars and drives around in a battered green Land Rover Defender. If my circumstances were different and I weren't her skivvy, I'd be interested to get to know her. I like people who defy conventions.

The Featherstones' bedroom is in the centre of the house, with views across the lawns at the rear. It's the largest of the six bedrooms and the one with the best views. There is an impressive bow window with a window seat curving underneath it, piled high with chintzy cushions in floral fabrics, mainly in dusty pinks and pale greys. It's not to my taste. The bed is unmade, with the large duvet left crumpled at the bottom of the bed, the pale grey linen pillows still showing indents where Robin and Tamsin laid their heads. I have to admit that I always feel a bit awkward coming in here, as if I'm snooping somehow, and it's even worse now Robin is newly married. Tamsin's bedside table is cluttered with pieces of jewellery, a glass of water with a lipstick mark, a packet of contraceptive pills, a leather-cased alarm clock and a pile of *Grazia* magazines. It's quite the contrast to Robin's bedside table, which is free from any clutter except a small leather-cased alarm clock. There's a heavily used Beethoven score on the floor next to the bed. The room smells of Tamsin's perfume. It's floral and spicy all at the same time, and from my description you might think it's nice, but for some reason I loathe the smell. Although I'm sure it's a very expensive scent, it reminds me of a cheap perfume that my sister wore, and that's not a good memory.

Hurriedly, I smooth down the sheets and pull up the duvet, and then I run the vacuum cleaner around the room, fortuitously avoiding hoovering up a diamond earring on the floor near their en-suite bathroom. Tamsin is so much younger than Robin, I wonder whether she's after his money or if it's genuine love. I don't know, because I've rarely seen them together, but I've no doubt that tongues are wagging.

There's really very little to clean, because I keep on top of the dusting and vacuuming, tidying up here three times a week. The bathroom requires a little more attention, particularly Tamsin's sink, which is tinted an orange-brown thanks to splattered makeup. When I'm done and the taps are sparkling and the mirrors spotless, I carry my cleaning materials downstairs in one of those little plastic buckets. The only room I've got left to do is Robin's studio, and most of the time he bats me away, saying he doesn't want to be disturbed. As I walk along the downstairs corridor, passing the wall covered with his certificates and photos of the famous actors, actresses and singers he's worked with, I'm surprised there's silence. Perhaps Robin is listening to music through headphones. I knock on the closed door.

There's no answer.

I knock again. Still there's no answer.

I open the door just a few centimetres. 'Hello, Robin, sorry to disturb you.'

Then I hear a gurgling sound. I push the door wide open and rush inside. My heart pounds as I process what I'm seeing. Robin is lying on the floor next to his grand piano, his eyes staring at me in terror, his hands clutching his chest.

'What's happened?' I yelp as I rush to his side, dropping the cleaning materials and kneeling down beside him.

'Heart,' he murmurs.

Oh. My. God. Robin is having a heart attack. I grab my mobile phone out of the rear pocket of my jeans and dial 999, all the while staring at Robin in horror, regretting that I never got around to doing a first aid course.

'What's your emergency?' the operator says.

'I need an ambulance. My employer is having a heart attack.'

I'm put straight through to another operator. After getting the essentials of my name and the address of Stave House, the operator asks, 'Is he unresponsive?'

'Robin, can you lift your arms?' I ask.

He mumbles something but doesn't move. and it's then that I realise his face is drooping on the left side. 'I think he's had a stroke. He's unresponsive,' I say, trying to keep my voice on an even keel. It feels as if *my* heart is going to pound out of my chest. Robin can't die. Not right here, with only me at his side. I take his hand and hold it in mine whilst clasping the phone to my ear with my other hand. Robin has long, thin fingers and neatly groomed fingernails, the hands of a professional musician.

'The ambulance is on its way,' I say, repeating the call operator's words. 'You're going to be just fine.'

But who am I to utter such a platitude? I have no idea if he will be fine or not. He tries to say something, but his words slur together incomprehensibly.

'Shall I get you a glass of water?'

He tries to speak again and attempts to shake his head, but drool slides out of the corner of his mouth as he makes a feeble attempt to grasp my hand.

'It's okay,' I say, stroking the back of his hand with my fingers. 'I'll wait with you until the ambulance comes. Don't worry, I'm going nowhere. Just try to relax.' I start humming the main tune from Tchaikovsky's Romeo and Juliet Overture. Robin was playing it a few weeks back, and he overheard me singing it quietly as I cleaned. We had a chat back then as to how a beautiful melody was the single most important thing to evoke feelings, but then we laughed about my singing it, because the tune is a bit of a cliché.

Please don't die, I repeat silently and continuously. *Please don't die.* My inept humming seems to relax Robin. I just pray that he survives. Why did this have to happen now, when both Pavla and Tamsin are out? I don't even have their mobile numbers, because the only contact detail I've ever needed is the house landline. The minutes seem to drag. I wonder if I'll need to call 999 again.

When I hear the siren of an ambulance, I feel an overwhelming relief and say another silent prayer. *Please let Robin Featherstone survive without any long-lasting effects. He's a good man.*

'I'm going to let the paramedics in,' I say as I release his hand. I rush to the front door, where two uniformed paramedics follow me in. One of them immediately sinks to his knees and assesses Robin whilst the other removes equipment from a couple of boxes. I feel like a spare part as they tend to him, talking in low, comforting voices and murmuring to each other medical terms that sound like a foreign language to me. Eventually they manoeuvre him onto a stretcher and wheel him out to the open-doored ambulance. This morning, Robin looked young for his fifty-eight years, with a mop of dark brown hair just tinged with grey at the temples and a tall, slender build. But now, with an oxygen mask over his nose and mouth, and skin a strange chalky pallor, he looks twenty years older, barely recognisable.

'Would you like to come with us?' the younger of the two paramedics asks.

'Should I?'

'It's normally a comfort for patients to have a familiar face with them.'

'Um, yes, of course. I'll just grab my things.' I hurry back into the house and leave a scribbled note for Pavla and Tamsin on the kitchen counter, asking them to call me urgently, and then I pull the front door to, locking myself out of the house.

I FEEL awkward as I travel in the back of the ambulance. It shouldn't be me who is accompanying Robin, but Tamsin or one of his children, Brooke or David. I've met Brooke a couple of times. She's late twenties, über confident, with poker-straight, long blonde hair and green eyes made to look catlike, due to the kohl she uses to create long lines like little arrows pointing up to her temples. Brooke has never deigned to talk to me. I've no idea what she does, but she keeps a bedroom here. Not that she's been around since her father remarried. I've never met David. Perhaps he only visits at the weekends, or maybe he's estranged from Robin, because no one talks about him.

The journey to hospital seems to go on for ever. Robin's eyes are closed, and he is being tended to by the kindly paramedic. I certainly hadn't imagined this to be in my job description when I started work at Stave House. It all seems so long ago, that interview.

I'm not one for complaining, but my life hasn't been easy. Ten months ago, I was desperate for money and willing to do whatever I could, so long as I was left a few hours so I could practice the violin and hopefully get gigs. A friend of a friend told me that Robin Featherstone was looking for a cleaner, and since I was a musician, perhaps it would suit me. Goodness knows how she found out, but I knew better than to ask. Nevertheless, I assumed the job might be through an agency and that it would require references and checks, and that I would have to be an employee and pay tax. Fortunately, I was wrong.

I turned up for the interview on a cool spring day and stood looking at the house in awe. It's an impressive Georgian house with pale orange-pink bricks and wisteria creeping up the central portion, clinging to the bricks and encircling the windows on the upper floor. On either side of the large white front door are two double-fronted patio doors, and on the first floor, there are five windows positioned neatly across the width of the main house, the panes of glass each crisscrossed in white. To one side is an extension, which, despite its flat roof, doesn't detract from the elegance of the design. To the left of the house is an open oak carport for three cars. Stave House is one of those English houses that makes you smile: traditional, symmetrical and very desirable. The sort of house that people like me never step foot inside. My trainers crunched on the gravel as I walked up the driveway and squeaked on the wide stone steps, and I straightened my coat and smoothed down my hair before pressing the shiny gold buzzer. I barely had time to step backwards when the door swung open.

I didn't know it then, but it was Pavla who greeted me, her eyes moving slowly from my head to toes before she stood back to let me in. I don't recall her being anything but civil; perhaps she even smiled at me. I followed her through the beautiful entrance hall with its large fireplace and sweeping staircase, down a long corridor into the largest kitchen I've been inside. She gestured for me to take a seat at the table, but she didn't offer me a drink.

'It's a pleasure to meet you, Mrs Featherstone,' I said.

'I'm not Mrs Featherstone,' she replied rather too quickly, and I knew I'd put my foot in it. 'I'm Mr Featherstone's house-keeper and have been running this household for the past twenty years.'

With hindsight, I wonder whether Pavla was quite flattered to be mistaken for Robin's wife, because she was surprisingly gentle in her interviewing. 'Tell me about yourself,' she said, leaning back in her chair.

And so I did. I was honest – well, mostly so. I explained that I was a trained musician, but was looking for cleaning jobs to supplement my paltry income.

'Mr Featherstone won't be giving you any music work, you do understand that, don't you?' she asked.

'Of course.'

'And he has very exacting standards. No hoovering around his studio when the door is closed, and you don't go in there without his express permission. Tell me about your cleaning experience.'

I didn't have much, or at least much that I could be up front about, so I expanded a little on the truth, because we all have to do that to get our feet in the door, don't we? I offered to do a couple of hours' cleaning at no charge so she could see how I worked, but she said that wouldn't be necessary. 'Mr Featherstone is a fair man. If you work hard, we'll pay you. When can you start?'

'Next week,' I said. I held my breath as I waited for her to talk about a contract or national insurance contributions, but she didn't. She told me I would be paid £14 per hour in cash. I was to work from 10 am until 3 pm Mondays, Wednesdays and Fridays, and my hours might be increased.

Just as I was standing up to leave, a tall, distinguished man walked into the kitchen. He had dark hair on the cusp of turning grey, glasses perched on the top of his head and was wearing a buttoned-down shirt and chinos.

'I need a cup of coffee.' And then he stopped. 'Oh,' he said, standing there awkwardly, as if he were the stranger in his kitchen rather than me. Then it was as if a switch flicked inside him and he remembered his manners. 'Sorry, sorry. And you are?'

Pavla's thin eyebrows drew together. 'This is Mia Benton. She's the new cleaner. Mia, this is Mr Featherstone.'

'Good to meet you, Mia.'

He extended his hand, which I shook. I immediately liked the look of Mr Featherstone. It sounds strange, but his symmetrical features, square jaw and very slightly hooded eyes suggested an innate kindness, so I was surprised by his next question.

'I trust Pavla has told you the rules?'

'Rules?'

He chortled. 'I'm very sensitive to sound. You have to be in my line of work. The damned vacuum cleaner that Pavla insists on us using is in the key of E, and I'm working on a piece in E flat, which is immensely frustrating, not that I need to bore you with that.'

'Actually, I'm a violinist with perfect pitch, so I totally understand.'

'You are?' He removed his spectacles and peered at me a little closer. 'Well, we'll have plenty to talk about, won't we.'

I wondered whether Pavla's nose was somewhat put out of joint, because she hurried me out of the house and told me to be at the back door of the property at 10 am sharp on Monday.

OVER THE PAST FEW MONTHS, I've talked with Robin about music on a few occasions. Once when I was cleaning the stove, he came into the kitchen and asked my opinion on a section for strings, seemingly genuinely interested as to whether I thought the harmonies worked. A couple of months ago, he was passing me in the corridor.

'I've been wondering, Mia. How did you get into music?'

'My grandmother was a musician, a cellist. So I suppose it's in the genes.'

'And your parents?' he asked with a smile.

I just shook my head. Dad's been as supportive as he could, but the music was on Mum's side of the family. I've often wondered how much I've pursued the career of a musician because I know it would have made Mum happy. It's silly, really, because she's long dead; it's not as if her approval would make any difference. I don't believe in life after death either, so I'm not expecting her to greet me with open arms at the pearly gates, telling me how proud she is of me. I suppose I'm doing it because I love playing, and in some little way, I want to carry on her family's legacy. Her life was cut short much too young. A life of such promise.

'Your parents must be very proud,' Robin said.

I tried to smile, I really did, but I expect my expression came out more like a grimace. 'I must be getting on,' I said, hurrying away.

I like Robin Featherstone. Pavla has warmed towards me, too, over the months, although I can't say I know her. Tamsin is just a distant figure who has started living in the house. All in all, it's an easy job.

THE AMBULANCE PULLS into the hospital. Poor Tamsin. She's only been married a few weeks. I wonder how she'll cope if Robin is left with a permanent disability. Life is so very unfair.

As I walk behind the paramedics pushing Robin into Accident and Emergency, my phone rings.

'What's happened?' Pavla asks. She sounds out of breath.

'I think Mr Featherstone has had a stroke. We're at the hospital.'

'O můj Bože, o můj Bože!' she says. 'I'm on my way.'

'Will you tell Mrs Featherstone?'

'Of course.' She hangs up on me.

I'm in the waiting room, wedged between people with various wounds and illnesses, trying to breathe as shallowly as possible, eager not to pick up any unpleasant diseases. No one pays me sick days, so if I can't work, I don't earn. Robin has been taken somewhere out of sight, and I have no idea what his prognosis is, so I just say some silent prayers and play a mindless game on my phone to while away the time.

About half an hour later, Pavla scurries towards me. She looks pale, and her eyes are skittish. 'You can go now.' She turns away, but then, as if remembering her manners, swivels around again. 'Thanks for staying with him.'

'Of course.' I stand up. 'I really pray he's okay, and if you and Mrs Featherstone require any more help, I'd be more than happy to up my hours. I do have some care experience, and I've become very fond of Mr Featherstone.'

'Yes, lots of people become fond of Mr Featherstone,' she mutters. 'I'll discuss it with Mrs Featherstone when we know what's happening. Turn up as normal on Friday unless you hear from me to the contrary.'

2

TAMSIN

A WEEK LATER

My heart is broken. I have been married for less than two months to the love of my life, and now he's been destroyed. Of course, I knew it was a risk marrying a man twenty-four years my senior, but to have a stroke at fifty-eight is just too cruel.

We all have moments in our lives – life shocks, I think they're called – when time stops and it's as if our minds have taken a Polaroid of that split second, a frozen image that we'll never be able to banish. I was in Freida's Boutique, my favourite designer clothes shop, standing at the counter about to buy a pair of black leather trousers that I knew Robin would love, when my phone rang. It was Pavla. I ignored it at first, but when she rang again immediately, I sighed and held the trousers and my wallet in one hand and the phone in the other.

'Robin's had a stroke,' she said. 'I'm at the hospital.' I dropped the trousers onto the counter, shoved my wallet back into my Prada bag and ran. I don't recall a second of the journey to the hospital, but what I can't banish is the image of my husband lying prone on that hospital trolley. His skin had a grey tinge, his eyes were closed, and there were machines everywhere. I broke down and sobbed.

A week later, and Robin is home, but he's not the Robin I married. This man has aged a couple of decades, and he's broken. There's something feeble about him that spears my heart, because the Robin I fell in love with was strong and powerful, a true patriarch. The new Robin has slurred speech, and although I'm beginning to decipher what he says, it's hard. The more I struggle to understand, the more frustrated he gets.

I'm sitting at the large oak-topped kitchen table, a steaming cappuccino in front of me, leafing through a plant catalogue. The succulents' section is sparse, so it's not holding my interest. I glance around the kitchen, which looks like it's been plucked straight from the pages of an interiors design magazine. It really is a dream kitchen, and my favourite room in the house. The units are Shaker style, painted in pale grey. There's a big black Aga on the back wall, and an impressive island unit topped with white-and-grey-veined marble that contrasts with the dark-grey-painted cupboards underneath. Robin has suggested that I might like to redecorate the house, to erase the memories of the first Mrs Featherstone, but honestly, it's not my thing. I'm just grateful to live in this beautiful home that requires nothing of me. It's such a step up from my rented one-bedroom flat, it's almost laughable.

'He's asking for you,' Pavla says as she scurries through the kitchen, filling up a water carafe at the butler's sink. 'He's asked if you can bring his manuscript paper and a pencil.'

I sigh. Robin's fine motor skills are returning slowly, but as he can barely navigate bringing a fork to his lips, I doubt he'll do well holding a pencil. I shove my chair back and get up.

'Mia's offered to help out more, with Robin's care and the like,' Pavla says with her back to me.

'She has?' That perks me up. I feel a bit bad that I haven't spoken to Mia. She seems nice enough, doing whatever it is that she does around the house. Up until now, I've been out most of the time she's been here. There's nothing for me to do during the day whilst Robin is working, so I made the most of being a lady of leisure, shopping with the platinum credit card that Robin gave me, meeting up with friends, visiting succulent nurseries, having the odd beauty treatment.

'That sounds like a great idea,' I say, trying to keep my voice nonchalant. 'I'm sure Robin will get fed up of just having you and me tending to him.' I ignore Pavla's tut as I walk out of the kitchen. She can be such a sourpuss at times. I wasn't expecting the full welcome with open arms from her, but she could make more of an effort with me.

Robin's study, which he calls his studio, is a small room tucked at the back of the house. It's jam-packed full of keyboards and music studio equipment and speakers and a load of complicated-looking machines that I haven't got a clue about. He's a very neat man, and his desk has two piles. A sheaf of manuscript paper lies on the top, and in a little wooden beaker to the side are several retractable pencils. I select one and pick up the pad of manuscript paper. Musical notes and notations are scribbled across many of the pages. I wish I knew how to read music, but to me, they're just a jumble of scrawls. Perhaps Robin can teach me. But then I stifle a sob; I doubt my Robin can teach anything.

As I walk slowly up the grand staircase, I think back to when Robin and I met. I had been working in PR for the past ten years. I fell into the job and discovered it suited me. I'm an organised type of person, with a good eye for detail, and I don't turn down any party invitation. My colleague, Annie, was organising a wrap party for a television production company. She asked for my help, but frankly it was the last thing I felt like doing. I'd just split up with Pierre, my boyfriend, the man I thought would put a ring on my finger. I wasn't in the mood for plastering a fake smile on my face. But I owed Annie, and when she said the ballroom of the fancy hotel was going to be packed with film stars, I agreed to help. As it turned out, I didn't recognise a single face. By the time the dinner and the boring speeches were over, all I wanted to do was call for a taxi and go home, but first I made my way to the bar and ordered a Cointreau. We're not meant to drink when we're working, but this was to be one for the road.

As the waiter was preparing my drink, I swallowed a yawn.

'You look as bored as I feel.'

I turned to look at the owner of the deep, honey-smooth voice and was surprised to see a distinguished-looking man wearing black tie.

'Haven't you enjoyed the function?' I ask.

'Nope. I attend because it's expected of me. And you, what are you doing here?'

'Helping organise it. I work for Cableknit PR.'

'I thought you might be an actress.'

I snorted. 'Flattery will get you nowhere. I can't act for life nor money. Are you an actor?'

He smiled wryly. 'No, I'm a composer. I wrote the music for the film.' He held out his hand. 'Robin Featherstone. It's a pleasure to meet you.'

I honestly thought that love at first sight was nonsense up until the moment Robin clasped my hand in his. But something magical happened. I know that he felt it, too. It was crazy, and still is. Robin, being the consummate gentleman, wined and dined me every night for the following week.

When he took me to bed (in a luxury five-star hotel, of course), I knew that I never wanted to leave his arms. Age is just a number, right? The only fly in the ointment was the fact that he seemed keen to keep me away from Stave House. I only visited his home twice before we married, but I fell in love with the property too. Who wouldn't adore a Queen Anne–style house, with its beautiful proportions and white sash windows and a fabulous wisteria creeping across the front?

Six months after we first met, following long weekends to European cities and lazy nights spent in his London club, he got down on one knee and asked me to marry him. I cried with joy.

'You know I can't do the big white wedding thing,' he said after a vigorous session of lovemaking. Age certainly didn't hold Robin back.

'It's fine. I'll do whatever you want.' I admit I was a little disappointed, because who wouldn't want to show off her handsome, older husband and the massive chunk of diamond on her finger? But it's not like I have a big family to accommodate, and there was no one to walk me down the aisle. Of course I understood that this wedding was the second time around for Robin, and he was very conscious of not wanting to upset his two adult children, neither of whom I had met. Instead, he presented me with two first-class tickets to Saint Lucia and we eloped, which is much more romantic. We got married on a white sandy beach, a pink-orange sunset setting a magical backdrop to the perfect December day. I wore a floaty white dress with bare feet, and Robin sported an open-necked shirt and chinos. It was truly idyllic.

I wish the memories hadn't been tarnished by our home-coming. The day after we returned, we were accosted by Robin's ex-wife, Claudia, and adult daughter, Brooke. It's understandable that they wouldn't approve of me, but I certainly didn't anticipate the insults and upset and the waves that rippled through all of our relationships. With hindsight, I suppose I was naive.

ROBIN HAS TWO ADULT CHILDREN, Brooke and David. It's slightly awkward because they are only a few years younger than me – not that I've ever met the elusive son. According to Pavla, he lives in Geneva, selling real estate in the summer and ski guiding in the winter. Whenever I bring up his name, Robin deftly changes the subject. The morning after we returned from our honeymoon, and just a few hours after we christened our new marital bed, Brooke stormed into the kitchen, where Robin and I were eating a lazy Saturday morning breakfast.

'I can't believe you did it!' Brooke exclaimed, standing there with her hands on her hips, her eyes welling with tears. 'How could you marry her!' she exclaimed, jabbing her finger towards me. Robin reached over towards me and clasped my hand.

'I have married Tamsin because I love her, and she loves me.'

'But can't you see she's just a money-grabbing b–'

'That's enough, Brooke.' Another woman strode into the kitchen, late fifties at a guess, wearing a torn anorak and jeans. 'Surely you know your father well enough to realise that direct confrontation is never going to work. Look where it got me in my divorce.'

Robin sighed. 'What are you doing here, Claudia?'

I realised with horror that this was my first meeting with Mrs Featherstone number one.

'I'm accompanying my daughter to enquire whether my ex-husband has totally lost his senses.' She stood with her hands on her hips. There was something equine about her face, with its long nose and pointed chin and thin silvery hair tied back in a ponytail. She had lots of lines around her lips, and I wondered why she had never considered Botox. I could see that she might have been an attractive woman once, but she certainly had let her looks go.

Robin dropped my hand and put his arm around my shoulders. 'I'm sorry, my love, that this is your first introduction to my ex-wife and my daughter.' His lips grazed my cheek.

I took a deep breath, squeezed Robin's hand and stood up.

'It's a pleasure to meet you,' I said, holding my arm out towards Claudia and smiling as sweetly as I could at Brooke, who was standing right behind her mother.

'Hmm,' Claudia said, rolling her eyes and stepping backwards, causing Brooke to yelp as she stepped on her daughter's toes. It was quite the comedic scene, except it wasn't. There was a glimmer of hatred in the green eyes of those two women. I let my hand drop to my side.

'Get out of my house,' Robin said quietly. 'Brooke, you're welcome to come back whenever you are ready to apologise for your appalling manners. Claudia, you need to book an appointment before stepping foot in here again. I've paid you off generously. I'm sure you don't want me to take out a restraining order.'

'Daddy!' Brooke exclaimed.

'Goodbye, both of you. Please leave Tamsin and me to have our breakfast in peace.'

IT CONFOUNDS me that Robin was married to Claudia, as they seem such an unlikely match. Everything about her is very strident, such a contrast to Robin's quiet, unassuming yet deeply confident manner. She's the type of woman who is a big presence: Not that she's large in size; it's just her voice is a little too loud, her manner overbearing. I imagine she was the head-girl type, very bossy and deeply conventional. I've felt a residual discomfort that she and I are sharing the same marital bedroom with the same man – and, of course, the same surname. That unease isn't helped by the fact that since his stroke, Robin has banished me from the bedroom, saying that he has insomnia now, and that I should sleep in the spare room for a while until he recuperates. It feels like I've been discarded. I tell myself that's a stupid thought because Robin is mine, but I'm lonely. I miss his arms around me at night, the gentle rhythmic breathing and the way he makes me feel so secure, yet desirable.

I knock gently on the bedroom door and push it open. My husband is propped up in bed, and he tries to smile at me, but his expression looks more like a grimace. I suppose I should count my blessings that he knows who I am. Imagine what it would be like if he had had memory loss. A little drop of saliva trickles down his chin. It spears my heart, and I have to look away, but at least he wipes it away with the back of his hand, turning his head from me in the hope that I didn't notice. That's considerable progress from a week ago.

'What you got?' he mumbles.

Pavla has left one of those tray cushions on the floor next to the bed, so I place the manuscript paper on it and put it on his lap. I hand him the pencil, but he drops it. I lean over him, pick it up off the bed cover and squeeze his fingers around the pencil. It stays within his grasp.

'You gonna leave me now?' he mumbles quietly. I think I see a tear in his eye. I drop down to my knees and place a kiss on his cheek.

'You're going to get better, Robin. The physio is coming this afternoon, and you'll be back to normal in no time. You're a strong, resilient man. With regular physio, your prognosis is excellent.' That's what the doctor told Robin when they discharged him from hospital, and I intend to repeat that statement one hundred times a day if I have to. I'm a firm believer in positive affirmations. My vision board got me to where I am today.

He squeezes his eyes closed. Of course, no one really knows whether Robin will fully recover, but when a few months ago, I told him about my daily affirmations, he said he also believes in the power of positive thinking, so I intend to reinforce that. Frankly, I don't know what I'll do if Robin doesn't improve. If this is going to be the rest of my life, a nurse to a much older, invalid husband, am I a good enough person to stick by him? I really don't know. Actually, I do know. I doubt it, but I'm not going to admit that to anyone, not even to myself.

I'm relieved when we're interrupted by the phone ringing. Despite all the modern equipment Robin has in his studio, he is antiquated in other ways and still has a landline. I pick up the phone next to his bed.

'Tamsin speaking.'

'It's Brooke. We need to talk.'

'You and me or you and your—'

She interrupts me. 'You and me.'

'Alright.' I blow a kiss at Robin and walk into the corridor. From the tone of Brooke's voice, if I want to keep Robin's stress levels down, this isn't a conversation that I want him to overhear.

'We need to sort out a new will,' Brooke says.

'Excuse me?' I can't believe my ears.

'Dad's will. As far as I'm aware, he hasn't updated it since he married you.'

'I don't know anything about your father's will.'

'Yeah, right,' Brooke says sarcastically.

I am perfectly aware that they all think I'm a gold digger, but I'm not. I love Robin Featherstone.

'Look, Tamsin. The way it currently stands, you will inherit everything. Assuming Dad's marriage to you is legal, then it supersedes his previous will, and you get the lot. Let's face it, he won't have had time to write a new one between tying the knot and having his stroke, and that's not fair. Not fair to David, me or Mum.'

'What are you trying to say?' My fingers clasp the phone tightly as my heart hammers in my chest.

'That I want to come and see Dad and bring along a solicitor or a wills person. Dad won't want me and David to be written out of his will, even though that's probably what you want.'

I feel fury bubbling up my throat. 'Listen, Brooke. You know nothing about me, but one thing I promise you is that I am no gold digger. Your father and I married each other because we're in love.'

'Yeah,' she mutters. 'I'll come tomorrow.'

'No. Your father is very unwell, and the last thing he needs is being pressured to change his will. Come in a week or so, when he'll be a bit stronger.'

I can't believe that Brooke is being so unsubtle about this. She's only visited her father once since he had his stroke, and as far as I'm aware, David hasn't even telephoned. I find it extraordinary that Robin has produced two such insensitive children.

'I knew you'd be like this. Taking control of Dad, trying to oust me. It was all so bloody predictable!' Then she hangs up on me.

I am shaking as I stare at the phone. I get that Brooke is angry towards me, but it's not as if I were responsible for breaking up her parents' marriage. They'd already been divorced for four years when Robin and I met. I've tried to be pleasant towards her despite her hostility towards me.

I pace up and down the corridor and think about what she said. Annoyingly, I agree with her that Robin should write a new will. It's not as if I want him to cut out his children; they're perfectly entitled to inherit their father's wealth, and I'm quite sure there's enough to go around for all of us. It's just that Brooke is so crass and money-grabbing. As I walk back towards the bedroom, I try to look for the positives. At least you get what you see with Brooke. How much worse it would be if she was conniving and secretly planning to stab me in the back.

3

MIA

The past four weeks have sped by, simply because I've been so busy. Pavla appointed me as Robin's temporary assistant, and I'm now working full time for the Featherstones, helping Robin when he's awake and cleaning when he's resting. A little over a month on from his stroke and he has improved no end, undoubtedly due to all the physio he's having and the fact that Robin himself is so determined to get better. His speech is almost normal, although he's still wobbly on his feet, and his fine motor skills have definitely suffered. The strange thing is that although Robin finds it difficult to notate his manuscript paper, he's perfectly able to play the piano. The curious workings of the human brain.

The good thing from my side, despite the cash, is that I'm getting an insight into how this esteemed composer works, and he seems genuinely interested in my musical opinions. It's a bit like doing a master's in music with a private professor. The life I thought I'd have before ... Oh well, I just need to make the most of what I've got. Right now, I'm sitting in

Robin's studio at a small, collapsible card table positioned between the grand piano and Robin's pedestal desk. He's reading something or other, and I'm notating a piece that he played on the piano, listening to it through a pair of over-ear headphones. He is composing a theme tune for a new four-part thriller that will be aired on Netflix later in the year. Although I'm no composer, I love listening to him trying out melodies on the piano, then adding in harmonies. I'm somewhat bewildered, though, as he builds on these using software called Logic, simulating all of the different instruments in an orchestra. Today, though, he has been unusually quiet, using his computer, rarely saying much to me.

So when he speaks, I'm concentrating on listening to the music and miss what he says.

'Sorry,' I say, pausing the recording and removing the headphones.

'I'm just moaning,' Robin says. 'They all want a piece of me, Mia.'

I frown. 'What do you mean? Have you got too much work on?' Perhaps he'll ask me to help him with some work. Maybe I'll even get credits. That would be too good to be true, although I'm not sure I have the ability to come up with original compositions.

He sighs. 'If only. No, it's not work. It's Brooke and Claudia. They're pressuring me to rewrite my will.'

I chew the side of my lip. This is the first time that Robin has mentioned anything not related to music. I have to admit that I've wondered whether Tamsin married Robin for his money, because no one lives in a beautiful house like this surrounded by antiques and silver and oil paintings without having plenty of money, but why would Brooke and Claudia be badgering him?

'By marrying Tamsin, my previous will is null and void, so

as things currently stand, Tamsin inherits the lot,' he explains.

So I was on the right track. I don't know anything about wills. When Dad passes, I've no doubt that the only things I'll inherit are debts. We're not the sort of people to worry about wills and working out ways to avoid inheritance tax. I wish we were. Poor Dad. I know he's doing everything he can to pay off our family's debts, but it's like climbing a mountain wearing a pair of flip-flops.

I say nothing, but pull what I hope is a sympathetic face.

'What do you think I should do?' he asks.

I stare at him. 'You shouldn't be asking me! I mean, what do I know about such things?'

'But I am asking you, Mia. What is morally right?' The left side of his lip curls upwards, and I see the old Robin. He tilts his head to one side and waits for my answer.

'Well, it's not really fair that Tamsin gets everything. She is your wife, and obviously you really love her, but I mean, you do have a responsibility towards your children.' It hasn't escaped my notice that Tamsin seems to be sleeping in a spare room. I assume that's because of Robin's stroke, and not due to any fallout in their relationship. I don't see her often, but when she's around, Robin's eyes soften; it's obvious he's in love with her. I wonder whether she feels the same way.

He sighs and shifts in his chair. 'My children are avaricious. You've seen how Brooke is, how bitter she is towards Tamsin.'

I haven't, actually, so I keep my face expressionless. Brooke seems to come and go from this house. Sometimes she's here for a week or so at a time, leaving her room in a total mess, but then she is gone for a couple of months. She hasn't stayed the night here since Tamsin moved in. I can't say I know Robin's daughter, because we've barely spoken a few words.

'If only Brooke would open her heart, she might realise that Tamsin is a good person, someone who could be a great friend to her. But no, my daughter is capricious and entitled. Sometimes I look at her and wonder where Claudia and I went so very wrong in our parenting.'

'I'm sure–'

He interrupts me. 'It was my fault, of course. I was an absent parent, too focused on my music, leaving Claudia to bring up the children. And then we sent them away to boarding school. Such a mistake. Why on earth do we think that an institution can do a better job in child-raising than we can?'

I have no answer to that. I don't know anyone who went to a boarding school, so it's a bit difficult for me to give an opinion. I suppose it doesn't matter what age you are; everyone is affected by their parents' marriage breakdown, whatever the circumstances. It can't be easy if your dad marries someone only a few years older than you. But surely that's easier than what I went through – your mother dying when you're just ten years old.

'I suppose Brooke is just struggling with someone else taking her mother's place in your affections,' I suggest. I have often wondered how I would feel if Dad remarried. I think I'd be grateful, but alas, I can't see that ever happening.

Robin harrumphs. 'Unlikely. Claudia's and my relationship broke down years ago. We stayed together for the kids and then remained living under the same roof until ...' His voice peters out. 'And as for David, he only ever contacts me when he wants something. I can't remember the last time he actually set foot in this house.'

I'm curious to know more about David. Robin has never talked about his son. I wonder if they're estranged, and if so, why. Has that got something to do with his parents' divorce?

'Pavla mentioned that he lives in Switzerland,' I say.

'Yes.' Robin rolls his eyes. 'But he's hardly a Swiss banker. He bums around on the ski slopes during the winter and supposedly sells real estate in the summer. They were such sweet children.' He stands up, levering himself by leaning on the grand piano. I move as if to help him, but he waves me away. He then shuffles across the room to the bookshelf on the wall behind the shiny black Bluthner grand piano. He reaches up and lifts a silver photo frame down from the top shelf. I'm pleased to see how much his balance and dexterity have improved in the last couple of weeks.

'Here,' he says, holding the photo frame out in front of him. 'They looked like little angels, didn't they?'

I have to agree. Aged four or five at a guess, they both have blonde curly hair, sparkling eyes and cherubic smiles. In the picture, Brooke is an inch or so taller than her younger brother, and she gazes straight at the camera. David looks as if he is desperate to be anywhere except in front of the camera.

'And this is David from a few years ago.' Robin picks up an unframed photograph of an exceptionally handsome, clean-shaven young man wearing a dark blue suit standing in front of a pale blue sky, the same colour as his eyes. It's interesting how Brooke's eyes are green, yet David's are blue. 'This was taken when he had a proper job,' Robin says wistfully.

'What did he do before he went to Switzerland?' I ask.

'Something in the city. I didn't understand it. He didn't last long there, but that's David for you. Flighty. He doesn't stick at anything for any length of time.'

'Are either of your children interested in music?'

Robin briefly closes his eyes. 'No. I made the classic parenting mistake. I forced them to have music lessons. Brooke learned the flute and David the piano, and then I stood over them whilst they practiced. The more I pushed them, the more they resisted. Both gave up learning instru-

ments by the age of twelve and showed zero interest in how I
made enough money to fund their luxurious lifestyles.'

'I'm sorry,' I say, although I'm not sure why. From the
sounds of things, the fact that his children aren't musical is
the least of Robin's worries. What upsets me is that neither
have shown the slightest bit of sympathy towards their father
and his ill health. I think of Dad then. He tries his best, he
really does, but he's a broken man. When you're so crushed
yourself, it's hard for you to be a rock to anyone else.

Robin turns and smiles at me. 'That's why it's a pleasure
to have you around, Mia. We speak the same language of
music.'

I feel a mixture of embarrassment and pride that the great
Robin Featherstone actually enjoys my company; I'm unable
to come up with an appropriate response. Fortunately, Robin
places the photos back on the shelf and walks back to his
desk, sitting down. I slip the headphones back over my ears,
but I can't help but think about Mum. I wonder how my relationship would have developed with her. I am sure she would
have been chuffed that I've chosen to carry on her family's
musical heritage, but would my life have turned out differ-
ently if she had lived? A mother's role is to support her
daughter, come what may, isn't it? But what if her two daugh-
ters give diametrically opposed versions of the truth? She is
meant to love them both equally, isn't she? Which daughter
does a mother choose? Would she have believed me?

Dad tells me that Mum would have been so proud of my
musical success, but he doesn't mention what came next.
Thinking about it, I can't recall the last time we spoke about
Mum out loud. My memories are scant, because Mum died
when I was ten, and since then, Dad has struggled along, all
alone. I'm not even sure whether my memories of Mum are
real or whether I've made them up based upon the stories
that Dad has told me when we looked through their old

photo albums. So really Robin asking me questions about families and inheritance is totally beyond my remit of experience. All I know is that despite living in opulence at Stave House, there's something very sorely missing in this household. I can't put my finger on it, but I will.

4

TAMSIN

I am walking past Robin's study, and the door is slightly ajar.

'I am asking you, Mia. What is morally right?' Robin says.

'Well, it's not really fair that Tamsin gets everything.'

What the hell! I cannot believe my ears. It's not like I mean to eavesdrop, but we're all programmed to catch the sound of our own names, aren't we? So when I hear Mia say my name, and then realise *my* husband is asking *her* advice about his will, I'm not going to ignore that conversation. The cheek of it! No, worse than that. How dare they! My husband is asking Mia what is morally right? And then she's replying that it's not fair that I get everything, and that Robin has a moral responsibility towards his children. This is a conversation he should be having with me, not her.

How dare Robin discuss our personal affairs with a cleaner, secretary, or whatever she is! And what right does she have to voice her opinion? Worse than that, my husband seemed to seriously consider what Mia said. It's as if he's able

to have more meaningful conversations with her than he is
with me, and that's cutting.

When they stop talking, I tiptoe away, but my heart is
thudding. I know people think I'm a money-grabber. What
they forget is that Robin and I fell in love, and that's why
we're married. His wealth is an added bonus. Okay, if I'm
being brutally honest, perhaps I wouldn't have fallen for him
in the same way if he'd been penniless, but that doesn't make
me a bad person. After all, he only brought me to this house a
couple of times at the weekends before we were married, and
although he paid for us to have lovely meals and stay in
classy hotels, he didn't flaunt excessive wealth. Robin doesn't
wear designer clothes or drive a fancy car, and he's said on
more than one occasion that Claudia took him to the cleaners
in their divorce. And if Robin had been worried that I only
wanted him for his money, he'd have asked me to sign a
prenuptial agreement, yet nothing was ever discussed. I
would have signed one if he'd asked. I would have carried on
working at Cableknit PR if he hadn't told me that I could quit.

I walk briskly out of the back door and down the garden
path, my eyes brimming with angry tears. Normally I pause
for a moment to admire the impressive structure that is my
greenhouse, but not today. I fling open the door and shut it
behind me, a little too strongly. It doesn't matter. The
building might be made out of numerous panes of glass, but
it's strong. The greenhouse was Robin's wedding present to
me. When I saw it for the first time, I was speechless. Even if
you're no horticulturalist, you'd recognise it as something
special. It's called a Lodge because it's the size of a small
house, with a thirty-feet glasshouse and a conservatory-type
room at the end. It looks like one of those Victorian greenhouses, with brick walls up to about two feet and numerous
glass panels in between powder-coated green aluminium
struts. Little metal arrows point upwards from the roof, giving

it a grandeur. Robin did his research and chose a model as close to the original structures created by the leading designer of greenhouses in Victorian England, Thomas Messenger. As he said, 'Only the best for my beautiful new bride.' It may, on a superficial level, have the look of an old glasshouse, but it has all of the latest mod cons. In fact, the building is more like a solarium with heating and cooling, the patented glass has some unique properties that I don't understand, and it's also got all of the must-have accessories. I won't bore you with them, because I know most people don't share my obsessive love of succulents, but if you were to visit, you'd appreciate the little garden room at the end with its bottle-green velvet sofa, drinks cabinet trolley and low glass coffee table. Robin even put in a coffee machine along with a miniature fridge. Yes, it's lovely to sit here and gaze at my extensive collection of cacti, but what I like most is getting my hands dirty, propagating and potting up, tending to my exotic babies. I don't tell most people about my passion because I get the strangest of looks. My carefully coiffured hair and designer clothes don't match with the image of a keen gardener, but that's what makes people interesting, isn't it? That dichotomy, which I rather revel in.

I stand inside the greenhouse and breathe in the warm, dry air, then I stride over to the bench where my newest cacti stand. Normally, I wear thick gardening gloves to protect my hands, but I want those sharp, barbed thorns to bite into my flesh, to feel some physical pain to dull the hurt of Robin's conversation with Mia. It might be masochistic, but I've noticed that my brain can only truly focus on one pain at a time, and physical hurt is better than the emotional hurt of betrayal. I pick up the latest addition to my collection, a *Copiapoa cinerea*.

It's quite the beauty, with long jet-black spines extending from its chalky grey-green body that is globular in shape.

Such a lovely word, *globular*. I love the symmetry of the plant and the way the spines are sparse, almost as if its maker considered exactly where each one should go. I let one of the spines dig into the fleshy tip of my right index finger and then pull the cactus away, watching as the pearl of blood rises to the surface of my skin, just like the globular shape of the *Copiapoa*. It's somehow more satisfying to be speared by this cactus, more so than the cacti with glochids, those short, hair-like prickles that can get stuck in your skin and cause irritation. I suck my finger and think.

Damn it. Mia is right. Of course Robin should change his will so that his children get some inheritance. Just because I married him doesn't mean I should get the lot. What's upsetting is that Robin should have discussed it with me, not her. What does that say about our short marriage?

I place the *Copiapoa* on the bench and glance around at my collection. It's expanded massively in the past few weeks. Thanks to Robin's credit card and his fabulous generosity, I've driven the length and breadth of the country, collecting rare succulents from specialist nurseries. My cacti come in every conceivable shape and size; if I carry on collecting and nurturing like this, I may end up with one of the largest private collections in the United Kingdom. The reality is, since his stroke, I've neglected Robin and used my plants as an excuse. I stare at my finger. The blood has gone, and I mustn't focus on it. Blood reminds me of my father; those are memories I like to banish. The truth is, I'm struggling with my husband's disability. I know it's a terrible thing to admit, but I fell in love with Robin because he was strong: my older, wiser, handsome protector. It wasn't meant to be like this, where I'm his nursemaid who has been chucked out of the marital bedroom. The situation has to change. It's up to me to take control.

I'm going to start with Mia. And she must go.

I remember what my therapist told me. *Say your affirmations. Speak them out loud.* And so I do. 'I am in control. I have a perfect life. I love my husband. Mia has to go.'

Okay, she didn't tell me I needed to get rid of someone, but if it means taking back control, then so be it. It makes me feel better already. I walk over to the coffee machine and switch it on, the gurgling noise blocking out my words as I repeat my affirmations. Then a shadow falls over me, and I swivel around, swallowing a lump in my throat.

'Oh, it's only you,' I say, relief making my shoulders sag. It's Marek, Pavla's son.

'Are you talking to yourself?' he asks.

I smile at him. 'Yup.'

'I talk to myself sometimes, too. Mum says it's the first sign of madness, but I think it's good.'

'It makes me feel better,' I admit.

'It makes me feel better too,' Marek says, repeating my words as he stares at me with his deep-set, unblinking eyes. I suppress a shiver. Marek is in his early twenties, and although no one has said anything, there is definitely something strange about the young man. He's a big lad with a thickset neck and patchy facial hair that gives him the air of someone slightly deranged. Despite his size, he's light on his feet and creeps around, forever startling me. I thought there might be something a bit wrong with him, learning difficulties or the like, because he's very socially awkward. Always staring, always the last person to look away. I thought about saying something to Robin, but Marek is such a hard worker, I have nothing to object to. He is one of those people who, when he's given a job, just gets on with it without so much as a question. Even when it's bucketing down outside, and the deer have eaten the roses and the squirrels have dug up all of the bulbs he just planted, Marek keeps his head down and doesn't complain. He is employed as the gardener's assistant, but as he lives here with his mum and dad in the small cottage at the bottom of the drive, Marek is always around. He does a bit of gardening and odd jobs, and more recently he's been helping me out in the greenhouse. I don't think he likes my cacti very much, but he's willing to clean down the windows in the greenhouse and sweep the floors, and although he's strictly forbidden from coming in here when I'm not around, more often than not he appears when I'm pottering with my plants.

They're a strange family, the Whittakers. Well, at least the mother and son are. Pavla has never been rude to me, but she's not exactly warm. I suppose her nose has been put out of joint a bit by me tipping up. Perhaps she was buddy-buddy with Claudia back in the day. I can imagine the two of them together, bitching about Robin, taking advantage of the man who supported them both. Thomas, Pavla's husband, seems to be the only friendly one in their family. He's Robin's gardener, maintenance man and general dogsbody. If a light bulb needs replacing, Thomas does it. When the irrigation system in the greenhouse stopped working, he fixed it. Thomas smiles at me when I pass him in the garden and nods his head in a rather quaint, deferential way. I get the feeling that he's trying to be the typical country gent with his tweed flat cap and navy guernsey and green wellingtons. The only problem is his strong Cockney accent, which is at odds with his sartorial choices.

'Mum wants to know if you'll be here for lunch,' Marek says, his eyes boring into mine.

'Yes, I will. And I'll eat it with Robin. Can you tell your mum that her cooking is the best?' Pavla's cooking is alright, and certainly not cordon bleu, but I'm grateful that she's there to cook for us, saving me the trouble. Besides, it's about time that I butter up Pavla, especially as her workload will be increasing once Mia goes.

'I'll tell her what you said.' Even a compliment doesn't warrant a smile. Marek just turns and strides out of the greenhouse.

I wonder what Mum would think of me now, being looked after by a caretaker, with a wealthy, erudite older husband. If only she'd lived long enough to see this, I think she would have been so proud. I give myself a mental congratulatory pat on the back. I've come such a long way, but I really must make sure that I butter up the right people so I don't suffer the indignity of a tumultuous fall. I like my way of life here, even without Robin being his normal strength. If Mia needs to go to maintain that, then I'm sorry, but I can't hesitate to take action.

5

MIA

For the first time in weeks, I'm able to clean Robin's studio. He's gone out this morning, to a doctor's appointment, driven by Pavla because, as he said to me last night, he's not quite up to driving the old Range Rover by himself yet. The truth probably is that his insurance company won't let him drive, but he hasn't shared that with me. For such a brilliant, independent man, losing his confidence like that must be an awful blow. I've just started the vacuum cleaner and am cleaning behind his desk when, for no obvious reason, the machine stops. I turn around and jump when I see Tamsin standing there. She's switched off the power at the mains.

I frown.

'What are you doing in here?' she asks with a scowl. She's wearing a white jumper shot through with silvery threads and white skinny jeans. Her toffee-coloured hair falls in waves over her shoulders, and she's crossed her arms in front of her chest.

'Cleaning. Robin ... Mr Featherstone said it was alright because he's out this morning.'

'You know perfectly well that no member of staff is allowed in here when he's not present. This really isn't working out.'

What does she mean? Is there something wrong with the vacuum cleaner? I stare at her. She reddens slightly. 'I'm sorry, Mia, but I need to ask you to leave.'

'Yes, of course. I'll do the living room instead.'

'No, you don't understand.' She can't meet my eyes. 'You need to leave this job and not come back.'

'But–'

'No buts. I'd like you to collect your belongings and be out of here in the next five minutes. It's for the best.'

'You can't just fire me!' I exclaim, anger knotting in my stomach.

'Actually, I can. We pay you cash, you don't have a contract, and we employed you to assist my husband, but now he is so much better, we don't need you any longer. I'll give you a reference if you want.'

'But Pavla–'

She cuts me off again. 'Pavla works for me, and she does as I say. We're overstaffed here, and it's my job to keep a lid on the household finances.' She stands to one side and beckons for me to walk through the door. 'Good luck with whatever you do in the future, and don't hesitate to ask me for a reference.'

I don't believe a word of what she's saying. Since when did she have to keep a lid on household finances? Are they really overstaffed? Surely Robin would have mentioned something to me. I open and close my mouth, but what else can I do? Tamsin is right. I don't have a contract, and even if I did, I'm not in a position to sue my employer. If she wants me to go, go I must. Or should I hold fire and hang around until Robin or Pavla return, because I'm sure that Robin, at least, doesn't want me to leave? Or perhaps he does? Perhaps he's just a very nice man who doesn't like confrontation, particularly with his ill health. Perhaps he's asked Tamsin to do this whilst he's out.

I hesitate for a moment, but then I realise dignity must prevail. I leave the vacuum cleaner by Robin's desk and manage to control myself as I walk past Tamsin, keeping my back rigid and biting the inside of my cheek to stop myself from sobbing. It suited me to take a job here, not just because of my admiration for Robin, but also due to me being paid cash in hand. I would never have gotten the job if Pavla had looked into my past and followed up references and realised just where I've been for the past few years. But perhaps Tamsin has worked it out and she's sparing me the humiliation.

I walk into the utility room, put my jacket on and grab my handbag. I stride out of the back door without glancing backwards. And then I let the tears flow. It's so damned unfair. The newest Mrs Featherstone is a stuck-up, privileged cow who has taken a dislike to me, probably because I get on better with her husband than she does herself. Other than for her looks, I can't imagine why Robin married her. It's obvious she's just after his money. I collect my knackered but trusty old bicycle, which I've leaned against the garage wall, and wheel it down the drive. I wonder if I should ring Pavla and tell her that Tamsin's fired me. I don't suppose she'll be too happy that her conscientious cleaner has been given the boot, or perhaps Robin has already discussed it with her. I let out a sob.

Marek steps into the driveway from behind a tree and gives me the fright of my life. I give out a little yelp, only just saving my bike from toppling over.

'Why're you crying?' He stares at me, his face expressionless.

'I had some bad news.' I sniff and wipe my eyes with the back of my hand.

'Dad says I need to hug people when they're sad. I'm not that keen on hugs, but I will give you one if you like.'

He marches forwards. I put my hand up in front of me to stop him.

'It's kind of you, but no,' I say. I think I see a flash of annoyance cross his face, but it's hard to tell with Marek. He almost always has an inscrutable expression.

'Tamsin has fired me.'

'Fired?'

'Taken my job away.' That's another thing he does; frequently repeats what someone has just said, as if he needs to say it aloud to comprehend it.

He stares at me.

'Goodbye, Marek. You take care.' I wriggle my fingers at him and hop onto my bike. When I reach the bottom of the drive, I turn around to have a final look at Stave House. Marek is still standing there, staring at me. I'll miss this place. Most of all, I'll miss Robin.

IT TAKES a good twenty minutes to cycle back to my bedsit in town, along narrow country roads not designed for cyclists. I've had a couple of near misses over the past few months, but on the whole, I enjoy the ride. The countryside is lovely, with verdant hedgerows and woodland and quaint chocolate-box type houses, but most of all, I love the freedom. The cold air that stings my cheeks, the wind through my hair and even the rain that soaks through my clothes so that I reach home a soggy mess. I don't mind any of that, because it's so different to where I've come from. It makes me feel alive, and I truly appreciate that sense of freedom that only someone who has had all their liberties taken away will truly understand.

As I cycle up a steep hill, I reason with myself. That job was too good to be true. I mean, I didn't want to be a cleaner, not after studying the violin for all of my life. But at least it was cleaning for Robin Featherstone; we could talk music, and I had the inside track as to what he was working on. Then there was the money. I needed that desperately. Now I've got nothing. I doubt I have sufficient to pay next month's rent. I'll have to move. I'll have to go back to menial cleaning jobs and focus on getting as many gigs as I can. I'll busk if I have to. Oh, it's so ironic, when I think back. I was the golden girl; everyone said so, so it must have been true. I had a talent for music, but I also worked incredibly hard, and when I got that scholarship to study under one of Europe's most esteemed violin professors, it seemed like the world was my oyster. The violin is still my greatest consolation; I will play it when I get home. Some Bach perhaps, and then I'll put on some heavy metal and stomp around venting my fury – assuming the neighbours don't complain, because most of the time they do.

I snort at the concept of home. It's a minuscule bedsit with a single mattress on the floor, a small sink, a grimy microwave and a camping stove, but at least it's all mine, and I can come and go as I like, answering to no one. And that's what matters the most to me: freedom.

And therein lies the nub of my problems. I can't get 'proper' jobs because I don't have any references. I won't pass all the checks that employers like to have. They'll want to know what I have been doing and why, and when I tell them that the gap in my CV was because I was in prison, their eyebrows will knot together, and the corners of their lips will turn downwards, and they will say, 'Thank you for your interest. We'll be in touch.'

But they won't be in touch. because who wants to employ a woman who has no job history and who has been in prison? No one. I can't even get decent violin gigs because the competition is too stiff, and my contemporaries finished their degrees, but I didn't. And that's why I can't tell the truth.

6

TAMSIN

There's a rapping on the glass, and Pavla pokes her head around the door to the glasshouse. 'Sorry to disturb you, Tamsin, but where's Mia?'

I pull off my thick gardening gloves and place them slowly on the bench. 'I fired her.'

'Sorry?' Pavla frowns, a look of incomprehension crossing her face.

'I let her go, told her she wasn't doing her job properly.'

Pavla opens and closes her mouth. I suppose it must be annoying for her to have a new 'lady of the house'.

'What did she do wrong?'

'She was nosying around Robin's study, rooting through his stuff.' A little white lie isn't going to hurt. Nevertheless, I do feel a twang of guilt.

'I'm surprised. She's always seemed very conscientious. I suppose I'll have to look for someone else.' She pauses, makes as if she's going to turn around, but then stops. 'What does Robin say about this?'

'I haven't had a chance to discuss it with him, so kindly refrain from saying anything.'

Pavla's thin eyebrows scoot upwards.

'And yes, please look for a new cleaner,' I say.

'And who will help Robin with his admin?' Pavla asks.

'I shall.' I smile at Pavla, tilting my head to one side.

Pavla's eyes widen, but wisely, she doesn't say anything.

I WAIT a couple of minutes and then follow Pavla back into the house. I'm having second thoughts about firing Mia now, as I know I should have discussed it with Robin first, but it's for the best, isn't it? I can hear Robin practicing his scales, so I knock gently and push the door open. He stops when he sees me, and his face breaks into a smile.

'How did the doctor's appointment go?' I ask.

'Well. Apparently I should make a full recovery so long as I continue with the physio. Well, almost a full recovery, because this limp might be here to stay, but it shouldn't affect my music.'

'Oh, that's wonderful news!' I say, rushing over to throw my arms around his neck. I nudge him sideways and perch on the piano stool next to him. I place my lips over his, but he leans away from me.

'Where's Mia?' he asks.

Now that is more than frustrating. He is asking me where Mia is when I'm trying to kiss him. I take a deep breath, because I don't want to lose my cool.

'I let her go. I'm sorry, Robin, but she really wasn't doing a good job. Besides, I thought I could take on some of her role, help you with your paperwork, keep your studio clean and the like. What do you reckon?'

Robin slams both fists down onto the piano keys, the sounds jarring and making me jump off the stool. I am totally shocked, because Robin has never lost his temper in front of me.

'How dare you!' He stares at me, his head is trembling on his neck, and his lip is still drooping downwards. Surely I haven't given him another stroke?

'Mia is employed by me. She is nothing to do with you.'

I swallow. 'She has everything to do with me, because I'm your wife, Robin.' I try to speak as gently as possible, recalling the client interfacing and negotiating skills training that I was forced to take as part of my old job. 'We share this house, and I have as much right to choose who I have in it as you do. I know it must be hard for you having me here and having to compromise, especially as you've had a few years alone to do as you please. You promised me that all that was yours was mine and vice versa. Have you forgotten our marriage vows already?'

'You do not lecture me on marriage vows.' His words are slurring slightly. 'Mia is a musician. She was helping me, doing a great job.'

'She was also nosying into our affairs, and I don't trust her one iota,' I say. I suppose I knew Robin would be annoyed, but now I'm seeing a cold fury that fills me with unease. 'Look,' I say, trying to adopt an even more conciliatory tone, 'I didn't mean to upset you. That's the last thing I'd want to do. Let me help out. It would be great for us to spend more time together, for me to try to understand what you do.' I stroke the side of his face, but he leans away from me.

'You're not a musician, Tamsin, and you'll never be able to help me in the way that Mia could.' He refuses to meet my eyes.

'Perhaps, but you could at least let me try. I only want what's best for you.'

'Do you? Sometimes I wonder. Why didn't you come to the doctor with me today? Instead, you got Pavla to drive me. Where have you been the past few weeks as I've tried to recover?'

Tears sting my eyes. I might not have been the nursemaid he was expecting, but I've tried. I really have.

'It's you who banished me from our bedroom!' I say, my voice rising. 'It's you who said it was okay for me to go out as much as I wanted and that Pavla would accompany you to your medical appointments. And not once has anyone asked how I am. Yes, I know you're the invalid, but this isn't what I expected within the first few months of marriage.' I regret my words immediately. Why do I always do that, say the first thing that comes into my head without filtering it first?

'Do you think I want to be like this?' Robin roars. 'Do you think I'm happy that all you do is go out every day and use my credit card? That I feel like an impotent old man?'

'That's not fair! You're not an old man, and I love you. But you told me I could buy whatever I wanted.'

'And that's what I am to you, isn't it? A source of money, so you can buy your hideous cactus. A sickly old husband who you wish you hadn't married. I tried to ignore the jibes, the disquiet from my family, but I was wrong, wasn't I? I should have listened to Brooke and David, who said you're just a gold digger. It's made me realise, Tamsin, that I really don't think I know you at all.'

He looks exhausted now as he slumps over the keyboard, leaning his forehead on the glossy black piano lid.

'I'm sorry,' I say as I step towards him and lay a hand on his shoulder. 'None of that is right. I love you more than life itself. I was wrong to fire Mia, and I'm sorry.'

'Leave me. I want to be left alone.'

'I love you, Robin. I couldn't care less about your money. It's just I've found your illness difficult, and I know that's selfish of me because it's you who are suffering ...'

'I don't want to hear it, Tamsin,' Robin says again, his voice a mere whisper. 'Just leave me alone.'

I back out of the room, my eyes overflowing with tears,

my heart pounding. I've played this all wrong. I should have discussed Mia with Robin first, got him to support me, and then *he* could have fired her. Surely he would have sided with me. I've been an idiot, and now I've got to work out how to make things better, to make Robin realise that I love him in sickness or in health. Because I do, I really do.

As I walk upstairs to the bathroom, relieved not to bump into Pavla, I can't help but think about Dad. I've never told Robin what a monster Dad turned into after he got sick; how Mum gave up her life, quite literally, to care for an angry, often violent man who could never accept his own disabilities. I was nine years old, and up until that point my brother and I had had a very comfortable, middle-class upbringing. Mum worked in a florist's shop, and Dad worked in insurance.

He was also a fitness freak, particularly loving his football, helping train at the local youth football club. Every morning, he would get up early to go for a run and then ride his bicycle to work, returning home for 5.30 pm sharp, eager to be part of Donny's and my lives. He was a fun dad, kicking a ball around our small garden, helping us with our homework and tickling me until I cried.

It all changed one November afternoon. Dad didn't come home after work. Mum said he had gotten sick and was being looked after somewhere special. After that, she wasn't around much either, and Aunty Sue came to look after us, but no one told me or Donny what had really happened. On Christmas Eve, Aunty Sue sat Donny and me down on the sofa and told us that Father Christmas wouldn't be visiting this year, because Mum and Dad didn't have any money. 'Why does that matter?' Donny squealed, and then Aunty Sue told us that Father Christmas wasn't real anyway, and we needed to cut Mum a bit of slack because of all the pressure she was under. Christmas was

awful that year; we didn't even eat turkey, even though it
was Mum's favourite. In the New Year, Mum was around
more, but she looked like an old woman. One day, many
weeks later, she sat us down and told us that Dad was in the
hospital because he'd had a very serious injury after being
knocked off his bike by a dustbin lorry. Donny demanded
we go and visit him, but Mum said no, it would be too difficult for us.

I just wanted my dad back and couldn't understand why
we weren't allowed to go and see him, and why our happy
home had had all its colour bleached out of it. Donny ran
away one evening and was returned by the police a few hours
later. Mum was quite hysterical, and Aunty Sue sent me to
bed even though it was two hours before my bedtime. Later,
Donny told me he had run away to the hospital, but they
didn't let him in to see Dad and instead called the police,
because he was only seven and a half years old. I thought it
was daring of Donny. I was rather jealous he'd had the
gumption.

Ten months and five days after Dad disappeared, he came
home. If I thought our household was colourless before Dad
got home, afterwards, it turned into shades of charcoal and
black. What a shock it was seeing this man who claimed to be
our dad. He was an amputee, having lost his legs from the
knees downwards. His upper body was partially paralysed,
too, and he couldn't do even the simplest things like cutting
up his food or navigating his fork into his mouth. His speech
was weird, and the left half of his face looked like it had
slipped downwards. This wasn't our dad. This was some kind
of monster.

With hindsight, Mum made a terrible mistake by not
telling us what had happened, or at least warning us that Dad
no longer looked like the man we knew. Donny and I took
one glance at him and ran away. I couldn't stop sobbing for

hours; it took months before I could bring myself to actually look Dad in the face when I talked to him.

Dad had turned into an angry man, frustrated with himself, furious with the unfair fate that had befallen him, the injustice of it all, and he took out his fury mostly on Mum, but often on me, too. Mum gave up everything to care for Dad. She quit floristry and took a job as a carer in an old people's home, working nights so she could be there for Dad during the day and making sure she kept up the mortgage payments. If he needed anything at night, it was me who had to respond, but mostly he slept, thanks to a cocktail of alcohol and painkillers. Mum gave up her friends and her hobbies, and she never smiled. Her life revolved around my dad's needs, but whatever she did was never good enough. And then, one September morning four years later, when he was watching *EastEnders* on the telly, Dad had a heart attack and died.

I know it's a horrible thing to say, but it was such a relief. Donny and I thought that Mum might find herself a new partner, move out of that oppressive house, return to floristry. But that wasn't to be. She died just five weeks later from undiagnosed pancreatic cancer. I've thought about it a lot over the years, and I think she sacrificed her life for my dad.

I always promised myself that I wouldn't play second fiddle to my husband, that I should remember that the needs of both partners are of equal importance. But I wonder if I've taken that too far. I denied it to myself at first, but if I'm being truly honest, that's probably why I haven't shown up for Robin. All I can think about is Mum and what a raw deal she got, and how I don't want to be like her. It terrifies me that I might give up my friends, my hobbies, my identity to look after Robin, and then when he dies, there'll be nothing left of me.

We went to live with Aunty Sue, which wasn't any fun.

Shortly before my sixteenth birthday, I read a newspaper article that explained the dustbin lorry driver's insurers had paid out an undisclosed sum to Dad. I asked Aunty Sue what had happened to the money, and she said that it was in the bank, available to Donny and me whenever we needed it. Half of what was left of that compensation money went to Donny, who gambled it away. My half paid for my education. I wanted to be more like the posh kids who wore clothes with logos and had fancy cars when they turned eighteen. Sure, I could have spent the money there and then, but I remembered the quote by Dr. Seuss: *'The more that you read, the more things you will know, the more that you learn, the more places you'll go.'* And I wanted to go places. So I took myself to a private sixth form college, where I learned how to speak with a plum in my throat, and I got a place at university where I worked hard for my degree in Communication Studies. Then I got a job in PR, where I never earned a lot, but sufficient to get by. And then I met Robin. Now my life is complete.

7

MIA

It's freezing cold. I'm standing just outside a shopping centre in Crawley, one of the few places that's under-cover so as to protect me – and most importantly, my violin – from the rain. I'm wearing layers of clothes and fingerless gloves, but it's still miserable, and I'm wedging my jaw downwards onto my violin's chin rest to stop my teeth from chattering. I've been here for a couple of hours and reckon I've earned about £1.20 from busking. I don't have a busking license, so I'm constantly on the lookout for any official who might move me on.

I catch the eye of a woman wearing a thick red beanie. There's something familiar about her, so I glance away and launch into Jealousy Tango, making it sound as showy as I can.

'Mia?' she asks, stepping forwards.

I stop playing.

'Oh my god! It's really you! What are you doing out here?' the woman asks.

It takes a long moment for me to place her. Then I recall that we were in a quartet together at music college.

'It's me, Lexi,' she explains.

'Hi, Lexi,' I say, reddening slightly as I recall what success she's had. She plays the violin in a gypsy jazz band called The Tangobles that's had loads of media coverage. How embarrassing that she heard me playing my version of such a well-known tango. I wonder whether she knows what happened to me. Probably not, as she would have hurried on by.

'It's so good to see you, Mia. Goodness, it's been such a long time. After you left college early, it's like you just disappeared into thin air. I'd love to catch up. Have you got time for a coffee?'

I'm really surprised she doesn't know what happened to me, but relieved too. I glance at my watch and pretend to think. But who am I kidding? I have no work and nowhere to be. But is it even a good idea to talk to Lexi? Perhaps she's pretending, and she really knows the truth.

'Come on. My treat! You look like you're freezing out here, and I could do with a caffeine kick.' She laughs.

'Sure, that would be great.' I bend down and place my violin in its case and hurriedly stuff the few coins into my jacket pocket. I've recited my cover story so many times, I almost believe it myself.

'Busking's great, isn't it,' Lexi says as I straighten up and hook my violin case over my shoulder. 'I busk sometimes when I'm putting together new repertoire.'

I nod, wondering what she would think of me if she knew this was my only source of income.

'So what have you been up to?' Lexi asks. 'I'm sorry we lost touch. I always thought you were one of the best violinists at college.'

'Really? That's very kind of you. I've seen some of your stories on social media, how you've been travelling the world with your gypsy jazz band. Congratulations.'

'You know what it's like. It all looks so glamorous from the outside, when in reality it's weeks spent in buses, living in cheap hotels, practicing in draughty acoustically poor halls, but at least we're making some sort of a living, however paltry it is, and visiting new places.'

She opens the door to a little independent coffee shop, and I follow Lexi inside, relieved to be hit by a wall of warmth and the delicious scent of roasting coffee. We walk up to the counter, and Lexi throws a smile at the barista.

'I'll have a Café Misto. And you?' Lexi asks.

I glance at the carefully written menu on the blackboard behind the counter and choose the cheapest item, just in case she doesn't pay for my drink. 'English breakfast tea, please,' I say.

The barista pushes the drinks across the counter. I make as if I'm removing my wallet from my bag.

'Put that away,' Lexi says, to my relief. I pick up my tea and follow her to a small table in front of the window, where we settle down opposite each other.

'You know that Roby Lakatos piece you were playing back there, and the Jealousy Tango, it's the sort of music we're performing on tour.'

'Yes, I know,' I say, imagining how wonderful it must be to play the upbeat music you love for an audience night after night.

'I'm only back home because Leah, our second violinist, has broken her arm. Don't suppose you'd be free to take her place, would you?'

I almost drop my teacup. 'Me?'

Lexi laughs. 'Come on, Mia. Don't tell me you've lost all your confidence. I don't know why I didn't think of you before when we were mooting names. I guess you've just totally disappeared off the radar. I thought you might have moved abroad or left the world of music.'

I smile tightly. There's no way that I'm going to tell Lexi where I've really been.

'The thing is, we're totally pressed for time. We need someone to take over, like, yesterday. We've had to cancel our performances for a fortnight, and our manager is getting antsy. We're meant to be in Paris next week, and he refuses to cancel. I need to find a replacement violinist urgently.'

'There must be loads of people who can fit in,' I say, drumming my index finger on my thigh under the table.

'You'd have thought so, but there's always a problem. The dates don't work, or they don't play gypsy jazz in the way we do, and we really wanted a girl, as we're an all-girl band. So far, no luck. Please say you'll consider it.' Lexi leans forwards across the table, her black, beaded hair flicking forwards. 'Can you come and audition tomorrow morning? I mean, it's not really an audition, just for the other two to hear you play and to make sure that you like our way of playing and you like us. Please say yes, Mia. I can email you the repertoire, but I'm sure it'll be easy for you to pick up.'

This seems like a dream about to come true. Could I really be travelling around Europe, playing in a quartet next week? I smile gingerly, because I can't let Lexi know that I want to stand on the table and scream yes.

'Where and when?' I ask.

THE NEXT DAY, I take the train to London, buying a ticket with the pittance I've earned from busking combined with the last few pounds I have. Next week, my money will have totally run out; I'll need to leave the bedsit and sofa-surf with friends or move back to Dad's flat, where I'll also be on the sofa. From Victoria Station, I walk all the way through Hyde Park and Kensington Gardens, relieved that it's not raining, because I don't want to waste money on the bus or tube. I walk briskly with my violin case on my back and enjoy the newly emerging daffodils and the blossom just starting to peek from the bare branches. On the other side of the park, I stride past Notting Hill Gate tube station and follow the satnav directions on my phone to a beautiful street with grandiose, stucco-fronted buildings. I ring the gold buzzer of the smartest London house I've ever stood in front of.

Lexi swings open the shiny black door. She's wearing black leggings and a cropped top, showing off her toned midriff.

'Come in, come in!' she exclaims. I follow her down a wide hallway and into a beautiful room with pale blue painted walls and ornate architraves and a parquet floor laid in a zigzag pattern. Light floods in through patio doors that look onto a small courtyard at the back of the building. The room is empty except for four chairs, four metal music stands, discarded instrument cases on the floor and foam acoustic panels attached to the walls and ceilings. Two young women are standing at the side chatting.

'Mia, this is Kira, our cellist, and Suzy, who plays the viola.'

Both the women smile at me warmly. I assume we're all a similar age, in our late twenties or early thirties, and I can immediately see why Lexi thought I might be a good fit. I know musicians should never be judged on their looks, but the depressing reality is that booking agents and managers are going to scoop up performers who are pleasing to the eye and tick all the diversity boxes, and this small group does just that. Lexi, the lead violinist, is tall, long-boned with ebony skin and numerous strands of black, beaded hair. Kira, who plays the cello, is a curvy redhead with titian locks that tumble over her shoulders and big dimples in her creamy cheeks. Suzy is of Chinese descent, a surprisingly petite girl considering she plays a full-sized viola, with rosebud lips, a ring in her nose and hair razored so close to her head, it looks like a tightly fitted sheer hat. And then there's me, who ticks the white Caucasian box, with my blonde hair and blue eyes. For a moment, this repels me. Do I want to be part of this wokeness? Shouldn't we just be chosen because of how well we play our instruments and how blended our sound is? But beggars can't be choosers. I need a lucky break, so I smile at them and take my violin out of its case, warming up with a few scales. We then take our seats, and Lexi hands out some sheet music.

'Let's start with some of the easier pieces,' she says. We tune up and start playing. There's tightness in my neck and tension in my fingers and shoulders. It's been so long since I've performed, and I feel judged, but after a few minutes, I lose myself in the music. Although I make the odd mistake, I'm good enough to improvise. Besides, I know most of these tunes, if not these particular arrangements. Eventually, Lexi takes her violin down from her shoulder.

'So, girls, what do you think?'

Suzy bursts out laughing. 'The last woman we auditioned was out of here in three minutes flat. How long have we been practicing for?' She glances at her watch, and I do the same, amazed that we've been playing for over an hour. 'Time flies when you're having fun, hey, Mia?' Suzy says.

'Welcome to the band.' Lexi leans over and pats me on the shoulder. 'All agreed?'

Suzy and Kia simultaneously nod and smile at me.

'We've got a four-week tour of Europe coming up, starting with Paris next week. Are you up for that, Mia?' Lexi asks.

'You bet I am!'

I walk out of that London townhouse with utter relief. I feel like dancing and singing and giving thanks that my luck has changed at long last. This is a new start for me. I'll be back doing what I love the most, travelling the world, and although the money is lousy, at least I'll be able to save, as all my living expenses will be paid for. And best of all, no one has asked for references. Of course this isn't a permanent post, just until the main second violinist recovers from her broken arm, but it certainly feels like my lucky break. Now, I've got four days to get my life together, practice the repertoire as much as I can and step into my future. A future where having a criminal record isn't going to be a problem.

THREE DAYS LATER, I've given notice on my bedsit, and I'm lugging two suitcases to Dad's place, with my violin case strapped over my back. Inside the bags are all my worldly belongings, most of which I'm going to leave at his flat. Lexi has explained that space is at a premium in the small six-seat tour minibus that their agent has rented. One seat for each of us girls, one for Kira's cello and another seat for the cases for our two violins and one viola. The paltry boot will fit our luggage, which includes our black concert clothes and toiletries. I'm not worried about the lack of space, because I don't have much stuff anyway. I'm just thrilled that I'm going to be travelling through Europe and playing the violin most nights with three other talented players. This is freedom personified, exactly what I dreamed of.

Dad lives in a tower block in Fulham. That's the thing about London: You have all the fancy multimillion-pound houses, and right next door is a tower block or two. I don't suppose the Fulham yummy mummies are too keen on the yobbos who live in the council tower blocks, but we've been here longer than they have. Dad's flat is small. He has one bedroom and a living room. When I stay over, I sleep on the sofa. I've just pressed the button on the lift – which today, fortunately, is working – when my phone rings, displaying a withheld number.

'Hello,' I say, wedging the phone under my chin.

'Mia?'

I recognise the voice immediately.

'It's Robin Featherstone. How are you?'

'Um, alright. And you?' This is awkward.

'I'm doing well, but I'd like to see you.'

'I'm about to go off on tour. I've joined The Tangobles, they're a gypsy jazz band.'

'Congratulations! I'm delighted for you. I've been wondering how you are. Do you think you could come and see me before you leave? It's important.'

I hesitate, because I only have one day left and I'd hoped to spend it with Dad.

'It's very important,' he reiterates. 'A private matter. And I want to apologise to you in person. Letting you go was not my decision. Please come and see me, Mia.'

'Okay,' I say reluctantly, agreeing only because Robin Featherstone is so influential in the music world, and a reference from him could be very useful. And, of course, I like the man, not that that counts for anything.

'Thank you, Mia. Come early tomorrow morning. Can you manage 8 am? I'll leave the door on the latch so you can let yourself in. I think it's best if you avoid seeing Pavla or Tamsin, don't you?'

'Yes,' I say cautiously. This is very weird. Why does he want me to go so early in the morning? I'm about to ask whether I can delay seeing him until my return, but Robin has already hung up. What does he want with me?

THE NEXT MORNING, I'm up at the crack of dawn. I hurry to Victoria Station, which is very quiet this early on a Sunday morning. I'm relieved that the train is on time. I take a taxi from Horsham station to Stave House using money that Dad insisted on giving me last night. I wonder if Robin has any idea how financially stretched I am. Just asking me to visit him puts me in the red. Maybe I can ask him to pay my travel costs.

It's a chilly but bright morning, and a low mist has settled across the fields, making it look as if the trees are hovering over a sea of smoke. I feel a weird nervousness as I ask the taxi driver to drop me at the bottom of the drive, worried that the crunching of the car tyres might wake up Tamsin or alert Pavla. I have no desire to see Tamsin again, although that feeling of anger has dissipated. She probably did me a favour by sacking me, as I wouldn't be in the position I'm in now, about to go off on tour.

It's strange walking up the driveway of the house I thought I'd never see again. Spring is late this year, and the trees are just beginning to bud, and daffodils are poking their heads out of the neatly maintained borders either side of the drive, at an earlier stage of growth than in London. I can't see Pavla's cottage from the drive, and I'm glad not to see Marek or her husband, Thomas, either. The curtains in the upstairs rooms of the house are drawn, and for a moment, I wonder whether I've been asked here on false pretences. I step up to the heavy white front door and see that it's very slightly open. I push it and walk inside, tiptoeing through the familiar entrance hall and down the corridor towards Robin's studio. Unusually, the studio door is wide open, and Robin is sitting at his desk, still wearing his pyjamas and navy dressing gown. He smiles broadly when I rap very gently on the door.

'Come in, Mia. Please shut the door behind you.'

I do as he says and sit down in the chair opposite him. I'm disappointed that he isn't looking much better. If anything, his face is more gaunt, the dark circles under his eyes pronounced.

'It's good to see you,' he says. 'I was very sorry my wife asked you to leave. It wasn't what I wanted.'

'Thank you. I'm really not sure what I did wrong.'

'Me neither.' There is sadness in his eyes. 'But as you'll learn when one day you get married, you have to pick your battles.' He rubs his eyes with his long, slender fingers, and I notice that his nails are no longer neatly trimmed as they used to be. Perhaps he doesn't have the dexterity to do it himself any longer.

'I won't deny I was very upset,' I say. 'But it's all worked out, because now I'm going on tour doing what I really wanted to do.'

'Indeed, and I wish you well for the future. You deserve success and happiness. But what a mess I've made.'

'Sorry?' I frown, wondering what he's referring to.

'The thing is, Mia, this may well be the last time we see each other, and I want you to know that I hold you in the highest esteem, and I'm sorry that it wasn't me who gave you your lucky career break. You're a good person, Mia, despite the adversity–'

I hold my breath, wondering with horror what he's about to say, but he immediately changes tack. Surely he doesn't know the truth?

'I'm also very aware that you saved my life.'

I smile with relief. 'I just happened to be there at the right time. It's not like I did anything special.'

He smiles wanly. 'Make your dreams come true, Mia. Use all of your inner strength. I'm just sad that this might be the last time I see you.'

I frown, shocked by his statement. 'I'll happily come back and see you, and if I don't have too much violin work, perhaps I could help you out in the future. That's if your wife wouldn't mind.'

He tilts his head to one side and sighs. 'I have my doubts that I'll be here when you return.'

'If you don't mind me asking, are you sick again?'

He shakes his head. 'No, but it's such a mess, dear Mia. Such a mess.'

Then there are footsteps from creaking floorboards upstairs. 'I think you should go now, Mia. Thank you very much for humouring me. I wish you health and happiness for the future.'

I stand up.

'Goodbye, my dear.' He stays seated in his chair.

'I *will* see you again,' I say, infusing my words with confidence.

He shakes his head ever so slightly, and I wonder what he knows that I don't. A sense of disquiet courses through me, an unsettling feeling as if something terrible is going to happen, but there are absolutely no indicators as to what that might be.

'Tamsin is getting up now, so please leave, Mia.'

I do as he says. With a quick glance back at him, I slip out of his study and tiptoe back the way I came, out the front door, which I close quietly behind me. As I walk down the drive, I look back up at the house, wondering if I'll see any faces at the windows. I don't. All is quiet. It isn't until I've reached the road and I'm pulling my phone out of my handbag to dial for a taxi that I realise I didn't ask Robin for any money. And I'm absolutely none the wiser as to why he actually wanted to see me.

8

TAMSIN

Last night, Robin and I went out for dinner. It was the first time we've been anywhere since his stroke, which seemed like a really big milestone. I wore a new fitted black dress that hugged my curves, and although it sounds vain, I really did look good. You know when you walk into a restaurant and all the diners turn around to gaze at you and your husband looks on admiringly? Well, that's what it was like. The men wanted me; the women wanted to be me.

The trouble was, conversation at dinner was stilted. It's as if Robin and I have forgotten how to talk to each other, and although I tried to initiate conversation, he spent most of the time concentrating on cutting up his food and navigating his fork to his mouth. I glowered at a neighbouring diner who was staring at me. I suppose she was wondering what I was doing with this older man. At the end of the meal, when the waiter presented us with the bill, I said very loudly, 'My husband will take care of that, won't you, darling?'

Robin threw me a strange look, because let's face it, I've never paid a restaurant bill since we've been together. Back at home, I put my arms around his neck and tried to kiss him, but he pulled away from me.

'I'm sorry, darling. But I'm not ready yet,' he said.

'But we had such a good love life before your stroke. I'm missing you,' I moaned, running my tongue up his neck.

'All in good time. I still find you beautiful, Tamsin, but you have to be patient with me.'

'Can we at least sleep in the same bed? I want to feel you next to me.'

Robin sighed. 'I've turned into an insomniac, and it would be better if we still sleep apart.'

I tried to protest, but he refused, point blank. My husband refused to sleep with me. Talk about a slap in the face.

'Do you want me to take a lover?' I asked.

He looked absolutely livid; I regretted my words immediately.

'I'm sorry, darling. I'd never do that,' I said, grabbing his hand, but he pulled his hand away and narrowed his eyes as if he didn't believe me. Then he turned and shuffled out of the room.

I SLEEP BADLY because I hate myself. I want to stay married to Robin, but I keep on saying the wrong thing, forgetting that recovery is possible, but it can be a long process. Just because Dad morphed into a bastard and never recovered doesn't mean the same will happen to Robin. I need to hold my tongue, to think before I speak, remember that he must be hurting too. Several times, I get out of bed and walk to the door with the intention of going to Robin to apologise. But what if I wake him up? Then he really will be annoyed.

Now that pale sunlight is seeping through the curtains, I get up and pad to the bathroom. Then I stop still. It sounds like Robin is talking to someone downstairs. I strain to listen, but there's silence. Perhaps he's talking to himself. It wouldn't surprise me, because he's been acting so strangely recently. I know he's angry with the world and taking it out on me, but it's not fair. I didn't handle things well last night, but there's got to be give and take. I don't care if there is some temporary disfunction in our lovemaking; we can get through that. I just want to feel his arms around me. I'm going to have to have a proper heart-to-heart with him later, but first we've got to get through Sunday lunch. Brooke is coming over, and heaven knows why, but Robin is insistent that we have a family lunch all together. Not exactly my idea of fun.

When I'm showered and dressed, I go downstairs, expecting to find Robin in his study, but he's not there. I tiptoe back upstairs and gently open the door to the master bedroom. Robin is in bed, his back towards the door. I whisper his name very quietly, but he doesn't stir.

As he's asleep, I don't suppose he'll mind if I'm in my greenhouse, so I spend the best part of the morning tending to my cacti. Around midday, I make my way to the kitchen.

'Something smells good,' I say.

Pavla is vigorously stirring a wooden spoon in a saucepan on the stove. 'Roast beef and my special Yorkshire puddings,' she says. 'Followed by treacle tart and ice cream, Robin's favourite.'

'He has such old-school taste.'

Pavla chuckles. 'It's something to do with British boarding school, I think. Such a strange thing, sending your children off to school, leaving them to the care of an institution.'

'You don't have that sort of education in the Czech Republic?'

'Goodness, no.'

'I rather wish I had been sent to boarding school,' I murmur.

Pavla stops stirring and raises an eyebrow at me.

'Not the happiest of childhoods, well, at least, after the age of ten. Unfortunately, there was no chance of me being sent off anywhere.'

'Me neither,' Pavla says.

I'm surprised by this bonding moment. Pavla and I have absolutely nothing in common – frankly, I've found it rather awkward having her around all the time. This woman with her strong accent, who knows Robin and his family so much better than I do. I get the feeling that she judges me and I've come up wanting. It's hard to put a finger on why I sense that, because she is always polite, but I definitely get the impression that she doesn't approve of me. Probably because I'm so much younger than Robin and nothing like Claudia.

'Would you like any help in preparing lunch?' I ask. I frequently ask the same question, even though she never says yes.

'Thank you, but it's all under control.'

Then I hear footsteps coming down the hallway, and Brooke strides into the kitchen. She's wearing tightly fitted brown leather trousers and an oversized cream jumper.

'Hello, Pavla,' she says, 'Tamsin,' muttering my name as an afterthought. 'Hope you've got enough food, because Mum's joining us. She's just nipped down to Dad's study to say hello.'

I can't believe this! Claudia has shown up, uninvited, treating this house as if she's still Robin's wife. Pavla throws me a glance, and I'm relieved that she looks as annoyed as I feel. I recall when Robin told Claudia that she needed to make an appointment before turning up at Stave House. I wonder whether that instruction still applies.

HALF AN HOUR LATER, we're all sitting at the table in the dining room. I'm trying to contain my annoyance that

Claudia has inveigled her way in yet again, and that Robin hasn't thrown her out. But after him rejecting me last night, I don't want to challenge Robin today, and certainly not in front of Claudia and Brooke. The atmosphere is horrible.

'How's the physio going, Robin?' Claudia asks, scooping several roast potatoes onto her plate.

'Fine.'

'Come on, Dad. We need more than a one-word answer.' Brooke stares at her father.

Robin ignores her and instead turns to Pavla, who is placing a bowl of Brussel sprouts on the table. 'The meat's overcooked, Pavla. Why the hell can't you ever get it right?'

Pavla purses her lips together, and the tension shows in her neck muscles. I can't believe Robin is talking to her like that.

'That's not fair,' I say, leaping to Pavla's defence. 'Look how beautifully pink it is in the middle.' I point to a thin sliver of beef on Robin's plate.

'The woman never gets it right, do you? You know it has to be melt-in-the-mouth; otherwise, I struggle with it.'

'Would you like another piece?' Pavla asks. 'Or I can cut it up into smaller slices.'

Robin waves her away. 'Go back to the kitchen.'

I squirm with embarrassment as Pavla returns to the kitchen. This behaviour isn't like Robin; it's horrible to watch. Claudia frowns slightly, while Brooke doesn't appear to notice.

'You need to be nicer to Pavla,' I say in a low voice to my husband. 'If you're not careful, we'll have no help at all.'

'What's happened to that other cleaning girl?' Brooke asks, in her strident voice.

'You mean Mia,' Robin says, pushing his food around on his plate. 'Tamsin fired her.'

'What did she do?' Brooke looks delighted. 'If you found her nicking stuff, we need to go to the police.'

'No, it was nothing like that. She just wasn't doing a good job,' I say.

'I disagree,' Robin retorts.

Claudia raises an eyebrow. For the very first time, I think I see some respect in her eyes. She probably assumed that I was the subservient second wife, pandering to all of Robin's needs. 'Trouble in paradise already?' she asks with a grin on her narrow face. Perhaps I got that wrong. Perhaps she's just waiting for a crack to appear in our relationship so she can step back in.

I don't say another word for the rest of the meal and just zone out as Claudia and Brooke talk between themselves, nattering about Claudia's horse and Brooke's plans to fly off for a spa break in Thailand. As soon as the meal is finished, I know I need to get out of the house, away from the toxic atmosphere. Once again, my cacti call me. Any discussions with Robin will have to wait until later.

I stride through the kitchen towards the utility room. Pavla is putting her coat on, and for one horrible moment, I wonder if she's walking out on us. Frankly, I wouldn't blame her after the way Robin talked to her. There's a pile of dirty pans in the sink that need washing. I don't mind doing it, but I have to admit I've become very lazy on the domestic front, and I rather like it that way.

'I'm sorry about that,' I say. 'Robin shouldn't speak to you in that way.'

She raises her shoulders but carries on doing up the zip on her coat.

'You're leaving?' I ask.

'Just nipping down to the chemist to pick up Robin's prescription before it closes.'

'Oh.' I breathe out a sigh of relief.

A flicker of a smile plays at her lips. I wonder if she realised what I was thinking. Of course Pavla isn't going to quit Robin's employment that easily. She's got what I assume is free accommodation in the cottage, and she, her husband and Marek are dependent upon the Featherstones' goodwill.

'I really am sorry Robin was so rude to you,' I say.

'He's angry with himself and the world.'

'Yes, but it's not right to take it out on you.'

'Don't worry. I'm used to it,' Pavla says. It's a strange statement because in the year I've known Robin, he has never been offensive like that. I would like to ask her some more questions, but she scuttles out of the back door.

I lose myself in the greenhouse for another couple of hours, by which time I hope that Brooke and Claudia have left and Pavla has returned. As the light begins to fade, I amble back to the house. The back door is unlocked, and when I walk into the kitchen, I see that the pots and pans are still in the sink. Perhaps Pavla decided not to return to Stave House this afternoon. I can't blame her, really; it is a Sunday, and she has every right to chill with her husband and son. I sigh. I'll do them myself, but first I want to talk to Robin. I'm going to be very conciliatory and explain to him why I'm finding his illness so difficult. He needs to know the full extent of my relationship with Dad, and I'll have to be unusually vulnerable. I'm ready for that, because this marriage has to work.

I hang my coat up on a hook in the utility room and walk down the corridor to Robin's study. The light is off and the door slightly ajar. That's strange. He normally only rests for half an hour or so after lunch. Perhaps he's still in bed. I walk back along the corridor and into the hall, and then time stops still.

Robin is lying crumpled in a heap at the bottom of the

stairs. His legs are bent at the strangest of angles, and he's totally still. I throw myself onto the ground next to him.

'No!' I scream. His glassy eyes are open and staring upwards. Unseeing.

'Wake up, Robin! Wake up!' I slap his cheek, shake his body. My hand comes away wet and slithery, and I scream again when I realise it's blood.

'Wake up, Robin!'

I am trembling and sobbing, and throw myself over my husband's static body. But I know it's too late.

Robin is dead.

9

TAMSIN

R obin is dead. My brilliant husband is dead.

I can never apologise to him. He died thinking the worst of me. And I am a widow.

I honestly don't know how I have got through the past ten days. It started off a confusion of paramedics and police and questions, which quickly gave way to sympathy. Thick, treacly sympathy from everyone and massive displays of exaggerated grief from Brooke and Claudia, full of heavy tears and snot. It's as if Claudia were still Robin's wife, the way she's been courting sympathy and hanging around Stave House. The only person who seems to be genuine is Pavla, who from time to time I've found bustling around, doing the ironing or the cooking, eyes brimming with tears, but ever efficient and determined to keep the show on the road.

Robin fell down the stairs. To think that one moment he was up there, eager to rebuild his health, following the strict regime given to him by his physiotherapist, no doubt hurrying downstairs to write out a melody, and the next moment he slipped. He tumbled down the whole flight, banging his head against the bottom step, landing with horrific force on the stone floor in the hall. And what is so heartbreaking is that not one of us was there to catch him. I haven't dared ask whether I might have saved him if I'd returned to the house an hour or so earlier. The grief is too immense and the blame too cutting.

I hate thinking about 'what if', but I do it all the time. What if Dad hadn't been knocked off his bike? What if Mum's cancer had been caught earlier? What if I had been clever enough to take a degree in Law rather than Communication Studies, then I might have been rich in my own right? What if I hadn't discovered my ex-boyfriend had been made redundant and I'd married him? What if I could have saved Robin? It's all futile, isn't it, those self-destructive thoughts that swirl around my brain. Robin's GP has given me a two-week prescription of diazepam, and thank goodness. At least it dulls those racing thoughts and the bone-shattering shock.

There have been so many decisions to make, many of which I am ill equipped to decide upon, both because I haven't known Robin for long and because my brain feels so sluggish and woolly. I have turned to Claudia from time to time, and she's lapped that up. I want to get it right for Robin, to make sure that we have hymns that he enjoyed, flowers that he loved, prayers that are infused with meaning, and that we play the compositions that he was most proud of. The lovely people at the funeral home have been accommodating, patient with me, despite my inability to make all the decisions in a timely manner. Grief hits everyone in different ways, they say. It's hit me like a sledgehammer.

TODAY IS ROBIN'S FUNERAL, and I am the grieving widow, the centre of attention. I am trying to forget the difficult, acrimonious few weeks of our marriage after Robin's stroke and to focus on the happier times. It makes the grief purer and less complicated. So here I am, a widow at thirty-four after the briefest of marriages. What will the future hold for me? I am alone yet again, and I so didn't want to be alone. The only consolation is that I should be well provided for. Wealthy, I assume. Yes, it's distasteful and avaricious even to think of such practicalities, but I have to look after myself. No one else will.

I put on a black shift dress with a matching black jacket over the top, black stockings and black shoes. My makeup is minimal. I considered buying one of those little pillar box hats with a veil, but that will probably be too much for a country funeral. Instead, I slip on a new black cashmere coat with fox-fur cuffs and look at myself in the mirror. My face is pale, made even paler by the all-black outfit. I put on a pair of sunglasses. Yes, I look the epitome of classy grief. I sigh as I stuff a couple of Robin's cotton handkerchiefs in my small black handbag. Taking a deep breath, I walk downstairs, avoiding the step where my beloved met his death and out to the waiting taxi. I have not offered Brooke, Claudia or Pavla and her family to come with me. I thought it only fitting that I arrive alone.

I have no idea how many people will turn up to pay their respects, but I assume many, if only out of curiosity. I can imagine what they're saying. *She's bumped off her husband. She only married him for the money. Her grief will be fake.* Claudia and Brooke are certainly acting that way; it sickens me. And today will be the first time I meet David. The elusive only son.

There are a few people hurrying into the crematorium, but I shall be the only person to walk behind the coffin. The funeral director asked whether Robin's family would wish to do that, and I said yes. I just haven't told Brooke, David or Claudia. That might sound mean, but at the end of the day, I am Robin's wife. His next of kin.

I stand at the door and look at the sea of heads. The

crematorium chapel is packed, with people wedged along each pew and stragglers standing at the back. And then the hearse arrives behind me, and the coffin bearers slide out the coffin, bedecked with a profusion of lilies. I stifle a little sob and am glad that I'm wearing dark glasses. My Robin is in that box.

'Are you ready, ma'am?'

I take a very deep breath and nod.

The music starts, a full orchestral piece that Robin wrote for a nature television programme, and the funeral bearers walk forwards while I follow a few steps behind. The hum of low voices fades, and I can feel numerous eyes on me, the grieving widow. I take a seat on the front pew, next to Brooke, and try to stop my shoulders from quivering. I glance along the pew, expecting to see David, but there is only Claudia, who throws me daggers. Pavla is seated on the row behind with Thomas, her oafish-looking husband, and Marek, who wriggles uncomfortably in an ill-fitting suit. And then the service starts.

I don't know how I get through it. I think it's because I pretend I'm on a beach in the Caribbean, waiting for Robin to emerge from the calm, turquoise waters. I know it's denial on my half, but if I really absorb what's happening, I'll break. But when they close the curtains and Robin's coffin disappears from view, I'm not the only person letting out a sob. Claudia is weeping openly, which seems rather ironic, since she's very much the ex-wife, and Brooke is inconsolable. I lift up my dark glasses and dab my eyes with one of Robin's handkerchiefs. When it's time to leave, I keep my head held up high as I walk out of the chapel, looking straight ahead.

I have organised limousines to ferry the family back to Stave House, and I'm relieved that the first one is for me and me only. I sink into the leather seat and close my eyes.

·   ·   ·

PAVLA HAS ORGANISED a catering company to prepare and serve the canapés and drinks, so all I need to do is make small talk with the guests. As soon as I'm home, I rush upstairs and touch up my makeup, removing all the smeared mascara from my cheeks. When I'm looking decent, I return downstairs and grab a glass of champagne. Filled glasses have been left on a side table in the hall. I tip back a glass and ready myself, walking into the living room, where all the furniture has been pushed back against the walls. The only person here is Brooke.

'Where's David?'

She sighs. 'Couldn't make it.'

I open my mouth, but Brooke speaks too quickly. 'You don't need to say anything. I'm livid and so is Mum. He has a big business deal going through in Switzerland that apparently he can't leave. It's bullshit, of course.'

'Surely he would want to pay his final respects to your dad?'

'You would have thought so, wouldn't you? But David is a shit. Only thinks about himself. Mum is really hurt.'

'I'm not surprised,' I say, my feelings softening towards Brooke and Claudia. I suppose David has come up with an excuse because he had such a bad relationship with his father, and he doesn't want to play the grieving son, but even so, it's utterly disrespectful. I feel a pang of hurt on Robin's behalf. Even if they'd fallen out, it doesn't mean he should avoid his father's funeral.

Then the rest of the guests start to arrive, and I recognise nobody, so I just stand there and nod demurely as they all introduce themselves to me and offer their sincerest condolences. I'm just about to seek out a waitress for another glass of champagne when I hear the clearing of a throat behind me.

'Mrs Featherstone?'

'Yes,' I say, turning to look at a balding man.

'I'm Timothy Carter, Robin's solicitor and long-standing family friend. I have a copy of his latest will. When would you like me to share the contents with the family?' His piggy eyes flit around the room. I can't decide if it's because I make him nervous or whether he's just the shifty type.

'By the family, I assume you mean Brooke, as David hasn't shown up?'

'Indeed. Obviously, there's no need to do it now. We can arrange it for another time, either here or at my office.'

'There's no time like the present. Why don't we congregate in Robin's study?'

'Very well,' he says.

'I'll go and get Mum,' Brooke says as soon as I tell her. I don't get the chance to say that the first Mrs Featherstone isn't invited, because she's already darted off through the throng of mourners.

Mr Carter follows me to Robin's study, where I pull out some chairs. I sit in Robin's swivel chair behind the desk, and Brooke, Claudia and Mr Carter sit opposite me. It's awkward.

Mr Carter clears his voice twice, then puts on a pair of metal-framed reading glasses, taking a document out of a large brown envelope. 'This is the final will and testament of Robin Featherstone.' He glances at me and then puts the document on his knee. 'There's no easy way of saying this, ladies. Robin has left everything to a woman called Mia Benton.'

We sit in silence for a long moment. *What the hell!*

'Everything?' I ask in disbelief.

Mr Carter nods. 'And he's made Mia Benton the sole executor.'

'No, that can't be right!' Brooke jumps to her feet. 'Dad wouldn't do that. I mean, I thought he'd leave everything to Tamsin, not to a bloody stranger. You must have it wrong.'

'I'm afraid I don't. Mr Featherstone came to my offices on 16 March.'

'Two days before he died,' I murmur.

'Mia Benton, did you say?' Claudia asks in a whisper.

'She's the blooding cleaning woman, Mum!'

'I know who she is,' Claudia spits. 'He must have lost it. I mean, he was on drugs after his stroke, wasn't he? He can't have been of sound mind.'

'I'm afraid that in my opinion, he was of completely sound mind and even had a note from his doctor, whom he had visited prior to seeing me, confirming that fact. He was perfectly cognisant that the contents of the will would upset you all, and even though I tried to convince him he should leave his family something, he was adamant that the complete estate should go to this Mia Benton. I'm very sorry. I trust you know who Mia Benton is?'

'She's the cleaner. A nobody. A nothing,' Brooke exclaims, and then she collapses back onto her chair, silent tears dripping down her cheeks. I can't work out if she's a total bitch or whether I actually feel sorry for her, until I realise what it means for me, too. I will get nothing. I gave up everything for Robin, my job, my flat – and now I have nothing. No savings, no property, no job. The bastard. I thought he loved me. I know I wasn't the best of wives these past few weeks, but I explained to him how I was struggling with his disabilities. Yes, there was tension, but we still loved each other, didn't we?

'She can contest, I assume?' Claudia says, throwing her head towards me. Her lips are puckered and lined, but of the three of us, she is the most focused. I suppose she wasn't expecting anything herself, so her disappointment is only for her children.

'Indeed, Mrs Featherstone can contest the will, although you will have to establish a valid reason for doing so,' Mr

Carter says. 'It certainly is a very unusual case. Do you, um, have any idea as to why Mr Featherstone should choose to leave everything to Ms Benton? Were they in some sort of relationship?'

'Most certainly not!' I exclaim. Although that is the only thing that makes sense. I know Robin liked Mia, and they had their music in common, but she was the cleaner, for goodness' sake! Who leaves their entire estate to the cleaner?

'I have an address for Miss Benton.' Mr Carter reads out a London address that means nothing to me. 'Do you know if that's correct?'

'Pavla might know what her address is,' Brooke says, wiping her eyes with the back of her hand. 'She employed her.'

'Ah, I see there is an email address, too.' Mr Carter squints at the piece of paper. 'I shall track her down.'

I'm rather hoping he fails to find her. How can this be right? I mean, I could have understood if Robin had left everything to Brooke and David, but Mia is a total outsider. Did he do that to get revenge on me because I fired her against his will? No, surely not. Robin wasn't a petty man. He might have left Mia something, but not the whole damned estate. It's hard to think straight as the shock grips me. 'How soon can I contest?' I ask, my voice quivering.

'As soon as you wish.'

'We'll support you,' Brooke says. 'Dad must have lost his marbles. There's no way that he'd leave nothing to me and David. We are his only kids. It's crazy! If you win, you'll give us a fair share, won't you?'

I nod. 'Of course. If you support my contesting of the will, I'll make sure that there is provision for all of you. You too, Claudia.'

10

MIA

I am lost. About ten minutes ago, I was in Prague's
Wenceslas Square, but I took a little back street, and
now I have no idea where I am. I need to find the
Charles River, and then I can reorient myself. Oh, how I love
this city. It's utterly charming with its stunning buildings,
fairy-tale-like castle, and Charles Bridge is so much more
breath-taking than the postcards suggest. Last night, we
performed to a sell-out auditorium in the most charming
theatre gilded with gold and ornately painted murals.
Tonight, we're playing in a club. The Czechs certainly appreciate our music; we got loud applause and shouts of *encore!*

As I carry on walking, the cobbled stones biting into the
soles of my feet through my worn-out trainers, my stomach
rumbles. Once again, I'm hungry. Despite having this gig,
money is so tight that I'm having to eat modestly. I thought
that I would be better off or that the band might pay for my
food *and* lodgings, but it appears they're only paying for my
bed at night. Why does making music earn so little? It's just
not fair, considering we all work so hard.

My phone vibrates in my pocket. It's a withheld number,

and for a moment I consider letting it go to voicemail. But what if it's for another gig? We've only got one more week to go, then I'll be back in England with no immediate prospect of work. I stop to answer the phone, standing back to let people walk past me on the pavement.

'Hello?'

'Is this Mia Benton?'

'Yes.'

'My name is Timothy Carter. I am Robin Featherstone's solicitor.'

I take a step backwards.

'Ms Benton, are you still there?'

'Yes, yes. Is everything alright?'

'I'm sorry to tell you that Mr Featherstone passed away three weeks ago.'

'Robin has died?' The street spins around me, and I stagger backwards a couple of steps to lean against the wall of a pale-yellow building.

'I'm afraid so. Are you able to come to my offices in Horsham?'

It takes me a moment to process this and to answer his question. 'Um, no. I'm in the Czech Republic, on tour around Europe. I won't be home until the week after next.'

'I see,' he says. 'In which case, can we do a Zoom call? I trust you have your passport with you.'

'Yes, but why? Why do you need to talk to me?'

'It's not something I can disclose in a phone conversation, but I will explain when we have our Zoom.'

'What happened to Robin? I only saw him just before I left the UK.'

'He fell down the stairs, and I'm afraid that death was instant. A terrible accident.'

I am in total shock, but just about coherent enough to agree to a Zoom in an hour's time. I can't believe it. Poor,

poor Robin. I knew he was wobbly on his feet, but that is terrible.

I AM GENUINELY GUTTED about Robin's passing. He was a good man; it's sad that such a genius died so relatively young. My thoughts are all tied up with Robin, so I only just make it back to my hotel room in time for the Zoom call, because I was more lost than I had thought. But the locals are patient with their directions, and most people speak at least a little English. The hotel room is small and basic but clean, with a single bed, whitewashed walls and a tall-backed chair. I sit cross-legged on the bed and fire up my old laptop.

Mr Carter appears on my screen, the light from his ceiling making his bald head shine.

'What's this about?' I ask, forgoing any niceties, because I still can't believe that Robin has died.

'It's regarding Mr Featherstone's will. Can you show me your passport, please, Ms Benton?' he asks.

I hold it up in front of the screen.

'Thank you. So–' He clears his throat. 'Mr Featherstone wrote a new will shortly before he passed, and he appointed you as the sole executor and beneficiary.'

'Sorry?' Has this solicitor said what I thought he did?

'In essence, Ms Benton, you will inherit everything that Mr Featherstone owned, and you have responsibility for facilitating his wishes. That will involve notifying all the authorities of his death, closing his bank accounts and taking on responsibility for his assets. As you may have guessed, he was a wealthy man.'

'This is a joke, isn't it?'

'No, Ms Benton. It is for real.' He holds a document up to the camera. I can see the words that say *Final Will and Testament of Robin Featherstone.*

I am silent for a long moment, still wondering whether this is a scam and if he'll be asking me for my bank account details in a moment so he can steal the paltry sum I have there.

'Ms Benton?' Mr Carter says. 'Is the Zoom connection still working?'

'Yes, I'm still here.'

'I realise this is a shock. I think everyone was–' He clears his throat again. 'Rather surprised.'

'But what about Tamsin and his children?'

'Unfortunately for them, there was no provision.'

'You mean they get nothing? That can't be right. Surely Robin wouldn't do that.' I shake my head and try to digest what the man has just told me. 'What is Tamsin saying about this?'

'The family are obviously quite upset. Mrs Featherstone will be formally contesting the will.'

So this *is* real. Of course Tamsin is contesting.

'What am I meant to do? Can I just, I don't know, take a little bit and give the rest back to them?'

'No, Ms Benton. That isn't possible. The full estate is your responsibility now, and any gifts would be taxable. May I suggest that you come back to the UK as soon as possible? I have the name of a good probate specialist who can advise you and help you fight your corner.'

Fight my corner? 'And if I don't come back?'

'That really isn't an option. You are set to become a very wealthy woman, Ms Benton, and you will need to claim it. I will forward you the details of Ian Dunworthy, who is a colleague and a probate specialist.'

'But where am I meant to stay?' I know that sounds like a silly question under the circumstances, but I gave up my bedsit, and Dad's place is so small. I can't stay with him for any length of time. I haven't really given any thought as to where I will live in the longer term. I was going to go with the flow, wherever the work took me.

'Stave House is your property. You have every right to reside there.'

'Live in that house?' I feel as if my head is about to explode. That beautiful Queen Anne–style house with all that land and the adjacent cottage is now mine. It's totally crazy, like winning the lottery when you haven't even bought a ticket. 'But what about Tamsin? She lives there.'

'You need to seek further advice, Ms Benton, as I am not a wills specialist, but you are probably aware of the saying that possession is nine-tenths of the law. You would be well advised to take possession of your property and administer the estate from there.'

'And what should I do about Tamsin and Brooke? I mean, it's their house, really. It doesn't seem fair.'

'As executor, you have the right to ask them to leave, but my off-the-cuff advice is to be as conciliatory as possible. Legal proceedings are going to be exceedingly costly to everyone concerned and will tie up the estate potentially for many years. I have seen too many litigation disputes bankrupt both parties. You may be well advised to negotiate and allow the ladies to stay in the property until probate is complete. I will email you further details.'

I blink a few times and barely register his goodbyes, and then he is gone. He hasn't asked for my bank account. He hasn't acted as if this is a scam or a spoof, so I assume this is all real. Yet I simply can't absorb what he has said. Have I really gone from being penniless to rich just like that? Is this some sort of sick joke?

Ever cynical, I look Timothy Carter up online. There he is, a solicitor in a firm in Horsham, his headshot confirming that he is indeed the man I've just spoken to. But why has Robin left everything to me? It doesn't make any sense. For sure, we had our music in common, but otherwise, I was just an assistant and his cleaner. I wasn't even his friend. I think back to that last strange meeting where he seemed to foresee his own death. Was he trying to tell me something that I didn't understand at the time? Or, for that matter, don't understand now? None of this makes any sense. Poor Robin.

I honestly don't know whether to laugh or cry. Yes, I'm sad for Robin, but at the same time, my life may be about to change beyond all recognition. I am totally conflicted.

My phone rings. It's Lexi. 'Hey, Mia, where are you? Thought you were going to join us for a drink?'

'Do you mind if I take a rain check? I've got a bit of a headache.'

'Sure. I'll pop in to check on you later.'

I'd like to tell the girls that my whole world might be about to change, but I know that I can't. Instead, I Google *wills* and *probate* and *contesting wills,* so that an hour later, I'm even more confused. One moment I'm excited, the next I'm hit by a wave of melancholy, and then my stomach is knotted with anxiety. I send Dad a text message and ask him to call me as soon as he's off his shift. Dad won't have any answers, but I need to speak to someone.

11

A week later, I'm back in London. To be honest, I wish I could have packed up my bags straight after Mr Carter's phone call, but I couldn't let the other girls down. I also couldn't tell them how my luck has changed and that my future is looking very different indeed. Can you imagine how difficult that was? You've just won the lottery and you can't tell a soul. The only person who knows is Dad, and I'm not sure he believes me.

'Nothing worthwhile in life is free,' he said. 'There has to be a catch, Mia. Perhaps the house is falling down and needs millions invested into it, or perhaps this Mr Featherstone of yours owes a fortune and all you're inheriting is debt.'

'You're such a cynic,' I said. 'Don't you think I've already paid my dues?' Dad had no answer to that, because he knows better than anyone what I've been through. 'Can't you just be happy for me?' I asked.

'Of course, love. I am. I just want to make sure you're not hurt.'

We were both silent for a moment. I wanted to add the word *again*.

. . .

AFTER COLLECTING my bags at Heathrow airport and hugging the girls goodbye, I'm tempted to take a black cab into London, but then have to remind myself that I don't have the money yet. I looked up online how long probate can take; it's likely to be at least five or six months, and could be up to a year – that's normal probate, not when it's contested. So I drag my bag and violin case onto the crowded tube and head to Dad's.

It might be a pokey one-bedroom flat with damp seeping through from the external walls, but Dad's place has a jaw-dropping view. From the living room window up on the eleventh floor, we can see all the way across London, towards the River Thames to the south. On a clear day, Dad – who is an ardent monarchist – reckons he can see Buckingham Palace to the east. I'm dubious, but if it makes him feel better to have a view of the queen, then I'm not going to burst that bubble.

The second I'm through the doors, Dad throws his arms around me. He must have changed shifts with someone so that he's here to welcome me.

'Welcome home,' he says, squeezing me tightly. 'I've made your favourite spag bol, and I want you to tell me everything. Every little detail of where you've been and the people you've met.'

I laugh. Dad has only been out of the UK once, and that was to Tenerife on his and Mum's honeymoon. Each summer for the first ten years of my life, we used to go to North Wales, where we stayed in a holiday park near the beach, sleeping in a static caravan and playing on the sandy beach whatever the weather. It rained most of the time, but my sister Sara and I didn't mind. I've got happy memories of those summers, except the last year. By then, Sara was thirteen and I was ten, and she absolutely didn't want to play with me. Instead, she hooked up with some mean-looking teens. I wonder whether that was the start of Sara's life going wrong. After Mum died, Dad couldn't afford to take us on holiday, and anyway, Wales was Mum's place, where her aunty Gwyneth was from and where, according to Dad, she had her own happy family memories.

Dad's tried so hard to be both Mum and Dad to us, but I'm not sure it has really worked. After the shock of Mum dying, he sank into a rut, which I've only recognised as depression with hindsight. He lost his job, put on a load of weight, and even now, so many years later, I don't know how truly happy Dad is. These days, he's a cleaner in a hospital in the evenings and does the occasional shift on the tills in Sainsbury's during the day. It's a far cry from the bookkeeper that he once was.

I follow him into the living room – which is also the kitchen and my temporary bedroom – and sink down on the worn sofa. 'You realise that next year you won't be here,' I say. 'I'll be able to buy you a new home. Imagine that! You owning your own place, or perhaps you'll move into Stave House with me.'

Dad looks at me with his serious face. 'Don't you go counting your chickens before they hatch. Just because some fancy solicitor makes you a promise doesn't mean he's right. I can't see the family giving up their inheritance without a fight. None of this sits easy with me, Mia. Anyway, it's time to eat. You can dream later.'

I take my place at the table for two. Dad brings over a steaming bowl of Bolognese with a pile of spaghetti. He's a lousy cook, and this is his only dish that is vaguely edible, so he's always assumed it's my favourite. I have no intention of ever disillusioning him.

'Oh, I forgot. There's a letter for you, over on the mantelpiece.'

I smile. Dad doesn't have a mantelpiece. Just a plywood shelf on which he keeps a bowl with his keys and a photograph of the four of us from happier times. I walk over and pick up the envelope. My name and Dad's address is typed, and I assume it's from the solicitor.

Eagerly, I open the envelope and read the typed letter.

Dear Mia,

I didn't get the chance to tell you when we met, and by the time you read this letter, I may well be deceased. I have changed my will, and I am leaving you all of my money, my house and everything I own. Also, I am making you the sole executor of my will, because I have no doubt that my family will contest the will and try to oust you from the house.

Dearest Mia, you and I speak the same language, that of music. I know you will put my wealth to good use and develop your own musical career, perhaps setting up a music charity to help young people access music lessons. May my legacy be music, continuing to bring you and others great joy.

I know you will question why I have chosen to leave everything to you, and it's just a visceral feeling that you are more deserving than my family. Does that make me a bad person, putting whims before blood? I don't know. But there is no law saying one has to leave one's wealth to family, just avaricious expectation.

It is very likely that by the time you read this letter, I will be dead. I think someone is trying to kill me, Mia. Just because I have suffered some disabilities from my stroke, it doesn't mean I'm stupid.

Enjoy your newfound wealth, Mia, and handle it wisely.
Look after your own family. The Featherstones will try to
bully you, but stand up to them. My solicitor, Timothy
Carter, will vouch that I was of sound mind when I
rewrote my will and that it is the final version.

Yours,
Robin Featherstone

'Shit.' I drop the letter onto the table.

'Language,' Dad says as he dollops some spaghetti into a bowl.

'I think Robin might have been murdered,' I say.

'Don't be silly, Mia. You and your overactive imagination.'

'Read it,' I say. My hand is shaking as I pick up the letter and pass it to Dad. I watch as the deep furrows on his forehead deepen.

'How do you even know that this Robin wrote the letter?'

'What do you mean?'

'It's typewritten. Is that his signature?'

I shrug. 'I don't know.'

'What state of mind was Mr Featherstone in when you saw him?'

'Not great,' I admit. 'The whole meeting was strange. For starters, I had to be there at the crack of dawn so that Tamsin and Pavla didn't spot me, and then he wasn't at all forthcoming as to why he had asked me to visit. He wasn't in a great space, that's for sure. He looked more ill than he had straight after his stroke. With hindsight, I think he was troubled, but was that a concern that his life was in danger, or a consequence of his illness? Surely if he was scared someone was going to hurt him, he would have contacted the police.'

'Perhaps he was delusional,' Dad suggests as he takes a big mouthful of spag bol. 'I mean, you don't know what damage the stroke did, or what medication he was on. This doesn't sit well with me, Mia. I said to you before, if something seems too good to be true, it normally is.'

'I don't know what to do,' I say. 'The solicitor suggested I go to the house and move in, because it's legally mine.'

'Really?' Dad frowns again.

I take a mouthful of Bolognese, but it burns my tongue.

'Why don't you go and visit and get a feel for the place? Take some more legal advice and then decide.'

I nod whilst I try to soothe my stinging mouth with cool water. Dad always worries about me, particularly after everything that happened. And I hate to worry him. As soon as I was released from prison, I was determined to do whatever I could to make Dad's life better. Right now, it looks like that might be a possibility.

'And don't count your chickens, Mia.'

I suppress a grin because Dad loves his idioms. My thoughts are in turmoil. On the one hand, I might be rich and never have to worry about money ever again. But on the other, what does that letter from Robin really mean? The solicitor says he fell down the stairs, but did he really fall? Could it be that he was pushed?

12

It has taken me a good week to get over the shock of Robin's will. Initially, I wondered whether Robin chose to leave everything to Mia out of spite towards me because I fired her without consulting him. But then I discounted that. It was a ridiculous thought, because even if he didn't want me to inherit, he would have left his estate to his children or even a charity. No, there must be something about Mia to make her more special than me, Brooke or David, and I am determined to discover what that is. I need to be resourceful, like I used to be in my PR job.

I have a huge advantage being blonde, blue-eyed and pretty, because people think I don't have much of a brain. I am frequently underestimated, and that's a very powerful position to be in. Yes, yes, I know that you should never articulate such a thought in today's day and age, but believe me, if you're an attractive blonde, you'll concur. I'm never going to be an Einstein, but I've got common sense and a dogged personality. I am organised and persuasive (although perhaps not as much as I had assumed, otherwise Robin wouldn't have left me in this position), and I intend to use every skill I possess. I am damned if this Mia Benton is going to get what is rightfully mine.

Firstly, I found myself a decent lawyer, not a provincial, doddery old man like Timothy Carter who has probably been lining his pockets off Robin's successes for years. I scoured the internet and researched which solicitors have won the most high-profile probate cases. I have chosen a woman called Shayla Chatterton. I like the alliteration of her name, but that's not the reason I've selected her. She won a massive victory on behalf of the fourth wife against the fifth wife of a Russian oligarch who was named the beneficiary of her new husband's will. Wife number four was able to prove that wife number five forged the will and made out that her husband wasn't of sane mind. Today, I am meeting Shayla Chatterton for the first time.

I take the train to London, and as the black cab drops me outside the imposing Mayfair town house where Shayla Chatterton is based, I take a deep breath and pat down my camel-coloured cashmere coat. I think it's fine to move away from wearing all black once the funeral is over. It's not as if colour is going to affect the grief. I flick my hair backwards and walk with a straight back up the steps to the shiny black door. I ring the buzzer and am let in. The waiting room is full of uncomfortable regency-style armchairs and sofas, and portraits of severe-looking eighteenth-century noblemen and noblewomen hang on the walls. I've never been in a solicitor's office before, but I assume that most of them don't look like this.

There is a pile of magazines and papers on a central table, so I flick through the *London Magazine* and the *Daily Telegraph*, but nothing is holding my attention. Even though I'm on time, Shayla Chatterton keeps me waiting. It's twenty minutes before her young secretary strides into the waiting room and calls my name. I follow her down the corridor and into a large room with cornicing and a vast dark wood board-room table. The window looks out onto a wall at the rear, which rather destroys the impressiveness of the space.

Shayla Chatterton is seated at the near end of the table, and she stands up when I walk in. She has dark caramel skin and poker-straight hair cut in a sharp bob. The only slash of colour is her deep red lipstick and the red soles of her Louboutin high heels. It's the skin on her neck and hands that belie her age. She must be late fifties, but looking damned good on it.

'Mrs Featherstone, it's a pleasure to meet you.'

We shake hands, and she squeezes my knuckles together painfully, her rings cutting into my fingers. 'Have a seat.' She points to the chair next to her. The assistant offers me a drink, and I request a latte. Shayla Chatterton chooses water.

'So how may I help you?'

As I explain my predicament and the fact that Brooke and David are supporting my contesting of the will, she steeples her fingers, listening intently. She has the ability to hold your gaze, making it seem like you're the most important person she has ever had the joy of listening to. It makes me feel comfortable and confident in her, but I bet she's a beast of an adversary. Exactly the sort of advocate that I need.

'Well,' she says eventually, leaning back in her chair, 'there are a number of avenues we can explore. Firstly, we will establish whether the will is valid. I shall know that very quickly once I have seen it.'

'I fear it is valid, because it was drawn up by my husband's solicitor, who declared that Robin was of sound mind.'

Shayla waves her hand in front of her. 'Not necessarily. I will decide whether that is the case or not. Assuming the will is valid, then we will establish whether your husband had a lack of testamentary capacity.'

'You mean if he was sound of mind? Because Robin did have a stroke shortly before he changed the will.'

Shayla licks her lip and smiles. 'Good.'

Wow, this woman really is the vulture the press makes her out to be.

'So then we assess whether he was of sound mind and had the memory and understanding as to what he was doing. If we can't get the medical evidence for that, our next step is to look at undue influence. Did this woman–'

'Mia Benton,' I add.

'Have undue influence over your husband? Did she coerce him to change the will? And that's where it becomes interesting. What was the true relationship between them? Can we prove that Mia was up to no good?'

'How do we prove that?'

'Good detective work.' She opens the black leather folder in front of her and slides a business card towards me. It reads 'Aiden Mitchell, Private Detective' and a mobile phone number.

'He's the best in the business. I suggest you give him a call and put him to work. If there's some dirt to find, Aiden will uncover it. Look, Mrs Featherstone, I need to be blunt with you. You must understand that it is very expensive contesting a will, and my hourly charge is high. On the other hand, if there's the slightest possibility that this will can be fought, then I am the best lawyer in the country to do it for you.' She hands me another sheet of paper. I try not to gasp as I see her hourly rate and the average fees for contesting a will. But it will be worth it. Even if I lose a big chunk to lawyer's fees, it's better to have a smaller percentage of something rather than a large percentage of nothing. And, of course, it doesn't help that I've no idea what Robin was worth. Perhaps Brooke can help me out on that one.

Shayla Chatterton stands up and extends her hand again.

I brace myself for another tight squeeze, but she's gentler this time. I guess she's already proven she's a terrier.

'Let me know how you'd like to proceed,' she says.

I FIND a coffee shop two streets away, order a double espresso and take a seat as far from the counter as possible. I send Shayla Chatterton an email from my phone, thanking her for meeting me and confirming that I wish to hire her, and then I dial the number on Aiden Mitchell's card.

'Hello.' The voice is gruff.

'I've been given your card by Shayla Chatterton. She said you might be able to find out more about a woman who has been named as the sole heir to my husband's will.'

'Has she indeed?' He has an estuary accent, more like the way I used to talk before I realised that talking the Queen's English is rather important in the world of PR. I give him all the details I have for Mia – which are simply her mobile phone number, the address on her CV and the fact that she's a violinist, or at least claimed to be. It's not like I ever heard her play. Aiden tells me his fees, and once again, I swallow hard. This is going to cost me a bloody fortune. I will certainly have to get some money off Brooke and David in return for giving them a cut when we win. I've got just under ten grand in the joint bank account I had with Robin, but after that, the money's going to run out. Before it was just an endless tap, drawing upon Robin's funds, but now it's all frozen. I simply can't think about it.

'How soon can you get me the information?' I ask Aiden.

'Should have the basics in a week's time. Depends what digging Shayla wants me to do.'

And so, by the time I am back on the train to Horsham, I have appointed Shayla Chatterton as my lawyer and Aiden Mitchell as my private investigator. I just pray we win so I've got enough money to pay them both, because in the meantime I'm going to have a very large overdraft.

THERE ARE two cars parked at the front of Stave House when I arrive: Claudia's silver Mercedes estate car and Brooke's pink Mini – a bespoke colour, of course. My heart sinks. It sinks even further when I see the pile of suitcases in the hall.

'What's going on?' I ask Pavla, who is attempting to heave a Louis Vuitton suitcase up the grand staircase.

'Brooke is moving back in, permanently.' Pavla has her back to me, so I can't see her expression, but I expect she's about as thrilled as I am. Brooke keeps a bedroom here and a wardrobe filled with clothes, but in the short time that I've lived here, she's rarely been around. Why is she moving back in now? Is she trying to put in some physical claim?

Claudia appears on the landing. 'Goodness, Pavla. That case is way too heavy for you to carry alone. Can't you get Marek or Thomas to help you?'

'It's fine,' Pavla says, but it clearly isn't. The woman's muscles are bulging on the side of her neck, and I can hear her wheezing from down here. I wait for Claudia to offer to help, but she doesn't, so I run up the stairs behind Pavla and try to lift the case from the bottom.

'You don't have to,' Pavla pants.

'I want to,' I say, glaring at Claudia. But Claudia isn't paying me any attention; she turns around and walks back towards Brooke's bedroom.

I let go of the case once we've reached the landing and follow Pavla as she wheels it towards Brooke's room. There is already a pile of luggage in the doorway.

'You've got way too much stuff for one room,' Claudia says. 'Why don't you take over the blue room, too. You can use it as your dressing room or a lounge.'

'Good idea, Mum,' Brooke says, catapulting over a couple of cases.

I open and close my mouth. I want Brooke and Claudia out of here, but right now, Stave House isn't mine, and I need to keep the two dreadful women onside if I want to collect what is my rightful inheritance. Before I can make any comment that I might live to regret, the phone rings. It's the landline, which Robin insisted on keeping, so I hurry to the master bedroom to pick up the handset.

'Hello,' I say.

'Um, Tamsin. This is Mia Benton.'

I take an audible inhale.

'I am very sorry about what's happened, that Robin died. And I'm in deep shock that he has left everything to me. It doesn't seem very fair.'

'No, it's not,' I say curtly.

'Um, I'm planning on coming to Stave House at the weekend.'

'Are you going to throw us out?' I clench my jaw.

'No, goodness. Well, let's talk about it when I get there. I assume Saturday is convenient for you?'

'And if it isn't?' I ask.

There's silence, which I break. 'Let's just get this over and done with.'

I hang up and sink onto the mattress. *Oh, Robin, what have you done?*

BACK DOWNSTAIRS, there are voices in the kitchen. Although I would prefer to ignore Brooke and Claudia, I'm gasping for a cup of tea, and I know that I need to get them onside. You know what it's like when you walk into a room and it's obvious that people have been talking about you? There's an awkward silence. It's Pavla, bless her, who breaks it.

'I've just boiled the kettle, Tamsin. Would you like a cuppa?'

'Please,' I say, inwardly smiling at the way Pavla has affected so many English colloquialisms. 'Mia is coming on Saturday,' I say.

'Bringing the bailiffs, is she?' Claudia asks.

'She says she wants to talk.'

'Of course she does. And then she's going to boot us. She can't really throw us out of our home, can she?' Brooke asks, with tears in her eyes, and actually I do feel sorry for her. This is the house she has called home for the best part of her life, the house that she associates with her father. I suppose she assumed that as her stepmother, I might still welcome her here, but Mia is a stranger. 'It's so unfair, isn't it?' Brooke sniffs.

'Yes, it is.'

Pavla passes me a mug of tea, but she is a bit careless as she hands it to me, and some of the burning liquid slops over the side, scalding my finger.

'Ouch,' I say.

'I'm so sorry,' Pavla says, grabbing me by the arm and leading me to the sink, where she opens the cold tap. 'It's all too much at the moment.'

'Yes, it is,' I agree.

'Well, the ball is in your court, Tamsin,' Claudia says, standing in front of the Aga with her arms crossed as she watches the cold water cascade over my sore finger.

'I've appointed a leading solicitor and a private investigator. I may need to borrow funds off you in order to pay them, but when we win, I'll give Brooke and David each twenty percent of Robin's estate. I think that's fair, don't you?'

'Quite a good payday for being married a matter of months,' Claudia says.

'Stop it, Mum.' Brooke says, surprising me. 'Tamsin has

every right to keep it all, so I think giving away forty percent is quite generous.'

'Really?' Claudia asks, rolling her eyes. 'You think twenty percent of Robin's wealth is going to fund your lavish life-style, keep you going until you find yourself a rich husband? Look at how I've had to downsize since the divorce. Most of the assets are tied up in this house. Your dad wasn't that wealthy, you know.'

'I can't take this anymore,' Brooke says, clamping her hands over her ears and stomping out of the room like a toddler.

I turn the tap off and catch Pavla shaking her head ever so slightly. In despair, I suppose.

13

MIA

Well, that was an awkward telephone conversation. I'm glad we both kept it short. I feel kind of sorry for Tamsin. I mean, she's a bitch, but I wonder why Robin married her if he didn't want her to inherit everything. And that's the trouble. One moment I am bursting with excitement that I'm going to be rich, that I'll be able to buy Dad a house, or perhaps he can come and live with me at Stave House or, better still, have his own place in Pavla's cottage, but the next moment, I feel terrible. It doesn't seem right that I'm going to be wealthy while Tamsin and Robin's children are being deprived of it all, and Pavla, Thomas and Marek homeless. I wonder if I should renounce the inheritance, whether that would be the morally honourable thing to do. But then I think about Robin's letter. I take it out of its envelope again, reading it for the fiftieth time in the past twenty-four hours. If he was genuinely concerned for his own life, then of course he wasn't going to leave anything to the people he thought were out to kill him. But why didn't he go to the police? Why didn't he discuss it with his solicitor?

Then it hits me. Perhaps he did. Perhaps Timothy Carter knows all about this. I dig out his email and telephone the solicitor before I can talk myself out of it.

'This is a bit awkward, but I've received a letter from Robin Featherstone, sent before he died.'

'Yes, he did mention that he was going to write to you.'

'Do you know the contents of the letter?'

There is a pause; I can imagine Mr Carter frowning. 'Only that he was going to notify you that you were his sole executor and beneficiary. I assume that's what you're referring to?'

'Yes, no. It's just he implied that he wasn't safe, that perhaps ...' And then I let my words die out, because I realise that this letter might be the very evidence that Tamsin needs to show that Robin wasn't of sound mind. Perhaps Robin really was delusional when he changed his will, and this paranoia that someone was trying to kill him was just evidence of that. And even though I don't think it's fair that I inherit everything, now it's been handed to me, I'm not ready to give it all back. I've been dealt a horrible hand in life, despite all of my hard work, and so has Dad. We've both had enough heartache and disappointment. We deserve a break.

'Ms Benton?' Timothy Carter asks.

'Yes, sorry. It's nothing. You mentioned that you might be able to put me in touch with a probate specialist.'

'Yes, indeed. Apologies that I haven't done that yet. I will email you straight away. Was there anything else?'

'No, no. Thank you.'

So NOW I really am in a quandary. I feel morally bad about accepting the inheritance, but if Robin was genuinely scared, then it's my duty to find out what was going on. I wonder if I should contact the police and ask if he let anyone know his concerns, but if so, then surely his death would have been considered suspicious.

I go online and search Robin Featherstone's name. There are several rather lovely obituaries, including a long one written in *The Times* newspaper, praising Robin as one of this generation's finest composers, insufficiently lauded during his lifetime, as many of the greats of the arts were. It just says that he died suddenly from a fall a few weeks after suffering a stroke. There is absolutely nothing online suggesting that Robin's death was anything other than a tragic accident. There was no inquest, and his funeral was held ten days after he died.

The only thing I can do is go to Stave House as planned and try to do a bit of discreet digging. In the meantime, I need to go to the shops and stock up on toiletries and the basics before my trip to Stave House. I also promised to pick up some food for Dad, who will be working late tonight and only eats ready meals when I'm not around.

Wearing my skinny black trousers, black boots and a royal blue faux fur jacket that I picked up in a charity shop last year, I lock up Dad's flat and take the many flights of stairs down to the ground floor. It's quiet at this time of day, but even so, I'm never totally comfortable walking through the concrete jungle of these blocks of council flats. Dad says it's better than it used to be, that there aren't so many junkies around, but even so I walk quickly, with my head down.

I hear footsteps behind me. That's not unusual, but it's the way they keep pace with me that is unnerving. When I speed up, the footsteps speed up. When I slow down, they slow down, too. I glance over my shoulder and see a man wearing a black hoodie, his face obscured by a thick black scarf wrapped around his neck and chin and the hood that covers his eyes. It's an ominous look.

My heart thumps as I break into a trot. There's no one

here; I need to get to the end of the road before I'm out onto the shopping street, where there'll be more people. But I'm not quick enough. The footsteps are right behind me, and then the man grabs my shoulder, tugging hard at my handbag.

'Get off me!' I shout, trying to keep hold of the handbag. In that split second, I know that's a bad idea. He could have a knife, in fact he probably does, but now the bag is cutting into my shoulder, and I can't release it. I try to kick out at the man, but I lose my balance. Then he's got his arm around my neck, and a hand is tugging so hard at the bag it feels like I'm strangling. I think of Robin in this split second; was this how he felt just before he died? Your life doesn't flash in front of your eyes; you just feel a sense of utter desperation. But then there are more footsteps and a thump. A grunt. Swearing and footsteps again. The mugger has released me. I stagger backwards until I'm leaning against the wall, my breathing ragged and spots dancing in front of my eyes. My legs feel like jelly. I don't know what happened, but the man in black is running like a maniac away from me. He disappears around the end of the street. I bend my head to my knees and try to calm my breathing.

'He's gone now.'

I look up into the face of a classically good-looking guy, about my age. He has honey-coloured hair that is a little too curly and unruly, sitting on the collar of his buttoned-down shirt. He sports a neatly shaven golden beard, a contrast to the mass of hair on his head. He puts his arm on mine and tilts his head to one side.

'Glad that I could put my kickboxing training to some good use. Are you okay?' His baritone voice is posh, full of rounded *ahhs* and *ays*. I suppose he lives in one of the fancy homes around the corner that sell for upwards of a million pounds.

'Yes. Yes, I think so. Thank you so much.' I'm still trembling though. 'I don't know what would have happened if you hadn't intervened.' Terrifying thoughts of being stabbed or raped flit through my mind. Or perhaps I wouldn't have made it that far and would have been strangled in seconds. I rub my neck where the strap dug into it.

'Honestly, I didn't do anything. I just rounded the corner, saw that bastard trying to attack you and kicked him in the groin.'

'I can't believe you did that.'

'He nearly got the knife into you,' this hero stranger says.

'What?' I gulp, my eyes wide as I stare at the man. 'He really had a knife?'

'Didn't you see it? All the kids do these days. It's so unsafe. Hey, you look really shaken. Try to take a few deep breaths. Breathe with me. Slowly, in through your nose and out through your mouth. And again.'

He's right. After three or four deep breaths, my head feels clearer.

'Are you a yoga teacher or something?' I ask.

He laughs. 'No. Are you feeling a bit better?'

'Yes, thank you so much.' Although I do feel a little better, my legs are wobbly, and I involuntarily reach over to grab his arm. 'Sorry,' I say again, embarrassed now.

'You could definitely do with a sugary drink. There's a coffee shop around the corner. Why don't we go and get you one?'

'I'll be fine, really. It's so kind of you.'

'Look, I haven't just saved your life for you to get dizzy and bash your head on the pavement. I'll take you to the coffee shop, and then I'll be on my way.'

I throw him another embarrassed smile and start walking alongside him.

'Do you live around here?' I ask.

'Just staying with friends for a few days, but I've been getting my morning coffees from the cafe around the corner, which is why I know it. And you, do you live here?'

'No. My dad does. I'm staying with him.' I don't mention that he lives in the council tower block, whereas undoubtedly this handsome stranger's friends live in one of the fancy million-plus houses. Dad remembers when those Fulham terraced houses were almost within the financial reach of ordinary folk like us. Shortly after my parents got married, they started saving up, and reckoned they would have squir-relled away enough to take out a mortgage on a three-bedroom terraced home somewhere off the North End Road.

But then Mum died, and our lives unravelled, and that was the end of that dream. I like to peek through the windows of the houses, with their basement extensions and large kitchens with marble-topped island units, and the white louvred shutters that allow tantalising glimpses of living rooms decorated with painted wooden bookshelves, flat-screen televisions and stone busts of the residents' ancestors.

'By the way, I'm Felix. What's your name?' the handsome stranger asks.

'Mia. Mia Benton.' I smile at him and wonder if we're going to shake hands, but he's got his hands in the pockets of his jeans. Then we're at the coffee shop, and he's holding the door open for me.

'What would you like to drink, Mia?' he asks as he steps in behind me. I guess he's staying. I'm rather relieved.

'Just an English breakfast tea, but what would you like? It's my treat,' I say. I hope I've got enough cash on me, as despite the tour with the gypsy jazz band, I'm still short of money.

'A double espresso, please,' he says, more to the barista than me.

'Do you need the caffeine?'

He laughs. 'No, it's just I've been travelling for work, and strong coffee takes away the taste of not-too-clean water. I've got rather addicted to caffeine.'

'Where have you been?'

'All over. The Far East, predominantly.'

'That explains the tan.'

His smile is rather lopsided and very cute.

'What do you do?' I ask, but he doesn't get the chance to answer, as the barista hands over our drinks. I get my wallet out of my bag and notice that the stitching on one of the handles of my bag has come loose, thanks to the mugger. It reminds me again of how grateful I am to this man, Felix.

'Put your wallet away,' Felix says.

'Absolutely not. The very least I can do to say thank you for saving my life is to buy you a coffee.'

He shrugs his shoulders as I hand over a ten-pound note. I may not be too keen on the shaggy hair and the beard, but Felix really is good looking, with an aquiline nose and impossibly white, perfectly straight teeth. He picks up both of our drinks, and I follow him to a table for two in the window.

'So, Mia Benton, what do you do when you're not being attacked by criminals?'

'I'm a violinist. Do you think I should have rung the police?'

He sighs. 'And tell them what? Did you get a good look at the guy's face? Because I didn't. All I can recall is that he's about six feet tall. It happened so quickly, I couldn't tell you if he was black or white.'

Felix is right. The mugger had covered up his face so well, and he was wearing black gloves. It would be impossible to give the police any type of description.

'It's how the bastards get away with it. Choosing a street

without any security cameras and chancing it,' Felix says. 'Tell me what it's like being a violinist.'

He leans forwards across the table and holds my eyes. I redden slightly. This man is flirting with me, and I'm totally out of practice. 'I've just come back from a tour around Europe. I play gypsy jazz – well, anything, really. It's hard to get work as a violinist. What about you?'

Felix shuffles in his seat. For some reason, he's not looking as comfortable as he was just a couple of minutes ago. Then he takes his mobile phone out of his pocket and frowns.

'I'm sorry, Mia, but I'm going to have to dash. Late for a meeting.'

'Oh, it's me who should be sorry,' I say. 'It's my fault.'

Felix finishes his coffee in one gulp. I've barely taken a sip of my tea; it's much too hot. 'No, not at all.' He stands up and shoves his phone into his back pocket. 'It's been a pleasure to meet you, Mia. Just stay away from strange men.'

'Thank you so much,' I say again, but there's something in Felix's expression that has changed, as if he's just desperate to get out of here. He gives me an awkward wave, and then he's gone.

I'm left sitting alone in the coffee shop, wondering what just happened. I thought we might have exchanged numbers, or I would have had the chance to find out a little bit more about him, but no. And now I feel strangely bereft. For a few short minutes, I was protected by a handsome stranger, and now he's vanished, and I'll never see him again. I take a sip of tea and burn my tongue.

14

TAMSIN

The dry warmth in my greenhouse normally brings me solace, but not today. I spent an hour or so in the greenhouse, but now I'm back in the house, standing in the kitchen and looking vacantly out of the window. I can't concentrate on anything, and all I can see in my mind's eye is Robin: His neck bent at a strange angle, his mouth wide open as if it was contorted into a scream. His blank unseeing eyes staring at the ceiling. As hard as I try, I can't dislodge that horrific last image of my husband, and although the few weeks of our marriage were so far removed from what I had hoped for, I am missing him terribly. It's as if I have no purpose now, wandering around like a broken zombie in a house that may or may not be mine, surrounded by strangers.

Last week, I met up with a couple of my girlfriends for supper in a newly opened restaurant in town. But we're at totally different places in our lives now. Lulu is expecting her second baby and fully immersed in all things maternal, whereas Sandy is dating and partying. They don't understand what I've been through, the quagmire of grief tinged with guilt that is my daily reality. The fact that I am a widow at thirty-four.

'Don't you think you're missing the man you hoped he would be rather than the person he really was?' Sandy suggested. 'I mean, you two weren't even together long enough to really know how the relationship would have panned out.'

'That's not fair,' I snapped, but perhaps Sandy was right. I think I am mourning the loss of my dreams. Because after his stroke, Robin wasn't the person I had fallen in love with.

'At least you're going to be a rich widow,' Lulu said, sighing wistfully. 'And you'll meet someone else soon enough.'

I considered telling the girls about Robin's will, but something stopped me. It doesn't reflect well on me, from whichever angle you look at it. Either Robin didn't value me and our marriage, or I look like a money-grabbing bitch for contesting the will, or – if he really wasn't of sound mind – why hadn't I done more to protect him? So for now, I'm not telling anyone that I potentially have no home, no money, no job and no man. In fact, I'm substantially worse off than I was before I got married. And it's a seriously crap situation to be in. Lulu and Sandy just don't understand; I've resolved to stay clear of my old friends for the time being.

I MAKE myself a cup of coffee and am about to carry the mug out to the greenhouse when I hear the crunching of tyres on the gravel driveway. Pavla isn't around, so I go to investigate. A white Luton van is parked in front of the house. To my dismay, Claudia is hopping down from the driver's seat, and Brooke clambers inelegantly from the passenger's side.

'Morning, Tamsin,' Claudia says breezily, as if it's perfectly normal for her to be driving a rental lorry.

'What's going on?' I ask.

'We thought we'd better remove a few of Dad's valuables before the Mia bitch gets here,' Brooke says.

'Brooke!' Claudia admonishes her. 'Language.'

Brooke is a grown woman, and I'm surprised she puts up with her mother's put-downs. 'I'm not sure–' I say.

But Claudia ignores me and strides straight in through the front door. 'I mean, we're all on the same side, aren't we?' She speaks over her shoulder. 'I'm going to take some of the better paintings and silver to my house for safekeeping.'

'It's the best way,' Brooke adds. 'Think about it. The cow has been working here, cleaning. She's probably made an inventory of everything we've got and had it all valued.'

'All of Robin's heirlooms will be up for auction in no time,' Claudia adds. 'The prospect fills me with horror.' She does a mock shiver. 'I mean, obviously I'd hoped that my children would inherit everything, but it's got to be better you having the lot than a total stranger.'

These two women really are a vile double act, but unfortunately, in this instance, they might be right. I am so conflicted. On the one hand, it's undoubtedly illegal to remove valuable items before probate has been completed, but on the other, I'd rather they had Robin's belongings than Mia. Then again, until the will has been proven to be valid, everything in the house belongs to me as Robin's wife. Should I be putting my foot down?

'It's illegal, what you're doing,' I say, standing just inside the front door and looking into the grand hallway and the staircase sweeping up on the left-hand side. Brooke is standing with her hands on her hips, gazing around the hall as if it's the first time she's entered it. Claudia is already upstairs, but she leans over the wooden railings on the landing upstairs to talk to me.

'Come on, Tamsin. We're doing this for you. Better to be

safe than sorry. Write an inventory of everything we're taking if you want. Remember, we're on your side. We're keeping it safe for you.'

I don't believe that for one moment, but that can be a battle for another day.

'By the way, Tamsin. David's coming over,' Brooke adds.

'Oh,' I say, surprised. Or perhaps I shouldn't be surprised. If they're ransacking the house of Robin's valuables, it makes sense for David to acquire his share.

I run my hands over my face. Damn Claudia, because this ruse is obviously her idea. I could chuck them all out, but I need their support in contesting the will.

Brooke takes a step onto the stairs and stands still on the exact spot where her father bashed his head in. I wonder if she is feeling a wash of sadness standing there. It's the step I always avoid now, hopping over it so as to avoid 'the killer step' as I've renamed it in my head.

But clearly not. Brooke turns to face the wall and then reaches up to remove a painting of a young eighteenth-century girl playing a violin. How can she do that, be so unfeeling standing where her dad died? Carrying the gold-framed painting, which is about a foot wide and two feet high, she strides towards me, and I have to stand to one side to let her pass. But no, I can't let that happen.

'Brooke,' I say, reaching out to touch her shoulder, 'you know what happened on that step, don't you?' I stare pointedly at the bottom of the wooden staircase. There is a faint outline on the wall, where the painting has discoloured the magnolia paint.

She looks at me as if I've lost the plot. 'Urgh, yes. Dad died there. This painting was quite possibly the last thing he saw.' And then she pauses for a moment and wrinkles her nose upwards. 'Oh. Did *you* want this picture for sentimental reasons?'

I don't really like the painting, but something breaks inside me, and I let out a little sob. I nod my head.

'Here you go, then,' Brooke says, thrusting the picture into my arms. 'I've no idea what it's worth, but you'd better hide it somewhere so Mia doesn't find it.'

I nod through my tears. 'You know, I'm not sure this is a good idea. Taking away the valuables. It could get us all into trouble.'

Claudia walks up behind me and makes me jump.

'Your intentions are good, Tamsin.' She laughs, but it sounds brittle and forced. 'Who would have thought I'd say that to my husband's second wife? Oh well. But the thing is, none of us know what Mia's intentions are. We need to join forces to do what is morally right.'

'Spot on, Mum,' Brooke says.

'You need to get your head around that, Tamsin. We need to stick together, us Featherstones.'

As much as I dislike Claudia, I can see that she might be right. As an unlikely alliance as it seems, I need to keep Brooke and Claudia onside, because the chances are high that I will need Claudia's help in paying the solicitor's fees. And if the three of us – plus David – are united, that must make my case much stronger.

'You're right,' I admit softly. But it doesn't mean I want to watch them ransack the house. 'Don't remove too much, because it'll be obvious to Mia that stuff is missing.'

'We've thought about that, Tamsin,' Claudia says. 'Don't worry, we'll be selective. I've got it under control. What you need to do is concentrate on assisting the solicitor, getting a strong legal case together.'

'I'm doing that, and I've got a private investigator on board, too.'

'Excellent,' Claudia says as she walks out to the transit van holding a particularly hideous pottery urn. I don't want to watch the two women any longer, so I turn around and walk through the hall and into Robin's study. This is where I miss him the most. I never paid much attention to the music he was making before, but now the house is so very quiet. It's so silent, even my light breaths seem much too loud. I walk over to the bookshelf and pick up a photograph in a silver frame of David and Brooke when they were young children. They look angelic, the perfect little golden-haired children, dressed in their smart party clothes.

'He doesn't look like that anymore.'

I jump, startled because I didn't hear Pavla walk into the room.

'Sorry, Tamsin. Didn't mean to give you a fright. I hope you don't mind, but I also sometimes sneak in here to remember Robin.'

I blink hard. I'd forgotten that Pavla, Thomas and Marek must be grieving Robin too. After all, they have known him for years. They must be feeling very insecure about their future.

'He was such a sweet little boy,' Pavla says, a hint of wistfulness in her voice.

I take another long look at the photograph. 'I'm looking forward to meeting David.'

'Ah yes. He is quite the charmer. Always has been, and especially as an adult. He's quite different to his sister. Brooke, bless her, has none of the charm. What you see is what you get with her, and if she doesn't like you, you'll know about it.'

I snort slightly, because I've certainly been on the receiving end of Brooke's venomous tongue.

'I know,' Pavla says. She places a hand on my arm. 'I'm aware that she's been beastly towards you, but she hasn't coped well with her parents' divorce, and even though she's pretending to be blasé about Mr Featherstone's passing, she's hurting on the inside.'

'And David. Do you think he's upset, too? It was strange that he didn't come to his father's funeral. I hate the way he's treated Robin, with such contempt and disrespect.'

'David is a law unto himself.' It never ceases to surprise me how very fluent Pavla is in English despite her strong accent. 'I've known him for so many years, but he's slippery. Very slippery. He's utterly charming when you first meet him, but is he trustworthy?' She shrugs her shoulders and looks away from me. I place the photo frame back on the shelf.

'You know that Mia is coming to stay.'

'Yes, Claudia has told me. The will was such a shock.'

'I am contesting it,' I reassure Pavla. 'And if I win, I won't chuck you out of the cottage. You can stay on and look after the house, and if I decide to sell it one day, then I'll give you plenty of notice.'

Pavla smiles, but it's so fleeting I can't tell if it's natural or forced, and then she turns and leaves the room.

HALF AN HOUR LATER, to my relief, Claudia and Brooke have left, and I have taken refuge in the greenhouse. It gives me some time to calm myself, to tend to my succulents and to try to plan what my future might look like. If I lose the case against Mia, I have to start all over again. I know I should be tidying up my CV, reaching out to my old colleagues to see if there are any vacancies in PR, but I feel so lethargic. I don't want to go back to my old life. I like being a lady of leisure, I like not having to worry about money, and I like living in this beautiful house. I even like having Pavla around, who bustles about as if she's the matriarch, making me supper every night, vacuuming my bedroom, collecting the dry cleaning. I pick up one of my newest cacti, a *Greenovia dodrantalis*, commonly known as the Mountain Rose. They're not that rare, as they're found in the Canary Islands, but what I love about them is how the fleshy green leaves make a perfect rose shape and they thrive and grow in the cooler months – a bit like me, really. I'm contemplating whether I should plant this little baby outside where it might be happier than inside my greenhouse.

'You look very sad.'

'Jeez, Marek, you've got to stop creeping up and scaring me.' I almost drop the *Greenovia*. What is it with Pavla and her family today? They're making me jump out of my skin.

'I'm sorry, Tamsin,' he says in a monotone voice.

I let out a whistle. 'It's alright.'

'Are you missing Mr Featherstone?' he asks.

I put the *Greenovia* on the bench. It reminds me of a beautiful bouquet of fifty pale pink roses that Robin gave to me when he asked me to marry him. 'Yes, I miss him very much.'

'Mum says Mia is coming back, and she might make us leave our home.'

'I very much hope we can stop that from happening.'

'Would you like me to do something about Mia?'

'What do you mean, Marek?' I ask, my heart beating a little too quickly. What is he suggesting? That he physically hurts her or what? Surely Marek isn't a violent person, but perhaps his moral judgement is a bit skewed.

'I mean, I like Mia, but if she's a bad person ...'

'No, Marek. Absolutely not. She's coming here tomorrow morning, and you just need to keep out of her way. Maybe you should go out for the day. Go to Worthing and have a stroll along the beach. I know you liked that the last time you went.'

He looks at me as if I'm demented. 'I can't drive.'

'Your dad could take you, couldn't he? You could do something fun with him.' Unlike Pavla, Thomas doesn't work at the weekends.

'Maybe.' Marek shrugs his big shoulders. 'See you, Tamsin,' he says as he ambles away.

THE NEXT MORNING, I find it incredibly hard to get out of bed. I moved back into the master bedroom, and although I've hidden it from Pavla, I sleep with the last pillowcase that Robin used. Any scent of him has faded now, but it still gives me comfort to know that he was here in this bed, that some of his cells are still on this piece of fabric. I can hear female voices downstairs. I suppose it's Pavla and Brooke chatting away, or perhaps Claudia is back, too. Apparently she gets up at the crack of dawn to care for her horses. I glance at my alarm clock. It's 9:10 am. I'd better get moving before Mia tips up.

Down in the kitchen, Claudia, Brooke and Pavla are seated at the kitchen table. Pavla jumps up.

'Would you like a coffee, Tamsin?'

'Thanks, yes.' I sit down at Robin's place. I can't believe I'm here, living with this cabal of women.

'Any news from your private investigator yet?' Claudia asks.

'No. But I'll chase him on Monday.'

'Right. Plan of action for today. We keep a united front. Tamsin is the rightful inheritor of Robin's estate,' Claudia says.

'Beneficiary,' I mutter.

'And although it pains me, we're in full support of you.'

Pavla hands me a coffee, and then the doorbell rings. We all freeze.

'Is she here already?' Brooke asks.

'Could it be David?' I suggest.

Brooke stands up, scraping the chair back. She harrumphs. 'David doesn't surface before lunchtime. I'll go and answer the door.'

A couple of minutes later, there are two sets of footsteps coming towards the kitchen. Brooke walks in, stony-faced, her arms across her chest. Mia is behind her, and she looks nothing like the Mia who used to work here. For starters, she's had a haircut – or a 'styling' would be more accurate. Her mousey hair is now a mixture of mid- and light blonde, and rather than being tied severely in a ponytail, it's shoulder length, lapping around her face in gentle waves. As if that wasn't transformation enough, she's wearing smart black trousers and a tailored grey woollen coat, and carrying a Mulberry bag. It might be fake, I suppose, because surely she can't be spending our money, not yet?

I glower at her, but she holds my gaze. 'I'm sorry for your loss, Tamsin. Robin was a very special man.'

'Mr Featherstone to you,' Claudia snaps. Mia just inclines her head towards Claudia.

'Mia has brought luggage,' Brooke says. 'She says there's more in her car.'

'You can stuff that back where it belongs,' Claudia mutters.

'This is very difficult, Mia.' I stand up. 'None of us want you here, and frankly it would be better all around if you stay away until the will dispute is resolved.'

'I'm sorry, but that won't be possible.'

Mia holds her ground. I have to admit I'm rather impressed, because it can't be easy standing there calmly in the face of all of our hostility.

'So we're going to play happy families, are we?' Brooke asks. 'You're just a thieving upstart who doesn't deserve–'

'Enough, Brooke,' Claudia interrupts.

Mia lets her bag drop to the floor. 'Look, I'm sorry about

all of this,' she says, glancing from one of us to the other. 'I didn't want any of this. The contents of Robin's will came as much of a shock to me as no doubt it did to you.'

'Yeah, right.' Brooke rolls her eyes, but Mia ignores her.

'We're going to need to be civil to each other, however difficult that might be.'

'You need to leave,' I say, but my hands are shaking, so I clench my fingers together behind my back.

'I'm sorry, but that's not going to happen.'

'Would you like me to forcibly get you to leave?' Brooke asks, taking a step towards Mia. 'This is my home, Tamsin's home, too. Pavla, can you get Thomas. He can escort Mia out.'

Pavla's back stiffens, and she busies herself with something at the sink.

'Actually, it isn't your home, it's mine. And against the advice of my legal team, I'm letting you stay here out of the goodness of my heart.'

'You what!' Brooke spits. She jabs a finger towards Mia.

'Look, we need to talk about this like civilised human beings. I think we all need to take some deep breaths. I'm sorry that this situation is so awkward. Why don't we talk over lunch?'

What does she think, that Pavla is going to make her lunch, too? She's the uninvited, unwanted guest here.

To my annoyance, Claudia agrees. 'David will be here later. Let's all talk then.'

Mia turns to me. 'Tamsin, you're the most important person in all of this. What do you think?'

'I think that I need to take legal advice right now.' I stride away, my jaw clenched together, my fingers curled into tight fists. And then I remember. It's Saturday. I doubt very much that Shayla Chatterton is going to answer my call at the weekend.

15

MIA

This is truly awful. I feel like the pariah, the unwanted guest in my own home. And I get it; I really do. Maybe it would be better if I walk straight back out of here, to my normal life, and forget that Robin has left me so much. I run my fingers through my hair. I can't. The solicitor explained to me that being an executor is my legal duty, but there's more than that. I need to find out what was really going on with Robin before he died. Did one of these horrible women cause his death? If I walk away now, no one will seek the truth, and I feel as if Robin truly trusted me, more so than his own relatives. Quite why, I've no idea.

As I stride away from them, out of the kitchen and back down the hall towards the front door, I wonder if somewhere as palatial as this will ever feel like my home. It seems almost impossible. I walk back out to Dad's old banger that he's loaned me for a few days. It's a battered Vauxhall Corsa, which used to be red, but these days is mainly rust. I open the boot, take out my suitcase and return to the house. As I go up the stairs, I can't stop thinking about where Robin fell. Was it here? A shiver goes up my spine. I can see that some of the paintings are missing on the wall next to the stairs. Even if I hadn't dusted every single one and admired them as I cleaned, I would have noticed, because they've left lighter squares on the painted wall.

I'm not going to make a fuss about that. If one of the Featherstones has taken them, it's fine by me. There are three bedrooms either side of the staircase. I turn right first and peek my head into Brooke's room. It looks as if she's reclaimed both her own room and the spare room next door to hers. Her clothes and shoes are literally spilling across every surface in both bedrooms. I ignore David's room, which looks exactly the same as it did when I stopped working here a few weeks ago, and walk across the landing. Tamsin has moved back into the master bedroom, and some of Robin's suits are laid out on the bed of the guest room next door, so that only leaves me the small box room with its single bed. I don't mind. It's still way more comfortable than my bedsit was, or the lumpy sofa bed at Dad's flat. I sit on top of the pink, floral bedspread and wonder what this room will become when the house is properly mine. A baby's room perhaps, perfectly sized for a cot, a changing cabinet and an easy chair. I laugh out loud. For heaven's sake, I haven't even got a boyfriend.

Then Felix flashes into my mind, and I laugh at myself. There's no point in thinking about that handsome hero stranger. I need to concentrate on the here and now.

I stand up and unpack a few things from my suitcase, and then I hear the telephone ring from somewhere down the hall. I grab my coat. It would be good to have a walk before lunch, to gather my thoughts before the onslaught from this family.

It's a cool, damp morning, the clouds a pale grey; the sky

is almost oppressive. I walk around the side of the house and into the garden, realising that although I looked out at it numerous times, I've never actually stepped foot here. It's a big garden that slopes downwards to a woodland. Large rhododendron bushes crowd the right-hand side of the lawn, beyond which there's a field that last year was planted with rapeseed plant, making it look like a sea of deep golden yellow. I wonder whether Robin owned any of the surrounding fields, and whether I might become a farmer by default. On the left side of the lawn is Tamsin's huge greenhouse. I can see her busying herself inside it, and am relieved that she doesn't look up and notice me. I stroll around the garden, admiring the mature trees and running the palms of my hands over the bushes.

Then I find myself around the other side of the house and walking down the drive. Pavla's cottage is set back from the driveway, hidden from view by a cluster of beech trees. It looks much like a coach house, and I suppose it was, many years ago. Thomas emerges from around the side of the cottage, carrying a basket of logs. I've only spoken to him once, shortly after I started working as Robin's cleaner. He had appeared at the back door looking for Pavla, with an expression of terror.

'Can you get Pavla now?' he'd said. 'Marek's hurt.' Thomas gripped the edge of the doorframe, and I noticed with a shock that he only had three fingers on his left hand.

'Is he alright?' I'd asked, concerned about the young man.

'Hurry and get me missus.'

I had rushed away, shouting Pavla's name up the stairs. She appeared holding a stack of towels.

'Your husband needs to talk to you urgently,' I said, preferring not to be the bearer of bad news. She dumped the towels and hurried downstairs, and I saw them both running down the driveway towards their cottage. An hour later, Pavla returned.

'Is your son alright?' I asked.

'A fuss about nothing,' she said, batting away my concern.

'What did Marek do?'

'Cut his finger; nothing that a plaster couldn't fix. Thomas panics about everything,' she said. 'And especially at the sight of blood. He can be such a wimp at times.' I'd wondered whether this had something to do with how Thomas lost his own fingers, but I never got the opportunity to ask.

On the few times I saw Thomas again, he either nodded at me so deeply it was a wonder his flat cap didn't fall off, or he muttered 'Day's dawning'. It took me a while to realise that it's Cockney for *good morning*. Now, I raise a hand in greeting. To my surprise he smiles, lifts up his hand at me and shouts hello. He's the only person who seems relaxed about my presence here.

AN HOUR LATER, after following a public footpath around the side of Stave House, my head feels clearer, but I'm dreading lunch. The Featherstones must hate me. I'd hate me if I was them, but I'm going to have to get them onside somehow. I recall those very dark years, and how I had to dig so deep just to survive; how I learned to stand up for myself in impossible situations. I take a deep breath. I can do this, and I will. I walk in through the front door and carry my boots and coat upstairs to my room. I'm not ready yet to hang my coat on the rack on the wall by the door, or leave my belongings scattered around the house; I wonder if I ever will. I walk back downstairs slowly, readying myself. Then I hear the sound of a car door slamming, a key jangles in the lock to the grand front door, and just as I arrive at the bottom step, the door opens.

When I see him, I have to grab the stair handrail to steady myself.

'What are you doing here?'

Felix looks panicked, his eyes glancing from side to side. He paces towards me and grips my elbow. 'We need to talk,' he says, in an urgent whisper.

Too bloody right we do.

He guides me towards the cloakroom, where guests use the toilet and where the family hang up their more formal coats in a large cupboard that spans the length of the room. Felix shuts the door behind us.

'Are you going to explain to me why you're here? Because I assume it's no coincidence.'

'No.' He runs his fingers through his curly hair, making it stand up on end. 'Look, I'm sorry, Mia, but I have been spying on you.'

'What! Why? Who are you?'

'I'm David Felix Featherstone.'

I take a step backwards. It makes sense now. I can see the family resemblance. It's not too much of a stretch to see how that cute little boy in the photograph in Robin's study has grown up into this handsome man. Why didn't I realise before? The shock of the mugging, I suppose.

'But why were you spying on me?'

The room is too small for Felix – or David, as I suppose I'll have to call him now – to pace very much, but it's obvious that he's agitated. 'I've been keeping an eye on you for a few weeks. Well, clearly only when you were at your dad's, because I wasn't going to waste money and follow you around Europe when you were on tour.'

'You know about that?' I gulp. I feel a bit scared now. The palms of my hands are damp. 'How did you know I had gone on tour?'

'Because I saw you on social media. You didn't exactly keep it quiet that you were playing in some gypsy jazz group.'

I lower my eyes. He's right. I was so excited about my first professional gig in years that I posted about it on Instagram and Facebook, reviving the accounts that had lain dormant for too long. I try to understand how long David has been watching me.

'I thought you lived in Switzerland. Have you stayed here since your father's funeral?'

'I didn't go to Dad's funeral.'

He must sense the disapproval on my face because he says, 'Look, things weren't good between me and Dad, and it would have been totally hypocritical of me to tip up at his funeral. I was never the sad, grieving son, so why pretend?'

'How long have you been following me?'

'That doesn't matter.'

'It does to me!'

David fidgets and paces backwards and forwards even faster.

'And how did you know where I was living?'

'I got your address from the copy of the will that the old geezer, Timothy Carter, sent me. I mean, you can't blame me, can you? First of all there's Tamsin, the greedy second wife, but it turns out she's not so greedy after all, and some stranger has got their hands on our rightful inheritance. Someone had to find out about you, and Brooke's bloody hopeless, so it was never going to be her. I needed to know what you're like, whether you're mixing in criminal circles and what you did to manipulate Dad into changing his will.'

'I didn't manipulate your father. Firstly, I didn't even know he'd died until your solicitor contacted me. Secondly, I never asked for any of this. It's as much a shock to me as it is to you.' And then it dawns on me, perhaps I wasn't in any great danger on that street after all. 'So that mugging, was it a set-up?'

'No, of course not. I was following you, but when that guy started attacking you, what was I going to do? Turn around and walk in the opposite direction, or step in and save you? Yeah, maybe I should have left him to it. I thought about it, wondering if perhaps he'd kill you and then you wouldn't inherit all this, but then I wondered if you had any close family and perhaps they'd get it instead. But the truth is, I couldn't stand back and just let him hurt you. I'm not a total shit, you know.'

'That makes me so grateful,' I say, my voice laden with sarcasm. I try to make sense of my racing thoughts. 'But why didn't you just do your Good Samaritan deed and then rush off? Why did you say your name was Felix, and why did you take me for a coffee? It was pretty obvious I was going to find out the truth sooner or later.'

David can't stand still or look me in the eye. 'It was a difficult situation. I mean, I was in shock, too. And then I wondered if I could get some more information about you from talking face to face, but I was getting into deeper and deeper shit, so I ran off. It's not like I could have told you who I was there and then. You were in enough shock as it was.'

'But why did you say you were called Felix? David is a common enough name, and it's not like I recognised you as Robin's son.'

'It's my middle name. I've used the name for years.'

I look at him dubiously. I'm not sure I believe a word he's saying.

'It's true,' he says, holding my gaze for the first time. That makes me feel uneasy because despite everything, David or Felix or whatever he's called is an exceptionally good-looking guy. 'Felix was my grandfather's name, and I got my mates at school to call me Felix, and all my friends have ever since. It's only Dad and the close family who call me David. I didn't want to use the name that Robin Featherstone gave me.'

It's almost like he is contemptuously spitting Robin's name out.

'Why did you dislike your father so much?'

'Dad was a shit, he was foul towards Mum, and then he cheated on her, broke her heart. Yet it was her who had to leave this house.'

'But I thought he'd been divorced from your mother for several years before Tamsin came along.'

'She wasn't the first blonde bimbo young enough to be my sister. And then it was how he behaved towards me. He couldn't give a toss about me, because I wasn't musical. Do you know that he never attended a single parents' evening, never came to see me play in a cricket match? It's like I was nothing to him because I didn't care about music. So the fact he's gone ... yeah, I really don't care very much. What I do care about is why you? Why has he left everything to you and not to Tamsin or Brooke or me? That's what doesn't make sense.'

'If it's any consolation, it doesn't make sense to me either. I suppose it's because I'm a musician.'

'Dad knew plenty of those,' he says, his lip curling upwards ever so slightly. 'Look, I'm getting out of here, because if the others catch us chatting in private, they're going to wonder what the hell is going on. Don't breathe a word.'

And before I can reply, David opens the door and disappears.

IF I WAS CONFUSED about everything before, now it's even worse. Has David discovered the truth about me, that I spent time in prison? If he has, why didn't he let me suffer at the hands of the mugger? Unlikely, then. I splash my face with cold water and stare at myself in the mirror. I'm looking okay, more polished than normal. I'm definitely not looking like Robin's cleaning lady any longer, but I'm far from comfortable. No one wants me here. I can understand why David might have been spying on me, but it makes me feel deeply ill at ease, sullied even.

I can hear voices in the dining room, Brooke's strident voice rising above the others. As I walk out of the cloakroom, Pavla appears in the hallway, a tea towel over her arm.

'Lunch is ready. I'm serving it in the dining room. I assume you're joining in?'

'Yes, thank you, Pavla. And I'm sorry about everything. It's all very awkward.'

She nods, but her expression is impossible to read.

THE DINING ROOM is very formal, with walls painted in a terracotta colour and still-life oil paintings on the walls. There is a large satinwood dining room table, which I've polished on numerous occasions, and matching chairs. Tamsin is sitting at one end, Claudia at the other; Brooke and David are next to each other on one side. The empty chair opposite them is obviously for me. Silence falls when I enter the room.

'So, Mia, it's a pleasure to meet you. Or not, as the case may be.' David grins at me, but I don't return the smile.

'Don't be facetious,' Claudia says.

'So here we have the first Mrs Featherstone, the second Mrs Featherstone and what I presume was meant to be the third Mrs Featherstone,' David says, his arms waving around the table.

Both Tamsin and I speak at the same time, but I stop talking first because Tamsin looks like she's going to explode.

'Your father and I were in love, and if you'd bothered to

come to visit him after we were married or when he was poorly, you'd have seen so for yourself!'

'So why is it that you get zilch and she gets the whole lot?'

I actually think that David is enjoying this.

Red spots appear on Tamsin's cheeks and splodges on her neck. 'Probably because the will is a forgery or that woman coerced Robin into signing it. You should be asking Mia that question.'

'Look, everyone,' I say. 'I'm really sorry about this situation. It's not of my choosing, but this isn't a legacy that I can afford to turn down.'

Brooke snorts, but I try to ignore her.

'I don't know why Mr Featherstone chose me, and I intend to find out. And I'll make sure that you all get something, because that's only fair, even if it goes against Robin's wishes.'

'Oh, how very noble,' Brooke butts in. I try not to let the sarcasm distract me.

'So, for now, we need to establish how we're going to work together,' I say.

'Work?' David exclaims. 'These ladies have never done a day's work in their lives.'

'That's not true!' Tamsin retorts. 'I had a very successful career before I met your father. But once again, you wouldn't know that, would you? Because you have shown no compassion towards the man who has financially supported you all of your life.'

Now it's David's turn to look as if he's going to explode, whereas Brooke is leaning back in her chair, her food forgotten, a smirk of amusement on her face.

'I don't mean "work" in that sense of the word,' I say, trying to break through the horrible atmosphere. 'I mean, we need to get through probate and resolve the will. I've been advised to live here whilst that process is ongoing.'

'And what about us?' The redness in Tamsin's cheeks disappears. Now she looks abnormally pale. I notice that she's wearing hardly any makeup, a contrast to when she was married.

'I have no intention of chucking you out. I already explained that. Let's get the paperwork all sorted, and then we can take stock. If the will is valid–'

'Which it's not,' Tamsin interrupts.

'If it's valid, then we will agree to a reasonable time period to allow you sufficient time to find somewhere else to go.'

'Whoopee-do!' David exclaims. 'We're being given permission to stay in our own home.'

'Do you view this place as your home?' Tamsin asks. 'Because you haven't stepped foot in this place for months, years even.' She's throwing David daggers. I'm surprised about the animosity between them.

'It was my family home, but as there's not much family left, not really.' He spears an asparagus and slowly chews on it. 'But it's my heritage, and just because you don't physically live in a place doesn't mean it's not your soul home.'

David is certainly a strange individual. It's like he's trying to wind up Tamsin, and she has certainly taken a dislike to him, yet he shows a weird sensitivity talking about his soul home. I wonder whether he set up the whole mugging thing, whether it was some kind of ruse to trick me into talking to him. Right now, it feels very much like I'm caught in some sort of dystopian domestic feud, an unwilling heroine with no idea whom to trust and which way to turn. Despite everything David said about Robin, I think Robin was the good person here. Perhaps he wasn't the best dad – I've heard that very successful individuals often aren't – but I saw nothing to suggest that he wasn't kind to Brooke and Tamsin, giving them all a very luxuriant way of life.

As for Pavla and her family, she and Thomas had secure

jobs for years plus accommodation and a car. It's David who has been behaving suspiciously. Where exactly was he when Robin died? Was he really out of the country, or had he snuck back into the UK? Perhaps David was the person threatening Robin. Perhaps Robin didn't fall down the stairs. Perhaps his very own son pushed him. One thing is for sure, I don't trust a word that David says.

16

It's late afternoon. Claudia has left, David announced he was off to the pub, and Brooke is watching Netflix in the living room. Mia's disappeared, upstairs I think. What a horrible day. It's already dark outside, but I'm tempted to go to the greenhouse. I'm at the back door, debating whether to put on some warmer clothes, when my mobile phone rings. It's a withheld number.

'Tamsin Featherstone.'

'Mrs Featherstone, this is Aiden Mitchell.'

'Hello,' I say. My pulse starts to increase, surprised that he's calling me at the weekend. 'Have you got some news for me?'

'Indeed, I do. I hope you're sitting down.' I steady myself by leaning against the wall, unwelcome thoughts racing through my head. Is he going to tell me that Mia was Robin's lover and they have a child together? Or perhaps she's his love child from a distant relationship. Or was my marriage to Robin a sham? What other horrors would mean that she was more entitled to his inheritance than me?

'I have discovered that Mia Benton has a criminal conviction for fraud.'

'For fraud?'

'Indeed.'

I would like to let out a massive *hooray!* and air punch, but I try to be mature about this. Even so, I can't stop my face from breaking into a massive smile.

'What did she do? Did she forge someone else's will and got caught for it?'

'She was convicted of fraud and spent two years in prison. I don't know too many details at this stage, but by the end of Monday, I should have more information for you. I just thought you'd appreciate knowing the news immediately.'

'That's amazing news and such a relief. I knew there was something off about her. I knew that Robin would never knowingly deprive me and his children of our inheritance.'

'I'll be in touch,' he says before hanging up.

'Yes!' I say out loud, doing a silly little jig around the room.

'Who were you talking to?'

'You startled me,' I say to David, who has crept up behind me. I flush red in the knowledge that he has just witnessed my ridiculous display of joy. 'I thought you were in the pub.'

'Just a quick pint, and now I'm back. Well?'

'Well, what?'

'Who were you talking to?'

I cross my arms in front of my chest. I can see so much of Robin in David, how my husband must have looked when he was a much younger man. But David is like an unrefined version of his father, more rugged, more confident of his physique and good looks.

I'm inclined to tell him that it's none of his business, but actually, it is his business too, and I want David on my side. I step behind him and shut the door into the utility room. The last thing I want is Mia overhearing this conversation. I speak quietly. 'As I explained to your mother and sister, I have employed a private investigator. It seems that Mia has a criminal record, for fraud.'

'Seriously?'

'She went to prison!'

'So sweet little Mia isn't what she seems.'

'I'm so relieved, David. Your dad and I really loved each other, and we never discussed his will. Why would we? We were just starting our marriage, planning our future together. When he died, I assumed that he might have left me the house and that you and Brooke would get everything else, or something like that. And then we discovered Mia was getting it all. Anyway, if your father's estate does revert to me, I'm going to make sure that you and Brooke get your fair share. I know it's what your father would have wanted.'

David looks stunned and surprisingly lost for words. 'You know, Tamsin. I think I got you all wrong.'

I laugh. 'Most people do.'

'I thought you would be the stereotypical money-grabber, out to snare the old man and then bump him off so you could live the rest of your life in luxury. I was so angry with Dad for marrying someone half his age.'

'You should have made an effort to meet me, and then you would have learned the truth.'

He glances downwards. I notice what long, luscious lashes he has, and then he looks up at me, his lips slightly apart. He reminds me so much of Robin – a younger, even more handsome version.

'Are you going to the police?'

'What?' I ask, bringing myself back into the moment and reminding myself that this is the son of my recently deceased husband, for goodness' sake.

'You need to tell the police your suspicions that Mia has

forged the will. If she's got form for this kind of thing, then it's up to us to let them know.'

'I suppose you're right.'

'Would you like me to drive you?'

'What, right now? It's the weekend.'

'The police don't work nine to five, Tamsin. Mia is a criminal, and she's living under our roof, trying to steal what is rightfully yours. Yes, you need to go now.'

'Alright, fair enough.' Although I don't relish the prospect. I don't trust the police; why would I after they failed me? It takes me back to when I was thirteen. One day I returned home from school, and Mum was sitting in the kitchen with an ice pack up against her nose and eye. I asked her what had happened, and she said she'd walked into a cupboard. When she removed the ice pack, there was already swelling and dark bruising under her eye, and blood encrusted around her nostril.

'Which cupboard did you walk into?' I asked, because I might have been young, but I was streetwise.

'Leave it, Tamsin,' she said.

'Tell me the truth.' I stood there, my hands on my hips, all sanctimonious.

'Keep your voice down. Dad is resting.'

'I'm going to tell the police what he did to you. And it's not the first time, is it? And it probably won't be the last. I don't want to come home from school one day and find you dead on the floor.'

Mum laughed then, but it wasn't a funny *ha ha* laugh. She sounded angry and hurt and annoyed all at the same time. 'You really think that the police are going to believe you?' Mum said.

But I was a silly young girl, and I went upstairs to my room, and I telephoned 999. I told the policewoman that my dad had assaulted my mum, and that no one would believe it possible because he was in a wheelchair. But he was still strong in his arms, and he chucked things at Mum, and now she was bleeding, and I was frightened. Twenty minutes later, the doorbell rang, and there were two police officers standing in the doorway. I was too scared to go downstairs. Mum took them into the living room and shut the door, so I couldn't hear what was said. Five minutes later, they were gone. Mum walked upstairs and flung open my bedroom door.

'If you ever do anything like that again, I'm throwing you out of the house,' she said. Mum was shaking with rage; for the first time ever, she terrified me. We never spoke about it again. Even after Dad died, she didn't say a word. Then she died, too.

I think the police let us down. I know I was only thirteen, but surely they just had to look at Mum and see that Dad was violent and had hit her. And now, here I am, all of these years later, having to report another crime and wondering if I'm going to be believed.

'Tamsin, are you going or not?'

I pull myself back into the moment. David is right. I need to report Mia to the police. This is nothing like the situation at home with my parents. Mia is a known criminal, and it's shocking the lengths of deception that people like her are prepared to go to. She's obviously been biding her time working as the cleaner and then the personal assistant – grooming Robin, preying on him when he was vulnerable. Now it's up to me to avenge my deceased husband. 'I'll go straight away.'

'Excellent. Give me a call if you need any backup. We might have something to celebrate this evening,' David says.

'Don't you think we should keep this under wraps?' I suggest. 'We don't want Mia getting wind of what we know.'

'Good point, Tamsin,' David says, looking at me intently. I have to shift my gaze away. 'In fact, I think we should keep this knowledge as our secret for now. Neither Mum nor Brooke can keep their mouths shut. Better to keep your enemies close and all that, isn't it?'

I smile awkwardly. 'Let's see what the police have to say and take it from there.'

'Fair enough. Come and find me later.' David puts his hand on my arm, and I have to suppress a shiver.

DAVID IS wrong about one thing. English police stations are not open twenty-four hours. The one in Horsham is shut at the weekends, and the Crawley police station is only open until 8 pm on a Saturday, so I plug the address into Google Maps and head over there.

On the drive, I spend more time thinking about David than I do about the implications of our discovery about Mia. He isn't at all what I expected. I guess I thought he would be a spoiled, arrogant and angry young man, but he isn't. There is something measured and sensitive about him. Once you peel away that external veneer of confidence, he reminds me so much of his dad before his stroke. I can imagine that he'd make a great lover, but then I feel utterly disgusted with myself all over again. I'm not concentrating sufficiently on the road and let the nearside wheel of the Defender catch the edge of the verge. I have to grasp the steering wheel tightly to keep the car on the road, and let out a short screech. The husband I love is barely cold, and I'm already contemplating what it would be like to be in the arms of someone else. No, worse than that: In the arms of David, Robin's son. I need to get a grip.

The police station is a massive red-brick building with lots of windows that look like peeping eyes with strange window slots above them, reminiscent of eyebrows. My heart is racing as I force myself to walk forwards through the large front door and into the entrance lobby. It's busy, but perhaps I shouldn't be surprised considering it's early on a Saturday evening. A drunken man is throwing his fists around and shouting. I skirt around him and make my way to the front desk. I'm glad I'm wearing an old jacket and jeans, having changed before coming out. I take a deep breath and smile at the man seated behind the Perspex screen.

'I'd like to talk to a police officer, please, about a fraud.'

'Is it urgent?'

'Of course it's urgent. It might be life-threatening.' I mean, who knows what Mia is capable of? She's a criminal living in my house.

He takes my name and address and tells me to wait. I'm not best pleased to have to hang around with the rabble in the front lobby, but of course, I have no choice. I sit on a plastic seat attached to the wall and play a word game on my phone. About twenty minutes later, my name is called. I feel self-conscious as I follow a woman of Asian descent, probably in her forties, through a set of locked doors and down a long corridor. She's wearing black trousers and a baggy grey jumper. She pushes open the door to a small room and switches on the light. There's something rancid about the room, even though it's spotless. Maybe it's the smell of stale sweat.

After we've sat down, she says, 'My name is DS Amala Chabra. How can I help you?'

'My husband died suddenly a few weeks ago, and we discovered to our dismay that he had left everything to our cleaning girl. It turns out that she has a criminal record for fraud. I think that she might have coerced him to change the will, or that the will is fraudulent.'

'That's normally something that will be decided as a civil

matter.' She rather unsubtly looks at her watch, and that annoys me.

'The thing is, the woman who has done this is called Mia Benton, and she has a criminal record and has been in prison for fraud. She's also staying at our house, and I'm very worried.'

'Do you have any reason to believe that she harmed a person or has acted maliciously?'

I think of Robin lying at the bottom of the stairs. Surely not ... Could Mia have pushed Robin? Did she set this whole thing up so that she was named as the sole beneficiary in his will, and then she pushed him down the stairs to his death?

'I don't know for sure what she's done, but that's your job, isn't it? To investigate.'

DS Chabra scribbles something in a notebook. 'I'm afraid that unless you have any proof as to what Mia Benton might have done, it really isn't a matter that we can investigate.'

Robin's death was ruled an accident. Call me naive, but it's never crossed my mind that it wasn't. After all, he was wobbly on his feet. It wasn't a stretch to think he actually tumbled. But what if Mia pushed him? What if Mia isn't only a fraudster, but also a murderer? I feel as if I've been doused in freezing cold water as the shock of that thought permeates through my body.

'My advice is to pursue this matter in the civil court. That way, if you have sufficient evidence, your husband's will would revert back to the previous version. But I'm afraid a suspicion that fraud might have been committed just isn't enough to warrant the police to investigate.'

'And if it's a possibility that she could have murdered my husband, what then?'

'Obviously, that is a very different matter. But–' She glances down at her notebook and then looks up again. 'Mrs Featherstone, bringing a vexatious complaint is a crime in itself. You can't just make a groundless objection against someone in order to harass that person; otherwise, you may end up being prosecuted yourself. That can result in a criminal record, along with a fine or even a prison sentence.'

I open and close my mouth. My initial thoughts about the police were right. This woman is never going to help me. I'm going to have to find out the truth about Mia myself.

'So you're going to do nothing?'

'If you can bring us evidence that a criminal offence might have taken place, then we will certainly help you.'

I purse my lips together and nod. DS Chabra passes a business card across the table. I pick it up and feel like spitting on it, but I drop it into my handbag and push my chair back. 'Thank you for your time,' I say curtly, not because I feel the sentiment, but because I intend to show this smug policewoman that she was wrong to dismiss my claims.

By the time I get home, I'm still raging. I want Mia out of the house, and I've no idea how to go about it. I need to get hold of Shayla Chatterton first thing on Monday morning, and perhaps we can stop the first solicitor's meeting on Tuesday. Shayla insisted I agree to it – a mediation meeting, which apparently looks good when we go to court, because it suggests that we have at least tried to resolve our differences. I stomp into the cloakroom, dumping my coat, and stride into the kitchen. To my surprise, Pavla is there, stirring a pot on the stove.

'Why are you working on a Saturday evening?'

'Just processing some of the leftovers from lunch. I'll pop them in the freezer for you. Would you like some vegetable soup?'

'Yes, thanks. Is Mia still here?'

Pavla sighs. 'I believe so.'

'I've just been to the police station.'

Pavla stops stirring and turns to look at me. 'You have? Why?'

'I think Mia forged the will. Worse than that, she's a criminal. She's been to prison. I've been thinking about it, but maybe Robin didn't fall. Maybe he was pushed.'

'No,' Pavla says, dropping the wooden spoon. 'You think Mr Featherstone was murdered?'

'Mia has done this sort of thing before, and now she's bloody staying in our house. She probably set the whole thing up and pushed Robin.'

'Oh my goodness,' Pavla says. She's gone very pale and grips the handle on the Aga. 'Mia was here the day that Robin died.'

'What?' I take a step towards Pavla. 'Here?'

'She came to Stave House very early in the morning. Honestly, I didn't think anything of it at the time. I mean, she used to work here, and it was obvious that Mr Featherstone had a soft spot for her. Then, with everything that happened, I didn't think about it again.'

'Are you sure she was here on the day that Robin died?'

Pavla nods. 'It was before breakfast, but for all I know, she could have returned later. Or perhaps she was hiding somewhere in the house and didn't strike until later.'

I shiver and then think of what DS Chabra said. 'Have you got any proof?' I ask Pavla.

She looks confused. 'What, like a photograph?'

I shrug my shoulders.

'What are you trying to say?' Pavla asks.

'I think things aren't necessarily as they seem. I think Mia killed Robin so as to steal his estate, but the police won't investigate unless we have some proof. I've no idea how to go about it.'

Pavla looks really shocked. I wonder if I should get her to

sit down. 'Nothing has been the same since Mr Featherstone passed away,' she says in a whisper. 'Nothing will be the same ever again.'

'So long as I am living in this house, you, Thomas and Marek have a home here. And I'm going to fight Mia in the courts to prove that she's a thief and quite possibly a murderer too.'

'And if you lose?' Pavla asks in a small voice.

'I suppose Mia might sell up and throw you out. But that's not going to happen, Pavla. We're all on the same side. David, Brooke, Claudia, you and me. You mustn't worry. I'm going to make this right.'

Pavla throws me a watery smile. 'Thank you, Tamsin. You're a good woman.'

I bite the inside of my cheek to stop myself from grinning. It's been surprisingly easy to convert David and Pavla into liking me.

17

MIA

I underestimated how hard it would be staying in a house where you're not wanted. Each time I walked downstairs, I could hear whispers. I've tried to stay out of everyone's way, but now I'm hungry. I go downstairs, along the corridor and into the kitchen, where Pavla and Tamsin are huddled together near the stove, their heads nearly touching, speaking in low voices.

'Hello,' I say. They leap apart. Tamsin throws me an evil stare, then turns back to Pavla.

'Oh, I forgot to tell you, Pavla, my car is going in for a service on Wednesday.'

I get the impression she's just saying the first thing that comes into her head in a pretence that they weren't talking about me. I don't know why she bothered. She refuses to meet my eyes, then strides out of the room while Pavla returns to whatever she is doing at the stove, vigorously stirring something in a pot.

'I've brought my own food, but was wondering if I could make myself a scrambled egg,' I ask.

'Your house. Do whatever you want.' Pavla doesn't turn to look at me.

'I'm very sorry about all of this. I have no intention of chucking you out,' I say, watching Pavla's shoulders stiffen.

'What *are* your intentions regarding the house?' she asks.

'Honestly, I haven't thought that far ahead. There are a lot of hoops to jump through first. Robin's inheritance has come as much of a shock to me as, no doubt, it has to you too.'

Pavla still doesn't say anything, and I'm not sure how to further ease this horribly awkward situation.

'We're having a meeting with our solicitors on Tuesday. Our first mediation session, which will be much more satisfactory than going to court.'

'Satisfactory for whom?' The stirring stops again.

'All of us. If we end up in court, then we'll be burning money. I'm sure Robin wouldn't have wanted that.'

Pavla turns around now and glares at me. 'You really didn't know Mr Featherstone at all.'

'Perhaps I didn't.'

So I back out of the kitchen, walk up the darkened staircase and return to my room at the end of the upstairs corridor. I'm trying not to cry when I call Dad. He's at work, and he isn't meant to answer his phone, but I know he always tries to pick up when I ring.

'I can't stay here. The atmosphere is too awful.'

'Oh, Mia, what did you expect?'

'But the solicitors have told me I should be here.'

'You have to do what they suggest, love. They're the specialists.'

'I want to come back to London. Can I stay with you? I'll bring your car back.'

'You can hang onto the Corsa, love. I don't need it. And of course you can come back here, but I do think you should follow the advice of your lawyer and try to stick it out a bit longer. Nothing worthwhile is ever easy.'

I sigh, because it's one of Dad's sayings that I wish wasn't true but probably is.

'I'll stay tonight, and then I'm coming back to you. We've got a mediation meeting on Tuesday with our solicitors. I'll take stock then.'

'That sounds like a good idea. Sleep well, love.'

I don't. I slip back down to the kitchen about 8 pm, by which time Pavla has left, and the only voices are coming from the living room, where I assume Brooke and David are watching television. After making myself a quick omelette, I wash everything up by hand and then slip back upstairs. I know it's silly, but I'm scared. If Robin was really pushed down the stairs, then perhaps one of the Featherstones will do something to me, too. What if I'm stabbed in the night? I try to tell myself that's a ridiculous thought, but after a couple of hours of trying and failing to get to sleep, I climb out of bed and shift the chest of drawers in front of the door. It makes me feel a little safer. Eventually, I drift off to sleep.

IT'S TUESDAY, and our very first round-table discussion to try to resolve the will. It seems ridiculous that we've all had to traipse to London when we could have sat around the kitchen table at Stave House, but Tamsin insisted if we were to meet, it would be at her solicitor's offices. I feel deeply uncomfortable as I walk along this smart Mayfair street. My solicitor is a chap called Ian Dunworthy. He was recommended by Timothy Carter, Robin's solicitor, and he's based in Crawley. How else is someone like me meant to find a probate specialist? Anyway, I've had a couple of phone calls with Ian Dunworthy. He has promised me that his fees won't be out of reach, and that he can be paid out of Robin's estate. Let's hope he's right and I win this fight; otherwise I might be saddled with debts for the next decade, all for nothing.

I ring the doorbell and am buzzed in. I've never worked in an office, but this certainly doesn't have an office feel to it. The hallway looks like the entrance to a fancy private house; in fact, it reminds me of Stave House. A receptionist, a young woman with strange matt skin, probably due to the heavy layer of foundation on her face, and thick chestnut hair piled high in a fancy updo, sits at a small mahogany table that has just enough space for a slimline computer screen. She is talking to a man, and only when he steps away and I walk forwards and say my name does he turn around.

'Mia, I'm Ian Dunworthy.' We shake hands, and I feel a sense of relief that I have someone on my side. He's a scruffy-looking chap in his mid-fifties with a balding head and over-sized thick-rimmed tortoiseshell glasses that I think are meant to make him look cool, but rather miss the mark. He's wearing a suit that is a little too tight and shiny, and the hem has come down on his left leg, but he has kind eyes and ushers me into the waiting room. It looks like the grandiose drawing room of a stately home. Now I'm feeling really nervous. It's not as if I wanted any of this. Robin may have meant well, but I'm very uncomfortable.

It obviously shows on my face, because Ian Dunworthy leans towards me and says in a whisper, 'Nothing to worry about. You just leave it to me.'

I smile gratefully.

About ten minutes later, the receptionist tells us to take the lift to the third floor. It's a small lift with a horrible wire cage inner door that shuts with a metallic thud, reminding me of jail. I dig my short nails into the palms of my hands. The whole mechanism creaks and groans as it slowly rises upwards, then jangles as Ian opens the inner and outer doors. I'll take the stairs next time, if there is a next time.

We're met by another young woman wearing a black suit and vertiginous heels. She leads us to a large meeting room. It is as grand as downstairs, with a shiny wooden table that smells of furniture polish, and big windows looking out onto a brick wall. There is ornate cornicing on the ceiling, and very large paintings hang on the walls. I suppose they're expensive pieces of modern art, but to me they just look like multicolour splodges in various shades of greens. A horrible silence falls as we walk into the room. Tamsin, David and Brooke sit on one side of the table. Neither of them acknowledges Ian or me, but a tall, attractive woman wearing a pillar-box red jacket and black skirt stands up and strides towards Ian.

'Shayla Chatterton. Good to meet you,' she says as she pumps Ian's hand up and down. She doesn't shake my hand, but just inclines her head towards me. Another woman stands up and introduces herself as Briony Kesler. A black woman with fabulous hair that makes her face appear small, she seems more friendly. At least she smiles. Shayla takes her place at the head of the table, with Briony sitting next to her. Ian sits at the opposite end, so I am between him and Briony. Unfortunately, I'm sitting directly opposite Brooke, who is staring at me with narrowed eyes. If I was nervous before, now it feels as if my heart is going to jump out of my chest.

Shayla Chatterton starts talking. 'As you are aware, we are contesting Robin Featherstone's will and have agreed to try mediation with the help of my colleague, Briony Kesler. Over to you, Briony.'

'First, I need to say something,' Brooke interrupts. 'Mia must have done something to coerce Dad. I mean, there's no way that he'd just hand over everything to the cleaning woman. He'd have been more likely to give it to Pavla than Mia. At least she's worked for us for twenty years and was trusted. And what about Tamsin – she was Dad's new wife!

Mia was fired by Dad. It's totally fishy, and this must be her way of revenge.'

'Actually I was fired by Tamsin and not Mr Featherstone.'

'Because you have a criminal record,' Tamsin says, through gritted teeth. 'You lied; you stole–'

'I certainly did not!' I exclaim. But my heart sinks. The Featherstones have found out that I have a criminal record. Here I am again, back in the same situation where no one will believe me. I can sense Ian Dunworthy's frown, but I don't turn to catch his eye. I'll have to explain later. I don't suppose he'll believe me either, because who trusts someone who was convicted of a crime and served time in prison? I wonder if I should stand up and walk out right now. It might be easier for everyone concerned, but then I think of Robin's letter, and I know I need to stand up for him and myself.

'Ladies, please,' Briony Kesler says. 'I will not accept a slanging match. From now on, your legal representatives will talk for you as we try to achieve some resolution.'

She then goes on to set out how the mediation process will work, how we can each go into our break-out rooms to discuss things in private with our solicitors, and how it is unlikely that we will come to a consensus today, but can have further mediation sessions if required. I zone out for a while, vacillating about whether I should ignore Robin's wishes and just say I'll renounce the will. Surely that's possible? But I can't stop thinking about Robin's letter and how he feared for his life.

'Mia is manipulative and controlling,' Tamsin says, totally ignoring Briony Kesler's instructions. I start listening again when I hear my name. 'For all we know, she might have been instrumental in my husband's stroke, too. She was the only person in the house at the time. The doctors would never have investigated him for unnatural causes.'

'That's outrageous!' I retort. Ian Dunworthy pats my forearm.

'Let me deal with this, Mia,' he says quietly.

I cannot believe the slurs that Brooke and Tamsin are saying about me. I look at David, who hasn't uttered a word. He's kept his eyes to the table the whole time. I can't work out whether he's uncomfortable or just bored. Which one of these three is the most contemptible? Could one of them have killed Robin in the hope of receiving all his wealth? Tamsin is the most obvious culprit, but I wonder if she's come to some kind of deal with Brooke, which is why they appear so friendly and united these days. I wish I knew exactly what Robin had been referring to in his letter to me when he said that he feared for his life. Tamsin could have easily hurt her husband, given him too much medication, perhaps. She wasn't even sleeping in the same bedroom. It certainly would have been easy for Tamsin to have pushed her husband down the stairs.

The meeting carries on for a few more minutes, with Briony Kesler trying to keep harmony, but it's perfectly obvious that Tamsin wants the whole lot and outright rejects any suggestion that Robin's inheritance is split. Shayla Chatterton has made it quite clear that her clients do not want me to get a single penny. I wouldn't mind, other than Tamsin and Brooke keep on interrupting, making outrageous slurs about me. And then Briony suggests that we take some time out to have private chats with our respective solicitors.

It's a relief to get out of that horrible atmosphere. Ian and I are directed to a small room with a table that seats four. I pour myself a glass of water from a carafe placed on a sideboard and walk towards the window, which I open despite the drizzle outside. I need some fresh air.

'I don't want any of this,' I say, with my back turned to Ian. 'Let them have it all.'

'Absolutely not,' Ian Dunworthy says, with surprising vehemence. 'If you are innocent of the slurs being made against you, then it is your duty to uphold the wishes of the deceased.'

'Do you believe me?' I ask, swivelling around.

'I believe that a person is innocent until proven guilty beyond reasonable doubt.'

'And my previous record?'

'It would have been helpful if you'd told me about that beforehand, but that conviction is spent and consequently not relevant. This is a civil matter, anyway.'

'I'm sorry,' I say, finishing off the water and pulling out a chair. 'I was framed. Yes, I was convicted of fraud, but I was innocent despite the court finding me guilty. That situation bears no resemblance to this one.'

'You've been staying at Stave House, I understand.'

'Yes, but only a couple of nights. The atmosphere was awful.'

'My advice is that you return there and make an inventory of all of the chattels, as best you can. I appreciate that the atmosphere might be difficult, but it is within your right to ask the Featherstones to leave the house should you so wish.'

'I don't want to do that.'

'That's what I assumed you would say, so I will suggest that they behave cordially towards you until this matter is settled; otherwise, you will evict them.'

'Alright.' I know that is the right thing. If I'm to discover the truth as to whether something sinister happened to Robin, then I will have to stay in Stave House. It doesn't mean I'm looking forward to it.

I DRIVE BACK to Stave House, arriving about 10 pm, having spent the rest of the day in London meeting up with friends and having an early supper with Dad. Somehow, Ian persuaded Tamsin to give me a key to the house during the unpleasant meeting this morning, so at least I'm able to slip in and out as I please. It didn't go unnoticed that she only gave me a back door key. I suppose she'll always see me as staff.

The next morning, I'm in the kitchen at 8.30 am when Tamsin appears, her car keys dangling from her index finger.

'Good morning,' I say, but she just scowls at me and walks outside, getting in her Defender and driving away. If that's how she wants to act, so be it. In a way, I don't blame her.

About a minute later, I'm standing in front of the window, waiting for toast to pop out of the toaster, when I see a silver saloon car pull up in front of the house. It's as if Pavla was waiting for them, because she appears immediately. A man and a woman get out and stand there talking to her for a good ten minutes. There's something about them that screams police. It could be the fact that the man is scribbling in a little notebook and that he looks very young but confident, or the way they're standing with legs planted firmly apart and shoulders back. The woman glances up at the window, and I step back quickly, hoping she didn't see me. I can't make out what they're saying, but I feel deeply uneasy. Then Pavla is leading them into the house. Before I know it, they are in the kitchen.

'Mia Benton?' the woman asks.

'Yes.' My cup of tea sloshes slightly as I put it down on the table.

'We're from the police and would like to ask you some routine questions. My name is DS Amala Chabra, and this is my colleague, DC Ben Degreen. May we sit down?'

I glance at Pavla, who is standing in the doorway with her arms crossed in front of her chest. She doesn't look at me, and a wave of defiance ripples through me. I don't need to check with her whether they can sit down, because this is my house for now – and, as strange a thought as it is, Pavla is probably my employee.

'What is this about?'

'May we sit down?' DS Chabra asks again.

'Yes, yes. Please take a seat. Would you like a tea or coffee?'

'Two teas would be great. Both white with one sugar, please,' she says.

'Pavla, would you mind shutting the door on your way out?' I ask, smiling as sweetly as I can. She scowls, but does as I request. I assume she's standing on the other side of the door with her ear pressed against it.

I fill up the kettle and switch it on, turning to look at them.

'We're here with regard to the death of Robin Featherstone.'

'Has a crime been committed?' I ask.

'What do you think?' she asks.

'I've no idea,' I say.

'Are you living here now?' DC Chabra tilts her head to one side. Her black hair hangs like a curtain.

'Yes. I assume you're aware that Robin made me his executor and beneficiary?'

I turn to take the milk out of the fridge, then glance out of the window. I'm wrong about Pavla, because she is walking briskly down the drive towards her own cottage.

'Thank you,' DC Degreen says as I place the mugs on the table. I'm trying very hard not to show how nervous I'm feeling. The trouble is, I don't trust the law, and the police represent the law. I smile, but it feels as if I'm stretching my face unnaturally, so I give up and sit down opposite them, my hands underneath my thighs to stop them from shaking.

'What exactly was the nature of your relationship with Mr Featherstone?' DS Chabra asks.

'I was employed as a cleaner, and then after his stroke, I became more like his personal assistant. I'm a trained musician, so was able to help him with notation and transcribing and the like.'

'When did you leave the Featherstones' employment?'

'February 27. Tamsin fired me.'

'You must have been very upset about that,' DS Chabra suggests.

'I wasn't happy, obviously. Robin wasn't at home, and she didn't seem to have a good reason for firing me.'

'Yet you didn't argue the point?'

'I didn't have an employment contract, so there was no point in me trying to disagree.' There's nothing illegal about that, is there? I mean, nothing the police could pounce on. If anything, it's the Featherstones who were in the wrong, not supplying me with a contract, not paying employment taxes. But, of course, it suited us both.

'You must have been upset and angry.'

'To begin with, yes. But as things turned out, it was the best thing that could have happened to me. I was able to get back to playing the violin and was picked up to go on tour with a band. I don't understand why you're asking me all of these questions. Do you think Robin's death wasn't an accident?'

She ignores my question. 'Were you in this house on the day that Mr Featherstone died?'

And here it is: the killer question. Because yes, I was here on that day, but it was early in the morning, and I had gone back to London before Tamsin or Pavla got up. Yet I can't tell the police that I was here, because that will look horribly suspicious. I can see that they'll suggest that I had something to do with Robin's death. What should I do? They've backed me into a corner. I am sure that no one saw me.

I panic and I lie: 'No. I didn't return to the house until last week.'

DS Chabra stares at me. Her eyes are almost black; I find her gaze so unsettling I can't help but glance away. Can she tell that I'm lying?

'It must have come as a great shock when you discovered that you were the sole beneficiary. Or had Mr Featherstone already told you that he had changed his will?'

I don't like DS Chabra. It's as if she's trying to catch me out, and I suppose it's because she knows about my criminal record.

'No, he–' But my thoughts are interrupted when I remember the letter.

DS Chabra and DC Degreen glance at each other.

'I need to show you something. It's important. Can I just run upstairs and get it?'

DS Chabra nods.

I am so glad that I brought the letter with me, stuffed into the side pocket of my suitcase, hopefully away from any prying eyes. I race upstairs, along the corridor and into my bedroom, relieved I haven't run into any members of the family. Grabbing Robin's letter, I return downstairs to the kitchen and hand the letter to DS Chabra.

'What is this?' she asks.

'A letter that Robin sent to me before he died. I didn't receive it until I got home from my tour, a few weeks after he died. He sent it to Dad's address. You can see the postmark on the envelope.'

DS Chabra reads the letter while DC Degreen studies the envelope. It's clearly postmarked with the date and the place, Horsham.

'Do you believe this letter is really from Robin Feather-stone?' DS Chabra asks.

That's what Dad asked, and no, I can't be one hundred percent sure. 'I think it is. I mean, that's his signature at the bottom, and it sounds like the sort of wording he would use.'

'So why didn't you bring this letter to the police? If Mr Featherstone was really concerned about his well-being, why didn't you say anything?'

'Because I wondered if his stroke had affected his mind. He wasn't himself after the stroke, and I thought it might be some sort of paranoia. If he had really been scared, wouldn't he have contacted you himself?'

Neither of them say anything for a long moment.

'Can we keep this letter?' DS Chabra asks.

'Yes. But can you tell me what this is all about, why you're investigating?'

'We will keep you posted, Miss Benton. And please let us know if, for any reason, you need to leave the country.'

I swallow. 'Is this to do with my previous criminal record?'

'We will be considering all the facts, and yes, Ms Benton, your previous conviction does give us considerable reason for concern.'

I open and close my mouth, because what can I say?

DS Chabra stands up, and DC Degreen quickly follows suit.

'We can see ourselves out,' she says, inclining her head ever so slightly towards me.

So I watch them as they leave the kitchen and then walk down the steps towards their waiting car. I am tempted to run after them and tell them that I lied about not being at the house that day ... because if they do find out the truth, then I'm finished, aren't I? It's obvious they're suspicious about Robin's death, or wondering whether I had influenced him to change his will. I groan. And now I've just cast doubt on

Robin's mental capacity. If he wasn't fully with it, then that might affect the inheritance. Tamsin may be able to argue that Robin wasn't of sound mind, and then I'm certain to lose.

I sink back down into the chair and wonder what the hell I should do now.

18

When Pavla told me that Mia had visited Stave House the morning that Robin died, I just knew that Mia had killed my husband, and now I have to collect the evidence to prove it. I'm pissed off with Pavla that she didn't say anything earlier, but I suppose so much happened that it was understandable it slipped her mind. But now it all stacks up. Mia forced Robin to change his will, and then she killed him. What a travesty of justice that I'm expected to live in the same house as my husband's murderer. Pavla and I had a good chat about it. I'm so relieved that she and I are on the same page. She even offered to come to the police with me as moral support and to give a statement that she had seen Mia that morning. In the end, I telephoned DS Chabra. I'm just hoping that they take Mia in for questioning.

This morning, I had to leave early to take my car in for a service. Now, a doddery old man from the garage is giving me a lift back home in one of those new Land Rover Defenders, possibly in the vain hope that I might want to upgrade to a new model. I'm quite happy with the old one, thank you very much. There is so much going on at the moment, it feels like my head is spinning. And all of the trouble is related to Mia. I can't believe that she and her miserable-looking solicitor gave Brooke, David and me an ultimatum. It was the ultimate humiliation – accept Mia in the house and treat her with respect; otherwise she'll throw us out.

I feel even worse for Brooke and David; after all, this is their family home. I had a real go at Shayla Chatterton after the meeting, but she told me in that head-girl bossy voice of hers that the law was on Mia's side and I needed to rein in my opinions. So much for my expensive London lawyer.

As I get out of the car, Pavla appears.

'The police have been to speak to Mia,' she says in a conspiratorial whisper.

I let out a whoosh of breath and smile. 'Thank goodness.' I'm so relieved that they took my call seriously. 'Has she gone, then?' I ask.

'What, Mia? No, she's still here.'

'Oh,' I say, the disappointment I'm feeling mirrored on Pavla's face. I had assumed they would have carted Mia off in their squad car and arrested her. I guess they need to pull together more evidence first.

'Would you like a coffee?' Pavla asks, in a surprising act of generosity.

'I'll make my own in the greenhouse, thank you.'

I walk towards the greenhouse and see Thomas, who waves at me from across the garden. A wash of sadness sweeps over me as I think of how terrified Robin must have been when he felt a hand shove him from behind. I pray that he didn't lie there suffering, that when his head smashed into the bottom step, he lost consciousness immediately.

Once I've made my coffee and taken a few sips, I telephone my private detective, Aiden Mitchell, and bring him up to date with the police involvement and my suspicions. I am feeling a lot more hopeful now that we will be able to successfully contest the will. Who would have thought that Mia – meek, ordinary Mia – had served time in prison?

I WATER my plants and rearrange some of my cacti. I know that most people don't understand my fascination with these plants, because they're not pretty and they grow so slowly, but what they don't appreciate is how extraordinary they are. Robin used to laugh at my obsession, but nevertheless, he humoured me. For starters, he built me this amazing greenhouse. Of course, he made those cruel remarks after his stroke, telling me that he was my source of money so I could buy my hideous cacti, but I have to forgive him for that. Robin was ill and no doubt scared of what the future might hold. I don't think that he really begrudged me my collection. I wish I'd told him how similar I am to my plants: resilient with hidden depths.

These plants are truly tough, adapted to thrive in the harshest of environments. Many can survive a whole year without any water, so the thing I have to be most careful about is not overwatering them. I also love the shapes and their symmetry, which often is almost architectural. But the most amazing thing about cacti is how quickly and magnificently they flower. When the conditions are absolutely perfect, they produce dazzling, exotic blooms that simply take one's breath away. I am a true xerophile and proud of it. If I have to leave this place, my heart will break even further, because it's not like I can lift up this glasshouse and take it with me. Where would I put my precious plants? I'd probably have to sell them off at rock-bottom prices, or leave them here to wither and die. It's too horrible to think about it.

An email pings through on my phone. It's a local nursery letting me know that the rare *Forbessi* 'Super Spiralis' has arrived and is ready for me to collect. It's a fabulous plant, over a foot tall, like a huge spiralling cucumber, worth several hundred pounds. Straight away, my mood lifts. I hurry out of the greenhouse and back into the main house, collecting my handbag. And then I remember. Damn, my car is in the garage having a service. I walk out to the large, three-bay open garages and curse as I see Robin's black Range Rover is missing, no doubt taken by David. Brooke's revolting pink Mini is on the far end, but there is no way that I will be seen in that. Quite why Robin permitted her to have such a ridiculous-coloured car is beyond me. Perhaps Claudia gave her the money for it, because I'm sure Brooke didn't earn enough to buy it herself. At least up until now, I've been self-sufficient, strong and resilient, much like my cacti.

Annoyed, I return to the house. Pavla is walking through the hallway, dragging the vacuum cleaner.

'I'd forgotten that my car is in the garage today, and I wanted to go and collect a new cactus from a nursery on the coast. Any chance I could borrow yours?'

'I'm sorry, but Thomas has taken it. He'll be out for a couple of hours, as he's getting the strimmer fixed.'

'You can borrow mine, or rather my dad's.'

I swivel around to see Mia walking down the stairs.

I hesitate. Why would Mia let me borrow her car? We loathe each other, don't we? Perhaps this is her way of trying to be nice to me. But then I think, why not? After all, she's borrowing my house, so why shouldn't I borrow her car? I've got that type of insurance that lets me drive any car.

'Alright,' I say.

Mia hands me a car key with a tacky Union Jack fob.

'It's not very glamorous, but it works.'

I nod at her and mutter, 'Thank you,' more out of habit than because I feel any real gratitude.

I climb into the driver's seat, turn the key, and the engine splutters into life. It's a rusty tin box, but not a million miles away from my Defender, just a lot smaller. I rather enjoy the looks of surprise I get when I slip out of my green, rusting farm vehicle, dressed up smartly and looking like a sophisticated model. I turn the Vauxhall Corsa around and steer it down the long gravel driveway to the main road. As I approach the road, I put my foot on the brake.

Nothing happens.

I'm not driving fast, but I need to stop. Now.

I slam my foot on the brake again, pushing it down to the floor. Nothing. I'm slipping forwards, right into the path of any oncoming traffic. I scream as I realise the brake pedal is doing nothing. Is this it? Is this my end? At least if I were in the Defender, I'd be high off the ground, but this car will offer zero protection.

And then I'm in the road. In that quick second, I brace myself for the impact of another vehicle slamming into the sides of this little red tin box. There's a bump, and the windscreen is right up against the hedge. I'm jolted forwards, but not severely, as I wasn't driving fast. Then there's silence. The car has stalled, and the bonnet is firmly wedged in the hedge.

Trembling, I open the driver's door and jump out, my knees giving way. I grip onto the side of the car and look around me. There's no traffic coming from either direction, and the Corsa is completely on the verge.

What the hell happened? I feel sick and have to take several gulps of fresh air and swallow hard to stop myself from vomiting. The brakes failed. The bloody brakes failed, and if a lorry had been passing just now, I would have been killed. A white van approaches and slows right down. The driver winds down his window.

'You alright, love?'

'Yes, thank you. The brakes failed.'

'Do you need a lift?'

'Um, no, thanks. I live right here.'

'If you're sure?'

I smile at him and give a feeble wave. He drives away.

A few more vehicles drive past, but none of them stop. I step away from the Corsa. On first glance, it looks as if the car is a farmer's vehicle about to drive through a gate into a field – except there is no gate here, just a very long, dense stretch of hedgerow, and what farmer would be driving a thing like this?

The back wheels are off the road, and the vehicle isn't obstructing anything. I grab my handbag and lock the car; then I cross the road and walk up the long drive towards Stave House, trying to stop my legs from wobbling. I swallow hard as I realise that the accident should have happened to Mia, not me. And then it hits me. Did she know something was wrong with her car? Is that the reason she was so happy for me to borrow her car? If so, that's attempted murder, isn't it?

I can still hear the blood rushing in my ears, and my heart isn't slowing. Nothing like this has ever happened to me before. I've never been in an accident, let alone have someone attempt to kill me. I must be overreacting, because as much as I loathe Mia, I can't imagine her tampering with her own car. I'm just going to have to be calm and logical here, not do my typical thing of jumping to conclusions.

A car crunches on the gravel behind me, and I literally jump.

David winds the window down, a cigarette dangling from his lips. 'You look like you've just seen a ghost!'

'Jeez, David. You scared me.'

'Are you alright? You look as white as a sheet.'

'The brakes on Mia's car just failed.'

'What were you doing driving that rust heap?'

'I borrowed it.'

David turns off the engine and hops down from the Range Rover. He drops the cigarette butt and grinds it out with the heel of his brown brogue.

I'm still shaking. David walks towards me and grasps both of my shoulders. 'Are you ok?'

'Not really.' I let out a little sob, and David hugs me tightly. I feel so safe in his arms, the first time someone has held me like this since Robin had his stroke. I know I shouldn't be enjoying this moment, but despite his breath smelling of cigarette smoke, it's just what I need.

He's the first to let go, and I reluctantly step backwards.

'Where's the car?'

'Wedged in the hedge on the opposite side of the road.'

'Bloody hell, Tamsin. You could have been killed.'

'I know,' I murmur.

'Right, I'll go and have a look at it. I can use Dad's Range Rover to tow it back here.'

'Is that safe if the brakes aren't working?'

'It'll be fine, don't worry.'

HALF AN HOUR LATER, thanks to Marek standing in the road to stop any oncoming traffic, David has towed Mia's Corsa back to the house. Mia isn't anywhere to be seen, probably hiding in her room, and I'm glad about that. David has the bonnet open.

'How do you know what you're doing?' I ask. 'Wouldn't it be better if you get Thomas to help you?'

'Don't you trust me?'

'What with your clean hands and neatly manicured fingernails, you don't seem the type to be tinkering about with cars.'

David chuckles. 'Looks can be deceptive, Tamsin.'

After a few minutes looking inside the bonnet, David

levers himself onto the ground and peers underneath the car.
I thought he would be more like his father, not wanting to get
his smart clothes dirty, but it really looks like David is
enjoying himself. Me less so. I hop from foot to foot,
replaying those couple of seconds in my head.

'Shit!' David exclaims.

'What is it?'

He wriggles himself out from underneath the car and
wipes his hands on his jeans, leaving black smears down each
trouser leg.

'Someone's tampered with the brakes.'

'What?' I choke.

'I think it's the master cylinder.'

'I don't understand.'

David puts a hand on my arm. 'Look, I'm not a qualified
mechanic or anything, but I think something was done to the
car.'

'On purpose?'

He shrugs his shoulders. I don't say anything to David,
but did Mia just send me off in her car knowing full well that
the brakes weren't working? Was this her way of getting rid
of me?

We walk together into the house just as Pavla is coming
out of the kitchen, holding a steaming mug. 'Marek told me
what happened,' she says. 'I've made you a hot toddy. A
special tea with a few drops of whiskey to calm the nerves.'

I take it from her gratefully. 'Thanks, Pavla.'

The three of us walk together back into the kitchen.

'Has anyone told Mia?' Pavla asks. 'After all, it is her car.'

'I think she did this on purpose,' I say, suppressing
another shiver.

'Oh, goodness,' Pavla says, her hand rushing to cover her
mouth.

'We'll need to tell the police.' I'm surprised how calm I

feel now, even with the thought that my life might be in danger, because we all know who's the culprit.

'Mia,' I say quietly.

'Mia,' Pavla repeats after me.

'What are you saying about me?' And there she is. Mia walks into the kitchen, a wide-eyed look of innocence on her face.

'The brakes on your car have failed. Tamsin nearly got killed,' David says.

Mia's mouth opens, and she looks deeply shocked, but I think she's the consummate actress, so that doesn't impress me.

'That's terrible.'

'Can something like that happen by chance, or do you think it was done on purpose?' Pavla asks, voicing my exact thought.

'Look,' David says. 'As I said to Tamsin, I'm not a trained mechanic, but I doubt this sort of thing just happens.'

Mia's expression changes from shock to indignance. 'First of all, I know nothing about the workings of a car, and secondly, why would I tamper with my own car's brakes?'

'You suggested that I drive it,' I say.

'Yes, but I didn't know you were looking to borrow a car. That's ridiculous!' Her voice rises, and her eyes dart from David to Pavla to me and back again.

'Where were you this morning?' I ask Mia.

'You can't accuse me!' she retorts, her denial morphing into anger as she jams her hands into the pockets of her trousers.

'You were outside early this morning,' Pavla says.

'I'm outside every morning. I was walking around the garden, trying to clear my head. Assuming I knew how to cut the brakes of a car – which is ridiculous because I don't even own a car, and the Corsa is Dad's – why would I want to hurt Tamsin?'

Pavla, David and I all stare at Mia. Isn't it bloody obvious as to why she'd want to get me out of the picture? Is she really that stupid? If I'm dead, then I won't be contesting the will. I take a step nearer to David because as I'm looking at Mia, I'm wondering whether it's really possible that this woman is capable of murdering me. And if so, should I be living here under the same roof as her?

'I'm calling the police,' I say as I remove my mobile phone from my handbag. I dial DS Chabra's mobile phone, and I'm relieved when I get through. All the time I keep my eyes on Mia. She is studiously avoiding looking at me. I wonder whether I see fear in her face, or am I just projecting my own feelings?

'How can I help you?' DS Chabra asks.

When I tell her about the brakes, the tone of her voice changes. For the first time, I think that she might actually be taking what I'm saying seriously. I say goodbye and place my phone on the table.

'What did she say?' David asks.

'Put the kettle on, Pavla. DS Chabra will be here in fifteen minutes.'

Mia walks out of the room.

'That wasn't a very subtle accusation,' David says with a snigger.

'I don't think she's as clever as she thinks she is,' I retort, finishing off the boozy tea that Pavla made me.

'It's all stacking up against her, that's for sure,' David comments.

'I never liked her,' Pavla mutters. 'Just because she is a musician, it's like she thinks she's above all of us. I don't know why Mr Featherstone employed her.'

'To be fair, Pavla,' I say, 'you were the person who recruited her.'

Pavla reddens slightly. 'A terrible mistake.'

'Let's just hope that the police take this seriously,' I say.

TWENTY MINUTES LATER, DS Chabra and DC Degreen are back at Stave House. Despite it being Mia's car being investigated, she has scarpered. For all I know, she's left and caught a train back to London. Good riddance. DC Degreen is checking out the Corsa while DS Chabra and I stand next to it. I explain to her exactly what happened.

'What's going to happen next?' I ask.

'We will talk to everyone who lives here, and have the car properly checked over to see if it has been tampered with. I trust this isn't a malicious complaint, Tamsin?'

'What?' I glower at the policewoman. 'I am not the criminal around here. We all know that it's Mia Benton.'

'I suppose you want to talk to me?' Mia appears in the open front door to the house. She walks slowly down the steps, wearing an anorak with her handbag strapped across her body.

'Indeed, we do,' DS Chabra says.

'What are you going to do with Dad's car?'

'We would appreciate if you could let us inspect it,' she says. 'Do you need to talk to your father?'

'No, it's fine,' Mia replies. I suppose she's too worried about what Daddy might say when he discovers what a murderous little cow she is.

'It might be more comfortable for you to talk to us down at the station,' DS Chabra suggests.

We all know what that means. The policewoman has phrased it as if they're just going to have a little chat, but she's obviously taking the prospect of Mia's involvement in Robin's death and my near-miss accident very seriously. Mia's face is expressionless as she walks towards the saloon car. I would like to do a fist pump as I breathe out a sigh of relief. At last, Mia is getting what she deserves. I hope that I never set eyes on her ever again.

19

I am terrified. I honestly never thought I would be in this situation again, yet here I am with a stack of evidence pointing towards me, all circumstantial of course, but will the police see it that way? What do they have evidence for? Murder? Attempted murder? It's a joke, suspecting me of tampering with the brakes on Dad's car. What on earth do I know about cars? I passed my driving test years ago, but I've never actually owned a car. And I certainly wouldn't do anything to endanger my own life or risk damaging Dad's car.

How was I to know that Tamsin wanted to borrow it? I know Tamsin thinks it's me behind everything, but I reckon that's a convenient ruse for her. I think she's the perpetrator. I reckon it's all a double bluff to set me up. She could have driven really slowly to the end of the drive and then, when nothing was coming, edged the car across the road. No one would ever think that she would have endangered her own life. How very clever of her to set me up.

She's certainly the most obvious culprit for murdering Robin. She obviously married Robin for his money and bumped him off when he fell ill. Or perhaps she caused his stroke by giving him some poison. Is that possible? Perhaps, but surely the hospital would have found some residue in Robin's blood if that had been the case.

No, I suspect she simply didn't want to be married to him anymore after he lost his virility and vitality. As his wife, she should have inherited the lot; that must have been oh-too-tantalising. It would have been so easy to give him a shove at the top of the stairs, act like the grieving widow for a few weeks and then pounce on the money. Poor Robin must have realised that she was trying to bump him off, which is why he wrote that letter to me and why he changed his will. He'd already shared with me what a disappointment his children were to him.

What a shock it must have been for Tamsin to discover she wasn't going to inherit a penny, and how very convenient for her that she can blame everything on me. The failing brakes was so expedient. Clever, clever Tamsin, setting me up as the perfect fall guy. Anyone with a criminal record is going to be viewed with extra suspicion, and I have been too naive and left myself wide open to blame. I have tried so hard to keep my criminal record hidden, but it's easy enough for anyone to find if they go looking. I'm listed on the Criminal Records Bureau; it will be another six long years until my record is spent.

I look out of the car window and see all those people happily carrying on with their everyday business. How I wish I were one of them. Ordinary. Far away from all of this. Without a label. I think of the solicitor I had all those years ago and how she failed me, and I wonder if this is it – where my short run of good luck runs out, and I'll be back in prison again by the end of the year.

At the police station, they lead me in through a back door. I haven't been to Crawley police station before. It's bigger than I expected, but it still has the same smell of sweat and fear and stale alcohol and vomit disguised with bleach. It makes my stomach heave. They take me into a small, cold room, but at least it has a view onto the car park, and the furniture isn't fixed to the floor.

'Have a seat, Ms Benton. Can I get you a drink? A water or tea?' DC Degreen asks, as if we're here for a friendly chat.

'I'm fine, thanks.' That's a lie. I'm far from fine.

DS Chabra settles into her chair. 'Right, Ms Benton. You are not under arrest, and you're free to leave at any time. You have agreed to be here to give a voluntary interview, and are also entitled to get legal advice should you want it, but I suspect you know all of that, as this isn't your first time in a police station, is it?'

Last time I was in this situation, I sought legal advice and was appointed the duty solicitor. She was a total waste of space. If I end up really needing a solicitor, then I'll do my research first and find someone who believes in me and is hungry to fight to prove I'm innocent.

'Well, Ms Benton?'

'You can call me Mia, and I don't need a solicitor. With regard to my conviction, as you know, I have served a sentence for fraud. It was a wrong conviction, and I wanted to appeal, but ...' I let my voice peter out. There's no point in going there. I take a deep breath and focus on the present. 'Why am I here?'

DS Chabra looks at her notebook and then looks up to hold my gaze. 'We have a witness that placed you at Stave House at approximately 8 am on the morning of Robin Featherstone's death, yet you told us that you weren't at the house that day, and you hadn't been back since the day Tamsin Featherstone fired you. What do you say to that?'

'It's true.' My voice is small. 'I lied to you because I was scared that you'd accuse me of something that I haven't done.

That's exactly what's happening now, isn't it? I shouldn't have lied, but I panicked. I'm sorry.'

DS Chabra stares at me. 'Why were you there?'

'Robin telephoned me and asked me to go and visit him. I didn't have much time because I was about to leave for a tour around Europe. He asked if I could be there for 8 am on the Sunday morning. He implied that he didn't want Tamsin to see me, and he left the front door on the latch so that I didn't need to ring the bell.'

'And what was it that Mr Featherstone wanted to see you about?'

'Honestly, I'm not really sure. It was a strange conversation, as if he just wanted to see how I was, and he implied that it would be the last time I saw him – which, of course, it was. But I didn't really think anything of it until I returned from Europe and found his letter. Only a few minutes into our chat, we heard footsteps upstairs, which I suppose was Tamsin getting up, and he rather ushered me out of the house. The whole thing was very strange. To be honest, at the time, I was a bit annoyed, because I had so much to do to get ready for the tour, and on top of that, I could ill afford the travel costs to go and see him.' I bite the side of my lip. Should I have told them that I was annoyed? Will they twist that somehow?

'What time did you leave Stave House?'

'Definitely before 8.30 am, and as far as I was aware, no one saw me come or go.'

'Except they did. The Featherstones' housekeeper's partner saw you "sneaking away", as the housekeeper described it. What time did you return to Stave House?'

'I didn't!' I exclaim. 'I got a taxi to Horsham station and caught the train to London. You'll be able to see me on the CCTV, and if you call the taxi company, they'll be able to verify the times. I got a taxi to and from Horsham station.'

DC Degreen scribbles rapidly.

'Did Mr Featherstone tell you that he was going to make you the sole beneficiary of his will?' DS Chabra asks.

'No. I already told you it was a complete shock. Do you think that Robin was pushed down the stairs, that it wasn't an accident? Because based on his letter to me, that's what I think.'

'We are investigating various different scenarios. The problem is, Mia, all roads lead back to you. I was looking through your original charge sheet and the court conviction, and everything suggests that you've been up to your old tricks, but worse this time. This time, one person is dead, and another had a lucky escape.'

I place my hand on my thigh to stop my leg from bouncing up and down and fix my gaze on DS Chabra, hoping that I appear more confident than I really am. 'That's not true. I had nothing to do with what happened to Robin or Tamsin.'

'And what about the forgery?'

I am beginning to hate DS Chabra. She thinks she knows it all, but she doesn't. She has everything wrong.

'I was found guilty of forging several cheques and stealing money from my elderly aunt. But, as I told the court, I didn't do it.'

'Except the jury found you guilty, and the judge sentenced you to three years in jail, of which you served just over half of that time. Who do you think I'm going to believe, the court or you?'

'My sister stole the money. She is a drug addict; she forced me into doing it. She set me up.' I give up. There's no point in telling them this, because they'll never believe me. How I wish I could go back in time and undo everything.

Sara is four years older than me. For most of our childhood, I adored her and wanted to be like her. When Mum died so suddenly, it broke Sara, but I only realise that now, looking back. It broke me too, but I think it was worse for my sister. We weren't exactly flush with money beforehand, but we never went without anything. Our parents always made sure we had new shoes and the latest toys, and I was rarely given Sara's hand-me-downs. But when Mum died, we had to move out of our cosy cottage on the outskirts of Horsham into a council flat, and Sara and I had to share a bedroom. I thought that was great, but Sara was livid. Back then, Mum had a good job as a sales rep for a pharmaceuticals company. She was away quite a lot for work, but she always came home laden with presents. Dad was the constant in our lives. For me, at least, he still is. He worked from home as a book-keeper, waiting at the school gates for us and making sure that we were well fed with the meals that Mum had prepared and popped into the freezer.

Looking back, I suppose Sara got in with the wrong crowd when she was about fifteen. I knew she was smoking and drinking, but I didn't realise how much drugs came to rule her life. At that point, I was too obsessed with my violin and fulfilling my dream of getting into music school ... and trying to forget that my mother was dead. I guess I was lucky. I had a music teacher at junior school who spotted a talent in me. After Mum died, Mrs Carter took me under her wing, made sure I was nurtured and had access to some great teachers. She made sure that Dad knew what potential I had, and she somehow or other got me free lessons and the loan of a stunning violin.

When I was sixteen, I was offered a scholarship at one of the leading music schools in the country. I loved it there. I was surrounded by kids with a similar passion, who came from different walks of life and even different countries. While I thrived, Sara sank, and Dad just struggled to survive. I went home less and less, not only because I couldn't afford the train fares, but also because there was such a horrible atmosphere. Dad was constantly exhausted, short of money and arguing with Sara. As far as Sara was concerned, I was a pain in the backside who ratted on her when she smoked and drank. When I got offered a place at the Royal College of Music in London, there was no way that I was moving back home, but Dad couldn't afford to help me pay for staying in a hall of residence. I thought I would have to saddle myself with debts, but then Dad came up with a bright idea. He contacted Mum's aunt, Miriam. I had no recollection of her, as we'd only met the once, and that was at Mum's funeral when I was ten. It didn't take much persuading for her to agree for me to live with her in her Chelsea mews house in return for keeping an eye on her. Aunt Miriam was showing all the signs of early dementia, but she didn't want to leave her home. It seemed like the perfect solution, I'd get free lodgings, and she would have someone around to do basic errands and the like.

I knew it was going to be the perfect set-up the moment I met my great-aunt Miriam. She was tiny, definitely less than five feet tall, and she wore a bright purple cardigan with a pillar-box red pair of trousers, with her fine white hair piled on top of her head to resemble a precariously perched bird's nest.

'Benji tells me you're the musician,' she said, staring at her hand. She'd written on her palm the words:

Benji says Mia musician coming to stay.

'Yes, it's a pleasure to meet you, and thank you so much for having me.' I was very polite in those days.

'And who are you exactly?'

'I'm Paul's granddaughter,' I said, hoping she still remembered the name of her long-deceased brother.

She nodded and let me in. Her house was chaotic. The surface of every wall was covered with paintings of different styles and shapes. Nothing matched, and I absolutely loved how the colours clashed and that the style of everything she owned was so eclectic. She also had little Post-it notes stuck everywhere, carrying a wodge in her pocket and her trusty biro in her bun, so she never forgot where she'd put them. Aunt Miriam had clearly been adapting to life with memory loss for quite some time.

She showed me her single guest room, and my initial reaction was, where was I meant to sleep? There was so much clutter in there, from hanging rails filled with clothes and piles of books and paintings and lamps and loose shades, but she just laughed and said, 'You can have it all. Do what you want with it, sell it, give it away, just make this room your own.'

'Are you sure?' I asked, flabbergasted.

'I'm as sure as I'm standing here.' She patted my hand, and her skin felt like fine tissue paper.

And so I did. I made a nice pot of money on eBay by selling some of her junk, and when I offered her the cash, she had no idea what it was for and just told me to keep it. We were good companions for those first ten months. I was working hard at college, practicing as much as possible, and Aunt Miriam didn't mind – I suspect largely because she was very deaf, although she refused to admit it. I made sure that she had food in the house, and most evenings I would cook for her. Her son, my uncle, (whom I didn't know very well and had probably seen once after Mum died) visited Aunt Miriam once a week and seemed to approve of me. Life was so good, I even started dating a boy in the year above at college. I allowed myself to dream that we might rent a flat together in my third year, and who knows where our relationship could have led?

Although most of my friends went home in the summer, I stayed in London. I knew Dad would have liked me home, but I said that Aunt Miriam needed me, and in a way she did.

One hot August afternoon, Sara rang our doorbell. I hadn't seen her in months, and I hardly recognised my sister. Her hair was lank and dirty, her eyes red and her face so pale it looked almost bruised. She was wearing a filthy sweatshirt, much too warm for the hot day, and ripped black skinny jeans.

'God, Sara,' I exclaimed. 'What's happened to you?' I thought she was ill. How naive I was.

'I need somewhere to stay.'

'I'll check with Aunt Miriam.'

'No. You don't get it. I don't want her to know I'm here. Just let me in.'

'But–'

'Look, Mia. I know she's out. I saw that carer woman bundle her into a taxi, so the coast is clear, okay?'

I gawped at my sister. Where had the gentle funny girl gone? 'But why don't you want her to know you're here?'

Sara didn't answer, but pushed past me into the house. 'Where's your room?'

'Upstairs, second door on the left.'

I waited for her to dump her bag and come back downstairs, but she didn't. Eventually I went up to my room, and Sara was lying under my duvet, fully dressed, shivering.

'What's the matter with you? Do you need a doctor?'

'Piss off.'

'No, Sara. You came here, so you need to tell me what's going on.'

'You wouldn't understand, you in your little stuck-up classical music world.'

I swallowed an appropriate retort and instead said, 'Try me.'

'I need a fix, and I need cash.'

That shut me up. I'd never met anyone who was hooked on heroin, and I had absolutely no idea what to do. I should have rung Dad or called the police, especially later, when I saw Sara rummaging in Aunt Miriam's dressing table drawers, but she was my big sister, and I'd always done what she told me. With hindsight, I've tried to justify my lack of action. Things would have been so different if I had stood up to her and done what in my heart of hearts I knew I should have. Back then I was the eternal optimist. If I supported Sara, she'd kick her habit. I was sure that I could help her.

She came and went over the next few weeks, appearing when Aunt Miriam was out. Then, when she realised how confused Aunt Miriam was becoming, she played her, pretending that she was Miriam's long-lost daughter, and how could Miriam not remember her? Sara was cruel, but it turned out she was even crueller to me. Because she had been so careful to make sure that no one except me and Aunt Miriam saw her come or go, all the thieving and fraud was placed firmly on my shoulders. Obviously it was me who emptied out Aunt Miriam's bank account, and it was me who sold off her jewellery, and it was me who forged her signature on cheques. And when someone from social services tipped up, and it came to light that Aunt Miriam only had two pounds seventy left in her savings and current accounts combined, they all pointed their fingers at me.

I tried to explain that it wasn't me, that it was my sister, Sara, but she vanished. No one believed me. and even Dad thought I was laying the blame at Sara's door because she was an easy scapegoat.

After charging me, they let me out on bail, and I stayed at Dad's flat, still practicing the violin, still hopeful that I could return to college with my name cleared, still hopeful that I could track down Sara and get her to admit that she had set me up. I failed on every count. Dad stuck his head in the sand and pretended none of this was happening. I think he simply didn't have the emotional bandwidth to support me. He moved to his current council flat in Fulham. No one believed my version of events. I was sent to jail. Justice was seen to be done, except they sentenced the wrong sister.

All this time later, Dad now believes me, because Sara hasn't been seen since. I suppose she knew that if she returned home, Dad might get her arrested. Of course it's frequently crossed my mind that my older sister might be dead. I know I should feel some degree of sadness, and I do for the young Sara, but not for my adult sister who threw me to the wolves.

'WHAT IS your relationship like with Tamsin Featherstone?' DS Chabra asks, bringing me back into the interview room with a jolt.

'Not great. She fired me, and now she obviously loathes my guts because I'm inheriting her husband's estate. But if you don't mind me saying, I think you should look more closely at Tamsin. She'd been married for barely five minutes, and then her husband was found dead. She wasn't coping well with the after-effects of Robin's stroke.'

Both DS Chabra and DC Degreen are looking at me with stony faces. I guess they don't appreciate me telling them how to do their jobs.

'You left the country the day after Mr Featherstone's passing.'

'Yes, I went on tour with the gypsy jazz band. I've already told you that. Look, have you given any more consideration to the letter Robin sent me?'

Then DS Chabra's phone buzzes. She stands up. 'DS Degreen and I will be back shortly,' she says.

I wonder if this is a tactic that the police use, because I remember after I was arrested for fraud how I was left for ages when they were interviewing me. The panic starts to churn at my stomach lining. If I thought I was in a terrible situation back then, it is way worse now. It makes sense that Tamsin was the person who pushed Robin down the stairs, but would she really have tampered with the brakes on my car? It was a very risky thing to do. If a lorry had been passing when she slipped into the road, then she would have been killed. She could have declined my offer of her taking the car, yet she put herself in danger.

But if it wasn't Tamsin, could it have been David, who certainly seems to know about cars? I wonder about David. Handsome, suave David – who, despite everything, I still find attractive. Is he in on this? Did he try to set me up? Because he seems to be the only person in the household who knows about the workings of a car. Could Tamsin and David have been in on this together, with Tamsin pushing Robin, then David tampering with the brakes? As I sit here in this stinking, freezing room, all I do is go around and around in circles in my head whilst trying to quell the terror in my gut.

20

TAMSIN

I t's such a relief that the police took Mia away. I'm allowing myself to hope that all will be well, that we may never see her again. Brooke reappeared briefly and then announced that she was going away for the night, and took off in her hideous pink Mini. I suspect she's gone for a shopping trip, in the expectation that I'll honour my promise and dole out some of my inheritance to her.

'There's a truck out the front to collect Mia's car,' David says. 'Would you like me to deal with it?'

'Thanks, David. I'll go and get the keys.'

I run upstairs into the bedroom and dig out the keys, which I put in my handbag. David is waiting for me at the bottom of the stairs. As I hand them to him, our fingers touch. A shiver runs up my arm and down to the pit of my stomach. I think he feels it too, because his bright blue eyes meet mine, and the hint of a smile edges at his lips. Damn him. I bet he can have any woman he wants.

Then he winks at me, and I know for sure that he's feeling it too, and even though it's the corniest thing ever to wink at me, it flicks a switch in my head. Everything is going to be alright. I am still young, and Robin would want me to be happy. I don't suppose he'd be too happy if I was hooked up with his son, but I remind myself that Robin isn't here to pass judgement.

Pavla is ironing in the utility room, and she smiles at me as I walk past.

'Have the afternoon off, Pavla. You've been working much too hard recently.'

'Really?' Her thin eyebrows are raised.

'Go and spend some time with your husband and Marek. It's been so stressful here lately, it's made me realise how important family is.'

She speaks hesitantly. 'If you're sure.'

'Well – as, strictly speaking, you're employed by Mia now, and she's hopefully banged up in a prison cell, I don't think anyone is going to mind!'

Pavla grins at me and switches off the iron. 'It's been awful these past few weeks. Do you really think that she pushed Mr Featherstone?'

I shrug my shoulders because I don't know for sure, but it certainly seems that way.

'It's just she seemed so mouse-like,' Pavla says as she folds up the ironing board.

'I know. Very ordinary. I never understood why Robin liked her.'

'I suppose they spoke the same language.'

'Oh, music, do you mean?'

Pavla nods.

'But it's a bit like you running into someone who is Czech and automatically liking them.'

'I suppose so. But she must be, what's the word? Conniv–'

'Conniving,' I suggest.

'Yes, conniving, because she's been to prison and none of

us knew. I've never met anyone who has been to prison,' Pavla says.

'Me neither.' We grin at each other. I feel a comfortable bonding with Pavla, along with a slight regret that I wasn't warmer towards her when I first arrived at Stave House.

'Right, I'll be off now. Thanks, Tamsin.'

Pavla passes David on her way out, and I can see them chatting to each other but can't make out what they're saying. I feel sorry for Pavla. She's worked here for such a long time, and it must be incredibly hard for her not knowing what the future will hold.

Eventually David saunters back in, by which time I'm seated at the kitchen table, flicking through an Ottolenghi recipe book.

'Mia's car is gone. When will your Defender be back from the garage?' he asks.

'I'm not sure,' I say. 'What's your favourite food?'

'Why?' David cocks his head to one side and looks at me with a glint in his eyes. I think he might guess my plan.

'Thought I'd make us some supper. I've given Pavla the rest of the day off.'

The tension between us is crackling. When David walks towards me and I stand up, any thought of food is forgotten. His lips smash down onto mine, and he pulls me tightly towards him, a fire lighting up in my belly and spreading through every vein in my body.

'We shouldn't,' I say breathlessly as I eventually pull away from him.

'Why not? You were way too young and beautiful for Dad, and you're free now, Tamsin. There's no one here telling you what you should or shouldn't do, and I want you.'

And then I'm back in his arms again, and he's leading me through into the living room, because there's no way we'll make it upstairs. We're both shedding our clothes as we go. I feel guilty for a nanosecond, but then I lose all sense of time and place, lost in the exquisite sensations. David is an extraordinary lover.

Later that night, I'm lying in my marital bed, feeling sore and satiated and wondering if Robin is looking down on us with dismay. I enjoyed myself, but I'm still racked with guilt. I didn't want David to sleep with me in the master bedroom, just in case Brooke or Pavla found us, but David was insistent, and my body betrayed my mind. So here he is, all tangled up in the sheets, that beautiful torso catching the first rays of early morning sunlight. I say a silent little prayer to Robin, asking for his forgiveness.

I nudge David, who turns over with a groan and opens one eye. 'Hello, gorgeous,' he murmurs.

'I think you should go back to your room, just in case Pavla comes in early.'

'Oh, do I have to?' he asks as he runs his fingers down my naked body.

'Yes.'

He moans and sits up, rubbing his eyes as his hair stands up on end. 'How about we go to London for a couple of nights? I can book us into the Ritz or Claridge's, and we can get away from prying eyes.'

'Really?'

'You can't expect me to go tiptoeing around Stave House, but I do accept it's probably not the done thing for us to be seen to be sleeping together quite so soon. The trouble is, now I know what you feel like, how very delicious you are, I think I'm going to be hooked.'

'Okay, sounds like a fun idea.'

'Good. I'll book something, and we can go up to town later today. Do I really have to leave you now?' His hand is where it shouldn't be. I stifle a groan.

I glance at the alarm clock. It's nearly 7 am, and I know

that Pavla keeps all sorts of strange hours, coming and going as she pleases. 'Go and have a shower, handsome,' I say, removing his hand and prodding him gently in the ribs.

AN HOUR LATER, David and I are eating breakfast together. It's so confusing, as I know I shouldn't feel like this, but the attraction is overwhelming, exactly as I felt when I first met Robin.

'I've booked us into the Grosvenor. Perhaps we can catch a show tomorrow night. What do you think?'

'That would be fab.' I'm about to lean in to kiss him when I hear a key in the door. We spring apart. I pick up the plates and put them in the dishwasher.

'Good morning,' Pavla says. She looks surprised to see us both in the kitchen together, which is fair enough, as I'm rarely up this early. Fortunately she doesn't say anything.

'Right. I've got a few things to do, and then I'm going up to town later this afternoon for a dinner. What are your plans today, Tamsin?' he asks. I see the twinkle in his eye, and I have to stop myself from flushing as I realise the game he's playing.

'Actually, I'm meeting an old friend for supper and staying over at hers.'

'In London?' he asks.

I nod but don't catch his eye.

'Do you want a lift? I thought I might take Dad's car if that's alright with you.'

'Sure,' I say. I glance at Pavla, but she's bending down to get some cleaning materials out of a cupboard, and I can't see her expression.

David runs his tongue slowly over his lips, and I have to turn away.

I leave David and Pavla in the kitchen and go upstairs to

rifle through my wardrobe, selecting a slinky black dress. I dig out the silk lingerie that I wore on my first date with Robin – my lucky set, as I call them. When, after much deliberating, I have lain out all my clothes, I go into the corridor and pull the ladder down that gives access into the loft. I've only been up here once or twice, because I find the space creepy. The loft extends the full width and length of the house, although it's only possible to stand up in the middle section. Unlike new houses that are carefully insulated, the roof space of Stave House is full of crisscrossing beams strung with cobwebs; Robin told me there's a family of bats up here. There are lots of cardboard boxes stuffed with Robin's belongings as well as some overflowing with toys and books, obviously owned by Brooke and David when they were young.

Just to the left-hand side of the ladder is where we store our suitcases. I stand at the top of the ladder and am about to grab one of my small black wheelie cases, but there's another navy-blue suitcase blocking mine. I nudge it to one side, and it topples over. When I pick it up, I see that it belongs to David. The airline luggage label is still attached to the handle, with the large letters of LGW on it. Unsurprising that David flew from Geneva to Gatwick, but what stops me still is when I notice the date. It's dated 13 March, just five days before Robin died. Yet David didn't come to the funeral, citing important business in Switzerland. He claimed that he hadn't been to England in months. Did he come back for a few days at that point? But if so, why isn't there a more up-to-date luggage label on the case? Or does he have several cases, and he took a different one back with him? I carefully check all the other cases, but either they have no label, or they belong to Robin. I descend the ladder slowly, empty-handed.

David is in the living room, his laptop perched on his knees.

'Hello, gorgeous,' he says as I walk in.

'Shush. Hey, I just wanted to check something with you. How often have you been back to the UK this year?'

'Why?'

'No reason. I was just thinking it might be fun if I join you on a trip to Switzerland some time.'

'You're right. That would be fun. I haven't been back in ages. I don't think I saw Dad for about eighteen months before he died.'

'Still don't understand why you didn't come to his funeral.' I try to stop my fingers from fidgeting and end up wedging them into my trouser pockets.

'Dad and I didn't get on, and I had a really important meeting to attend in Geneva. Look, I'm sorry. I know you think badly of me because of it, but I really couldn't get away from Switzerland.'

I look David straight in the eye, and he doesn't flinch, not an iota. This man is a liar. Why would he pretend? And then I doubt myself. Did I misread the date perhaps, or get the year wrong? It doesn't make any sense as to why David is pretending he hasn't been back to the UK.

'Are you okay?' he asks, peering at me.

'Just feeling a little queasy,' I say, turning away and hurrying out of the room.

I go straight back up to the loft and reach for his suitcase. I unpeel the label and study it. It's very clear that David flew into Gatwick airport on the thirteenth of March this year, just a few days before Robin died. I don't know why, but it's clear to me that David has lied. Why, I don't know, but it begs the question – what else has he lied about?

I slip out of the house and into my greenhouse, where I try to lose myself in my plants, but I can't stop thinking about David. What is going on? The fleeting dismay that I felt after our first kiss turns into disgust the more I think about it.

What was I doing, betraying the memory of the man I loved? The more I think about it, I realise I cannot go to London with David. Instead, I am going to have to keep my distance for a while, just until I can work out what is going on. As I walk back towards the house, Thomas appears, pushing a wheelbarrow.

'Hello, Mrs Featherstone,' he says cheerily. 'You feelin' better?'

I tilt my head to one side.

He scratches his head. 'It'll be the shock. You have shock, like Uncle Dick.'

'Your uncle?' I ask, confused.

He laughs, a big belly guffaw. '"Uncle Dick" is "sick" in cockney. I always say that shock's like an illness, yeh know?'

'Oh yes, but I'm feeling better now. Thank you, Thomas.'

'If you need anything, I'm here to 'elp.'

'That's kind of you.'

He doffs his hat at me and carries on pushing the wheel-barrow, humming tunelessly.

Back in the house, I hear David in the kitchen, chattering away to Pavla. I poke my head around the door.

'I'm afraid I'm going to be bailing out of supper with my friend tonight. I don't feel at all well and wonder if I've picked up some sort of sickness bug. I'm going to bed.' I turn and walk away before either David or Pavla can speak.

'Tamsin!' I hear David say.

I turn around. 'Sorry, David, I need to go to bed.'

'Get better soon.' I don't turn to see his face, to work out whether he believes me.

21

Having missed out on eating any supper, by 8 am the next morning, I'm starving. I am putting marmalade on my third slice of toast when David comes sauntering in.

'Feeling better, babe?' he asks, ambling up to me and bending down to give me a kiss on the lips. I had hoped he might have gone to London without me.

I turn my face away, so he gets a mouthful of hair.

'What's up?' He sits down on the chair next to me.

'I've been thinking, David, and I don't think we should pursue this ... this thing between us. It's not going to work. It's too complicated.'

'That's nonsense. We are so good together.' He tries to take my hand, but I pull it away. 'We just need to be subtle about it for a few weeks, but soon enough no one will mind. It's perfectly normal for a young woman like you to want to get back onto the dating scene quickly. You've got the fertility window to think about, haven't you?'

I see now what a jerk David is. He may have the ripped body of a strong young man and the chiselled lines of his father's face, but he has none of Robin's gravitas and sophistication. But worse than that, this man is a liar. I don't doubt he is attracted to me, because even the best actor couldn't have performed as well as he did – and besides, I know I'm beautiful with a great figure – but he's talking as if we are committing to a long-term relationship. He must want something from me, money, I suppose. Perhaps he thinks that if he offers me babies, then he might get his hands on his dad's fortune. He's barking up the wrong tree there.

'I've made up my mind, David. We shouldn't have slept together, and it can't happen again.'

'You don't mean that,' he says, tracing a finger along my lips. I try to shake him off.

'I do mean it. I'm totally serious. It was a moment of weakness and loneliness, but I am not ready for any kind of relationship.'

'I'm not looking to marry you,' he says. 'I just want to feel that beautiful body against my bare skin, to feel myself inside–'

'Enough.' I cut him off. 'I'm sorry, David, but it's not going to happen.'

He narrows his eyes at me and stands up, his limbs all rigid. For a moment I am fearful. Is he going to pounce and attack me? But instead he just curls his lip, shakes his head and storms out of the room, letting the door slam behind him.

I let out a breath I didn't know I was holding. I know he's hurt and angry, but there's nothing I can do about that. I made a mistake.

Lighter footsteps enter the room from behind. 'What was all that about?'

Oh no. It's Mia the criminal. What is she doing back in the house, loitering in the corridor? I thought the police had arrested her, that she was out of the picture. What did she overhear? That's just what I don't need.

'Why are you back here?'

'The police had no evidence to hold me.'

'Really?' I can't help but sneer. 'Have you got better at pulling the wool over the police's eyes? I suppose it helps having all that practice.' This woman is a fraudster; she's spent time behind bars. I need to chuck her out of here. Mia steps forwards and pulls out the chair next to mine, the one that David has just vacated. I refuse to meet her eyes.

'I know what you're thinking, Tamsin. Because I was convicted of a crime, I'm up to no good. I don't expect you'll believe me, but I was set up by my sister. She stole a fortune from my aunt to feed her heroin habit, and made it up to look as if I did it.'

'So why didn't the jury believe you?'

'Because my sister was cleverer than me, and by then, she'd disappeared. I didn't have the funds to mount a legal challenge. It ruined my life.'

'How very convenient for you that doddery Robin Featherstone was open to your charms and that you convinced him to leave you his money before you killed him. Your previous conviction might have ruined your life, but now you're trying to ruin mine.'

'That's not true, Tamsin. I didn't ask for any of this, and if I'm allowed to, I'll share the inheritance with you.'

'Really?'

Mia looks at me with big eyes, but I don't trust a word she's saying. 'Are you and David romantically entangled?' she asks.

I let out a snort. 'My private conversations are none of your business, and for that matter, you're not wanted here.'

'David is a piece of work,' she says.

'What's that supposed to mean?'

'Did you know that David was spying on me?'

That gets my attention. I frown at her.

'When I returned from touring with my band, I stayed with my dad for a few nights. David had been keeping tabs on me.'

'What's that supposed to mean?'

'Someone tried to mug me, to nick my handbag. David happened to be watching, and he saw the mugger off. We went for a coffee, and then it got awkward, and he left. Imagine my shock when I arrived here and David turned out to be Robin's son. I'm not sure if he really saved me–' Mia uses her fingers to suggest the word 'saved' is in inverted commas – 'or if he'd set the whole thing up. He called himself Felix.'

'That's his middle name,' I say.

'Anyway, he admitted that when he found out that I had inherited everything from Robin, he researched what he could about me and then spied on me.'

If I hadn't caught David lying about when he had been in England, I would have thought that Mia was spinning some yarn to deflect suspicion off herself. Now I'm not so sure. Perhaps David really did spy on her.

'When did he say he'd come back to the UK?' I ask.

Mia frowns. 'I'm not sure, but a while.'

'He's been lying to me,' I say quietly. 'Did you know he didn't turn up to Robin's funeral.'

'Why not?' Mia looks shocked, but then again, I already know that Mia is like David, an accomplished liar.

'He said he was out of the country and couldn't get back in time. It was no secret that Robin and David had a difficult relationship.'

'Robin implied as much.'

That grates, because she's making it sound like Robin opened up to her, and based on that conversation I overheard when Robin asked Mia for her advice on his will, perhaps there might be some truth in that.

'It's obvious that he's here now because he's after his share of the money,' Mia continues.

I fear she's right.

'I absolutely promise that I had nothing to do with the brakes failing on the Corsa. The car was working perfectly when I came here from London, and Dad said it only passed its MOT three months ago. If the police do think it's malicious, it definitely wasn't me. I'm not in the least bit mechanical, and as a violinist, I have to look after my fingers.' She clearly sees the doubt in my eyes and changes the subject. 'Look, it's none of my business, but *are* you two together, you and David?'

'He's not my type,' I fib.

'I know you probably won't believe me, Tamsin, but I had nothing to do with what happened to Robin. I had no idea that he was leaving everything to me. But obviously David knew, which is why he was following me. But it's all rather odd, isn't it?'

We both sit there in silence. I wonder, could David have sneaked back here and pushed Robin down the stairs? He was in the country, and of course he has a key to the house. Could he have slipped in and out without any of us knowing? Or worse still, could he have been in cahoots with Brooke? I quickly discount that, because despite her being obnoxious and spoiled, I really don't think Brooke has evil in her. But what was David's motive? He clearly hated Robin, although I'm not really sure why, and I'm positive he resented my marriage to his father.

'Do you think David could have tampered with my car?' Mia asks gently. She's articulating exactly what is going through my mind.

'But why? Why would he do that?'

'If I'm out of the picture, then you get all the money. He either shacks up with you to lay his hands on it through a relationship, or he murders you, too. Eventually David and Brooke would get it all. Money and jealousy are the strongest motivators.'

I stare at Mia, shocked not only at how much sense her words make but also that against all odds, we might end up being on the same side. My horror is reflected in her face, but it's worse for me. I slept with David. I might have lain in the arms of a man who committed patricide. Is that the right word?

'Where is he right now?' Mia asks in a whisper.

'I don't know. You saw him storm out. What should we do? Should we tell the police that David has been lying?'

Mia scoffs. 'They're not going to believe a word I say. In their eyes, I'm already guilty of murdering Robin, of undue influence regarding his will and your attempted murder. The police have let me down before, and I'm sorry, but I don't trust them now.'

'Me neither,' I murmur.

Mia looks at me with wide eyes.

'A story for another day,' I say. 'Anyway, even if we do go to them, they'll just say we've got no evidence, that it's all speculation. That's what they said to me before. And it's true. We've got a hunch that David might be up to no good, but absolutely no proof.' I want to add that I'm still not sure if I trust Mia, but I turn my head away from her and swallow the thought. Whom on earth can I trust? Is Mia spinning me lies just to get herself off the hook? I really don't know whom to trust. Only myself, I suppose.

22

MIA

The thought of Tamsin and me sitting down and having a non-confrontational conversation would be unimaginable, except I think that's exactly what's happening. Up until now, the whole Featherstone family has been gunning for me, blaming me for all their woes – totally understandable, of course. Has Tamsin changed her tune because she has an ulterior motive, or does she genuinely suspect David of being up to no good?

I don't trust David. He's too smarmy and pleased with himself, happy to step into the 'man of the family' shoes, and that whole business of spying on me and then stepping in to appear like the hero smells like rotten fish. There must have been a good reason why Robin was so disappointed in his son. I wonder if there was a breakdown in their relationship far beyond the ill feeling that arises when the son doesn't match up to the father's aspirations for him.

Tamsin is boiling the kettle, standing next to the Aga, her back to me. I wish I could read her better.

'If only there was CCTV, we might be able to see who tampered with my car's brakes,' I muse.

Tamsin's back stiffens. She swivels around to face me. 'We've got security cameras above the front and back doors of the house,' she exclaims. 'It's not on all the time, as it's triggered by motion sensors, but it might have picked something up.'

'Haven't the police asked you for footage from those?'

'No. I'd totally forgotten about them. I don't know if the angle would pick up the garages, but it's worth having a look.'

'Does David know about the cameras?'

'I don't know, but probably not. Robin got them installed before we went to the Caribbean at Christmas, because Pavla and her family were going to be away at the same time. You wouldn't know they were there unless you were really looking for them. I'm not sure how long the footage is stored in the cloud, but it's worth having a look.'

I feel a little surge of hope that this might clear me from suspicion.

'I'll go and get my iPad.'

Tamsin leaves the room, and I dare to hope. I wonder whether Tamsin and I can come to some sort of agreement. I need to speak to Ian Dunworthy – but no, I'm getting ahead of myself. Firstly, we need to establish whether Robin was pushed and if David is behind everything.

Tamsin reappears quickly and places the iPad on the kitchen table. She holds the device in front of her face so it recognises her, and then she's in.

'What's the password?' she murmurs to herself. 'I thought these things were meant to remember passwords.' The wait is agonising, but eventually she's in the app. 'Here we go,' she says. 'What time did you get back from London?'

'About 10 pm, which means the brakes must have been tampered with between 10 on Tuesday evening and when you borrowed the car at around 11 am on Wednesday. Does it record what happens at night?' I ask.

'I'm not sure.'

I can't see exactly what Tamsin's doing, but she sits up straighter at one point.

'1.04 am,' she says, her eyes wide.

'What is it?'

'Oh, nothing. A bloody fox.' She turns the screen so I can see a big fox, the white tip of its tail catching the low light, stroll down the drive. Then Tamsin turns the screen back towards her again.

She inhales loudly. '8.36 am in the morning. There's someone there. A shadow. The trouble is, we can see the driveway in front of the carport, but not the carport itself. That's so frustrating. It's a person.'

'Who?'

'I can't tell. Oh yes!' she exclaims. 'It's Marek. Look, he's in the shrubs. What's he doing pruning shrubs at this time of year?'

'He's the gardener's assistant. That's his job, isn't it?'

Tamsin rolls her eyes at me. 'Of course not. You don't prune in the spring just when the buds are coming out.'

'Do you think Marek was up to no good?' Marek is socially awkward, but that certainly doesn't make him a bad person.

'According to the camera, he was there for ages, right up until when I came out and drove the car.'

'Do you remember seeing him?'

Tamsin shrugs. 'He's part of the furniture around here. He comes into the greenhouse to help out, but to be honest, I don't really clock him.'

'You don't think it's Marek, do you?' I ask dubiously. Tamsin shakes her head. 'But he might have seen if anyone had been behaving suspiciously around my car?' I suggest.

'True. Let me double-check I haven't missed anything.'

I wait whilst Tamsin rewinds the recording and watches it again.

'Nothing else. I mean, the car thing could have been a fluke. Brakes just fail from time to time, don't they? And your dad's car *is* rather knackered.'

'But David said–'

'Perhaps he's wrong. Perhaps he's trying a double bluff, letting us know the brakes were tampered with so we'd never suspect him.'

I can sense Tamsin closing down towards me again, doubting that David had anything to do with the mess we're in. I need to redirect her quickly.

'Why don't we go and have a word with Marek, just to find out if he saw anyone loitering around my car?'

'Sure. No harm in that.'

We both stand up and walk towards the back door. Tamsin stands in the doorway and hollers at the top of her voice. 'Marek! Marek!'

And then he appears in front of us, silently, quickly, as if from nowhere. Tamsin jumps. He must have been just around the side of the house.

'You startled me,' she says. 'Come in, Marek. We want to ask you something.'

Marek stands very still for a long time, then bends down to remove his muddy wellington boots, letting them drop onto the step. There is definitely something very odd about him. He is wearing thick grey socks, and his right big toe pokes out through a hole. I wonder how often he's been inside the house. We stand awkwardly in the utility room, where the space feels cramped with big Marek standing here.

'Did you see anyone doing anything to Mia's car on Tuesday night or Wednesday morning?' Tamsin asks.

'No,' he says, too quickly.

'You were spending a lot of time pruning the bushes near the carport on Wednesday morning. Did you see anyone?'

'No.' But Marek's lying. His eyes dart everywhere, and he tugs at his earlobes, runs his fingers through his hair and then keeps his head down, looking at his socked feet.

'Who told you to prune those bushes?' Tamsin asks. 'Look at me, please,' she says, her voice a little harsh. That makes Marek even more uncomfortable.

'No one,' he mutters, still refusing to look at either of us. 'Did I do wrong?'

'No, it's fine.' Tamsin sighs. 'But you shouldn't be pruning in the spring. That's not the issue. What we want to know is, did anyone touch Mia's car?'

Marek keeps his eyes to the ground, but shakes his head and continues shaking it so much that I wonder if he's getting dizzy.

'Marek?' Tamsin says, softening her tone, putting her hand out to touch his shoulder. Marek flinches.

'No, no, no, no, no, no,' Marek says, his voice getting louder as he clenches his fingers into fists. 'Can I go now?'

'Yes, you can go now,' Tamsin says wearily.

'What's going on? Marek, why are you in the house?' Pavla opens the back door and almost slams straight into her son.

Marek pushes past her and darts out of the open door.

'Marek!' Pavla shouts, running after him. I watch them for a moment as Pavla catches her son and then puts her arms around him. Even though he's twice as big as her, he seems to melt into his mother.

'Shit,' Tamsin says, shutting the door and turning back towards me. 'I didn't mean to upset him. I'm sure Marek means well, but ...' She groans.

'That was weird behaviour,' I say. 'Obviously, you know

Marek better than me, but it seems like he was hiding something.'

Before Tamsin can reply, the back door swings open, and Pavla strides back in. Her face is pale, but she has two red blotches on her cheeks, and her eyes are flashing with anger.

'Tamsin, can I have a word?'

I slip out of the room, but stand just behind the door so I can hear what's being said.

'Why were you questioning Marek?' Pavla asks.

'We wanted to know whether Marek saw anyone tampering with Mia's car.'

'He's really upset. I've sent him home to put the kettle on and watch some TV. What did you say to him?'

'I'm sorry if I upset him, it's just that he was out near the garage for ages, and I just–'

'Surely you're not accusing Marek of getting up to anything? You know he wouldn't do anyone any harm.'

'No, of course I know that.'

'Marek is special, Tamsin. You can't talk to him in the way you'd talk to me or anyone else. He's sensitive.'

'I'm really sorry, Pavla. I'll apologise to him.'

'No need, but I'm going to the cottage now to make sure he's okay.'

I WAIT a few seconds until I'm sure Pavla has left and then slip back into the kitchen.

'We've upset Pavla,' Tamsin says. She looks flustered.

'I always thought Pavla was a bit cold,' I say. 'I'm not sure why, but I think I got her wrong.'

'I felt the same, but now I reckon she's the only honest person here. She was gutted that Robin died, but she never shoved her grief in my face like Brooke and Claudia did.'

'How long has she worked here?'

'Goodness, I don't know. Twenty years or so, certainly since Brooke and David were little.'

'It must be very hard for her,' I say.

We're both silent for a moment, but then Tamsin turns to look at me, her eyes narrowed. 'I don't trust you, Mia. I still think you're playing me, and that there's lots of stuff you're not being honest about.'

Yes, this is exactly as I feared. Tamsin and I had a momentary bonding session, but once again she's turned against me. I'm on my own. There is no point in me trying to convince her, so I get up and leave the room without another word.

Back in the small bedroom, I telephone Ian Dunworthy. I really don't want to carry on living here, and I need to discuss it with him. Unfortunately, his assistant tells me that he's in court all day and won't be free until the morning. I suppose I'll have to sit tight until then. Instead, I take out my violin and play for a couple of hours. If it disturbs anyone in the house, I don't care.

LATER THAT NIGHT, something wakes me. I turn over in the narrow, single bed and press the top of my alarm clock. It's just gone 2 am. Something catches the back of my throat, and I start coughing. And then I smell it.

Smoke.

The acrid smell of smoke.

My heart pounds. There is nothing that scares me more than fire. I used to have nightmares about it when I was a child, sleeping with the light on until the first rays of sunshine broke through to banish my fears.

I jump out of bed, grab a sweater and pull it over me, then desperately try to get my legs into my jeans that I'd discarded on a chair. I shove my bare feet into my trainers. Gingerly, I

open the door onto the corridor and immediately cough. The
choking smell of burning is stronger here.

'Tamsin!' I yell. 'Wake up, everybody! Fire!' I'm screaming
now and coughing. The bathroom. I need to get a towel from
the bathroom. I dive inside, grab two towels from the rail and
run them under water.

'Help!' I hear Tamsin's voice, but the smoke is getting
denser, rising up and up, and I'm not sure where she is. I
wrap the wet towel around my head and dart out into the
corridor, bashing straight into someone. We both scream.

'Mia?' Tamsin gasps.

I shove the towel into her hands. 'We need to get out of
here, now!' I wheeze.

Will that even be possible?

'Are we going to die?' Tamsin's voice sounds so very
distant.

23

TAMSIN

'Not that way!' Mia yells, shoving a wet hand towel in my face. I follow her lead and wrap it around my nose and face; then she grabs my free hand, pulling me away from the staircase. 'Bend down. Keep down low.' She tugs me along down the corridor to her bedroom and slams the door shut behind us. It's smoky in here, but bearable. Although my eyes sting and everything hurts, at least we can see.

Mia flings open the window. 'We're going to have to jump.'

'What!' I exclaim. 'No. Absolutely not. We have to wait for the fire brigade.'

'I haven't even called them yet.'

'I have,' I gasp. 'I don't know if they heard what I was saying, though. I hung up on them when you screamed.' We stare at each other, the horror of what we're facing reflecting in both of our eyes. I think we're going to die in the most horrible manner possible. I double over and try not to vomit from fear.

Mia drags a chair across the room and places it underneath the windowsill. 'Look, this is the only window we can jump out of. The flat roof to the kitchen is directly underneath, and it's not that far to jump. Four feet, five at the most. It's got to be easier here. If we make it back into your bedroom, it's a double height drop down. I think we'd break our legs or worse, jumping from there.'

'I don't know if I can do it,' I mutter.

'You can, Tamsin, and you will, because this isn't your time to die.'

I stifle a sob. Where is Mia getting her inner strength from?

'How long do you think the fire brigade will take to get here?' I ask, and then I cough again. The smoke is creeping underneath the door.

'I'll go first, and then you follow,' Mia says.

'No,' I say. 'Let's jump together.'

'You sure?'

I nod. Mia lifts the sash window upwards as far as it will go, climbs on to the chair and swings her legs outwards so she's sitting on the ledge. She turns towards me and holds out a hand. There's barely space for the two of us to sit next to each other, but her body warmth gives me some comfort. At least she had the presence of mind to put on clothes. I'm just in my pyjamas, my feet in my sheepskin slippers. It's freezing cold out here.

'We'll jump on the count of three,' she says, and then she grabs my hand, clutching it really tightly.

'One, two, three.'

And we jump. It's dark outside, but there's enough low light from the moon to see the flat roof. I let go of her hand and bend my legs, the impact jolting up through my knees and causing me to stumble. But we make it. Mia grasps my hand again and we gingerly walk towards the edge of the gravelly flat roof, and then we sit down, our legs dangling over the gutter. It's damp from yesterday's rain, and the little stones dig into the fine cotton of my pyjama bottoms. I'm trembling now. Really shaking, my teeth rattling, freezing cold. Mia puts her arms around me; we cling to each other. I can feel her heart thumping rapidly, and she coughs from time to time. She smells of smoke, as no doubt I do too. I don't know how long we stay clinging to each other, neither of us saying a word. I listen for something. The roar of the fire, which, as of yet, isn't audible. The sirens in the distance. Shouts from neighbours – but, of course, we don't have any around here. Even Pavla's cottage is out of sight. The night is totally silent.

And then I hear it. Very distant wails that rapidly get closer and closer. The lights of two fire engines swing into the drive, their blue flashing lights catching the tops of the trees, throwing strange shadows across the front of the house. I stand up and wave.

'Up here! We're up here!'

A fireman throws a ladder against the side of the house. Before we know it, we're in strong arms, back on the ground, those metal blankets around our shoulders. I'm crying, truly crying, while Mia is just staring at the horizon, a blankness on her face as if she's retreated from our reality. We sit there on the wooden bench at the side of the house, staring up at Stave House. There are no flames licking at windows or the crashes of ceilings collapsing. From this side of the house, you would have no idea that it was burning from within.

'I think you saved my life,' I say quietly to Mia. She stares at me for a moment. Then it's as if she's being brought back into our present.

'No. We saved each other,' she says, and I lean into this woman who I thought was my foe, and wonder now whether she is my saviour.

'Ladies.' One of the firemen strides over towards us. 'Were you the only two sleeping in the house tonight?'

Mia and I look at each other. I glance at the carport. The pink Mini is gone, and I've barely seen Brooke since Mia has been around, even though her belongings are scattered throughout the house. I reckon the moment she realised Mia was back here, she got into her car and drove away.

'Brooke isn't here, but David ...' I say.

'David?' Mia looks at me with horror and then focuses on the fireman. 'Haven't you found David?' She gets to her feet and addresses me: 'Wasn't David staying here last night?'

I open and close my mouth. 'I don't know.' David hasn't spoken a word to me since I told him I didn't want a relationship with him. Could David be trapped inside?

'Frank!' The fireman shouts to his colleague and runs back towards the house. 'There's another person inside.'

'Oh my god,' Mia says quietly. 'Is David dead? Have we left him to die?'

Now I am trembling so severely, my teeth are chattering, and I'm quivering from head to toe. Mia puts her arms around me again, and I'm so grateful for her. 'I didn't want him to be dead,' I say.

I DON'T KNOW how long we sit there, but it probably feels much longer than it really is, because then two firemen are back in front of us.

'We searched the house, and we can't find anyone else. In fact, the fire was not as severe as it could have been. Fortunately, you called us in good time. There's an ambulance on its way, as we'd like you two ladies to get checked over. You'll be in shock, and you could have smoke inhalation.'

'Can we go back inside?' I ask.

'You can't go in the section of the house where the fire

was, but you're alright to be in the kitchen. We've turned the electrics off for now, but we'll check the fuses and double-check if it's safe to turn everything back on in the undamaged side of the house.'

'Do you know how the fire started?' Mia asks.

'No, there's nothing obvious. The fire investigators will be out to have a look. Do you have any ideas?'

Mia and I look at each other, but neither of us say a word. Could this be something more than a horrible accident? By the look on Mia's face, I reckon she's thinking exactly the same as me. It's not a happy thought.

By THE TIME the sun has come up, Mia and I have drunk litres of tea, and we are both exhausted, each of us yawning and setting the other one off.

'What was prison like?' I ask.

'Horrible. I was at an open prison, so it wasn't too bad in terms of comfort, and some of the other prisoners were quite interesting, but I didn't belong there. You know, just because you're convicted of a crime by a judge and jury, it doesn't always mean you're guilty. I didn't do it, Tamsin. My sister set me up, yet no one except Dad is prepared to believe me.'

'Nice sister,' I murmur, thinking of Donny, my brother, and wondering where he is these days.

'She got hooked on heroin and got desperate.'

'Where is she now?'

Mia turns her head away from me, and her eyes glisten with tears.

'Sorry,' I say, assuming her sister is dead.

'I don't know where she is. She could be alive, she could be dead, but I doubt I'll ever see her again. I know they say blood is thicker than water, but I don't agree. Robin didn't, either.'

'You discussed your sister with Robin?' I ask, that familiar stab of jealousy poking me in my sternum.

'Not in detail.'

'Did he know you were in prison?'

Mia shakes her head slowly. 'I don't suppose he'd have liked me so much if he had known. It probably would have been him firing me rather than you.'

I look away sheepishly. 'I wouldn't count on that. Robin said he liked to give people a second chance. Perhaps all of this was his way of doing that.' At least that would give some context as to why Robin deprived me of his legacy in favour of Mia. 'How did your parents cope with what happened to you?'

'It's only Dad. Mum died when I was ten.'

'I also lost my parents when I was young,' I say, realising that Mia and I have much more in common than I could have imagined.

'What happened?' Mia asks.

'Dad was run over on his bike, lost his legs and turned into a bitter, disabled man. He died when I was fifteen, and Mum died a few weeks later from cancer.'

'Weeks? That's awful,' Mia says. She looks genuinely distressed.

'And you? What happened to your mum?'

'Car accident. She was killed outright.'

'I'm sorry.'

Mia shrugs. I guess we've both learned to live with our tragedies in our own ways. But then we're interrupted by Pavla.

'What's happened?' she exclaims. She looks harried; I feel a bit guilty that we didn't wake her and tell her about the fire. Her cottage is set back from the driveway, and she wouldn't have been able to see the blue flashing lights from her house, even if she had been awake in the middle of the night.

'There was a fire. It's okay. Not too much damage.'

'We thought it was worse than it really was,' Mia adds. 'The smoke was awful.'

'I could smell it from down the drive. Oh my goodness, this is terrible. How did it happen? I need to call Thomas to assess the damage.'

'We don't know. An electrical fault probably. They're sending out a fire investigator later today.'

'And David, where is he?'

Mia and I both shrug our shoulders.

'As if there hasn't been enough tragedy or enough upheaval in this family,' Pavla says, and for the first time since Robin died, she seems truly upset, wringing her hands, swiping away tears from her pale cheeks. 'But, David, he is staying here at the moment. Where is he?'

For a horrible moment I wonder if the firemen have missed David's room, or he is lying unconscious in a cupboard somewhere, overcome by smoke. Have we all got it wrong?

'The firemen say he's not here,' Mia says.

'But have you looked?' There's a horrible edge of panic to Pavla's voice. I get up from my chair too quickly and knock it over. Could the firemen have made a mistake?

Mia grasps my arm. 'We're not allowed up there,' she says firmly. 'It's not safe, Tamsin.'

'But how do we know? Maybe they missed him,' I say breathlessly.

Pavla's eyes flash with fear. I realise that despite everything, despite warning me off David, she loves the boy that he once was.

'Relax, Tamsin. The fire brigade are never going to leave a property without properly searching it,' Mia says.

'Have you called him?' Pavla asks. Once again, Mia and I look at each other. We haven't called anyone, because both our mobile phones are in our bedrooms, and we're not allowed upstairs until the fire investigator has been. To be honest, it simply hasn't crossed my mind to try calling from the landline.

'Do you know David's number?' I ask Pavla.

'Of course.' She strides to the utility room, returning with her scratched brown leather handbag. She removes her phone, and I can hear ringing tones. Then there is a louder ringing tone, with just a hint of delay between Pavla's phone and the other one.

'Why are you calling me?' David says, holding his phone aloft. 'And who burned the bloody breakfast?'

The three of us stare at David. Then I can't stop myself from throwing myself at him, my arms hugging his solid back, my wet cheek pressed against his chest.

'Whoa! What's going on?' he asks. I step backwards, embarrassed now, because it was me who distanced myself from him. While there's a heavy smell of acrid smoke in the air, he stinks of sweat and beer. As I look at him, I notice the bloodshot eyes.

'Where've you been?' I ask.

'None of your business.'

'Actually, it is our business,' Mia says, standing up. 'There was a fire last night, and we didn't know whether you were alive or dead.'

'Shit,' David mutters. 'That's what the stink is. What happened?'

'Where were you?' I ask again. Even Pavla looks angry now, her concern morphing into frustration. David doesn't stand much of a chance with us three women glaring at him.

He holds his hands in the air. 'I stayed in the village last night, okay?'

'Where? With whom?' I ask.

'As I said, it's none of your business. But if you must know, I spent the night with someone.'

Another woman, I suppose. I sink back down into the chair. Of course David slept with someone else last night. Although I feel totally wounded about it, he has every right to. I rejected him. So why is it that I feel so desolate and betrayed? It's not like I had any hold over him. It just goes to prove that David was using me. Perhaps he set fire to the house as revenge, a quick easy way to get rid of Mia and me in one fell swoop.

'I need a coffee,' he says as he strides over to the Nespresso machine.

'If you're not allowed into your bedrooms, what are you going to wear?' Pavla asks. I'm still dressed in my pyjamas with an anorak over the top. Not a stylish look.

'Brooke's room is on the other side of the staircase. I suppose we could borrow some of her clothes,' I suggest. Mia looks doubtful.

'Let me have a look in the laundry basket and in the drying cupboard,' Pavla suggests. 'I'll iron some of your clothes, and if you don't mind, Mia can borrow them.'

'Good idea,' I say.

Mia and I nap in the living room for a couple of hours, woollen blankets thrown over us as we sleep stretched out on the large sofas. The sound of the vacuum awakens me. I see that Mia is already awake, sitting up with her back leaning against the sofa, staring out of the window.

'I suppose Pavla is on a clean-up mission,' I say, yawning. I walk out into the corridor and see her vacuuming outside Robin's study. She switches the machine off when she sees me.

'David's gone back to London, and there's been some

water damage in here,' Pavla explains.

My heart plummets. I've barely touched Robin's study, but I know how devastated he would have been if any of his manuscripts were damaged. Mia appears at my side and follows me to Robin's study.

'I wouldn't know what to do with his stuff anyway,' I say, mainly to myself.

'I can help you,' Mia suggests. Pavla switches the vacuum back on and drags it towards the utility room.

The room looks untouched, with the exception of the corner wall where Robin's manuscripts are piled on a bookshelf, and there are rows and rows of CD cases from the predigital days, when he kept all his recordings on CDs. Here there is water damage, and as I look up at the ceiling, I see that there is a large damp patch that has seeped down the wall. I can't tell if it was caused by the firemen or a burst pipe.

'Oh,' Mia says. 'Do you mind if I pick up some of these?' she asks, pointing towards the stacks of paper.

'They don't mean anything to me. They're just the old stuff that Robin used to work on, aren't they?'

'Yes, but some of these might be valuable, especially if they are the original manuscripts or recordings of the pieces that he's most famous for.'

'As I can't read music, the papers mean nothing to me. Sort through them, Mia. And to be honest, you can have them.'

'Are you sure?' Her eyes widen.

I nod. I may be resentful that Robin has left everything to her, but I can't get away from the fact that Mia saved my life. If she was really evil, she could have left me to die.

LATE MORNING, two cars arrive, and the doorbell rings. I walk to the front door.

'Good morning, Mrs Featherstone.' It's DS Chabra and DC Degreen. The man standing next to them extends his hand. He's tall, probably six feet four inches, and sports a small grey moustache.

'I'm Steve Fitzgerald, the fire investigator.'

'Please come in,' I say, although I am wondering why the police are here. Yes, it's crossed my mind that this fire may not have been started by accident, but how would they know?

'I'd like to inspect the damage,' Steve Fitzgerald says.

'Up the stairs and to the right,' I say, indicating upwards. 'Do you need me to come up with you?' I ask, wondering how I'll cope when I see the blackened interior of the upstairs hallway.

'No, no. I'll just have a look around and will come and talk to you when I've finished.'

I turn my attention to the police officers.

'We would like to talk to Mia Benton,' DS Chabra says. They follow me as I walk towards Robin's study.

'Why?' I ask.

DS Chabra looks at me as if I've lost my marbles. 'Because of the fire. We will know more when we receive Steve's report, but with everything else that has gone on in your family, Mrs Featherstone, when there is a fire that may or may not be suspicious, we have a duty to investigate.'

'Are you suggesting that Mia had something to do with this?'

Mia is standing in the living room doorway, looking worryingly pale.

'We are not at liberty to discuss our lines of questioning,' the policewoman says.

'Which means yes, they suspect me of everything.' Mia speaks quietly, standing there as if there are blocks of iron on her shoulders.

'We only just got out alive!' I exclaim. 'Mia saved my life.

If she hadn't shouted, then had the presence of mind to get a wet towel and pull me to safety, I could be dead and this whole house burned to smithereens.'

'This fire was nothing to do with me,' Mia says, catching my eye. I know we're both thinking the same thing.

'You might want to question David Featherstone,' I suggest.

'Robin's son?' DC Degreen asks with a frown.

'Yes. Look at his alibi. He should have been here last night, but he wasn't. He is the only person here who knows how a car works. He said he was out of the country at the time his father died, but he wasn't. Talk to him rather than Mia. If anyone was responsible for this fire, it would have been him.'

'And why would David Featherstone want to set his house alight?'

'Because if both Mia and me are out of the way, then he and his brattish sister would inherit half each of Robin's estate, which is no doubt what they hoped would happen all along.' But as I say the words out loud, doubt settles on me. When I look at Mia, I see that she also looks dubious. However ghastly Robin's children really are, would they kill to get their hands on the money? As much as I would like Mia to be the innocent party here, simply because she saved my life, the evidence isn't nearly conclusive enough to shift the blame away from her and onto David. Robin's death, the failing of her car's brakes and this fire could just be a series of unfortunate accidents. And perhaps Robin simply changed his will because he fell out of love with me. I try not to remember his words when we had that awful fight, but it's hard to forget when your husband calls you a gold digger and says 'I really don't think I know you at all'.

24

MIA

The police leave, but not before requesting I attend yet another interview at the station. It's obvious that they haven't got any concrete evidence against me, otherwise they would have charged me by now, but I'm the easy culprit around here. I'm grateful for Tamsin's support, but it's making me suspicious. The woman hated my guts twenty-four hours ago, and now she's acting like I'm her best friend. It's weird; I don't buy her line that I saved her life. She was already awake by the time I shouted for her. It was Tamsin who called the fire brigade.

I think that Tamsin is playing a very complicated game here. I reckon that it's either David or Tamsin who pushed Robin to his death, and who also started the fire. Perhaps they were even in cahoots. She may have come to my defence when the police accused me, but at the same time, she cleared herself of any suspicion. Perhaps she wanted to claim the insurance money, or perhaps she really wanted me out of the way – not dead, because otherwise she would have started the fire outside my bedroom – but sufficiently scared to scarper. There's nothing I would like more than to get out of this place, far away from all the Featherstones, but Tamsin has misjudged me. I'm shrewd, and despite everything, I want some of the money. I know that I wasn't so bothered before, but for everything they've put me through, I think I deserve it.

I take my violin out of its case and tune it up. The acoustics are poor in this small bedroom, but at least playing brings me some solace. I've had the window open all day, and although it's cold, the smell of smoke has gone. I warm up with some scales and a couple of studies and then decide to have a look through the pile of manuscripts that I've brought upstairs. Most of them are handwritten, with Robin's spidery writing and notations throughout. I play a couple of the pieces, but they're written for piano mainly, so just extracting the tune from the treble clef line doesn't sound great. I lay my violin on the bed and rifle through the whole pile.

The second-from-bottom manuscript is a piece I don't recognise, and at the top is scrawled the sentence 'On the birth of my second son'.

What?

Is this *Robin's* second son, or did he compose this for someone else? Did he and Claudia have another child, perhaps a boy who died at birth or in childhood? Or perhaps they had a child and put him up for adoption. But why? Could the child have had a disability that they felt they couldn't cope with? I scramble for my laptop and do a search for Robin Featherstone's children. He has a Wikipedia entry, but there is only mention of David and Brooke. I spend unnecessary money on Ancestry and type in Robin and Claudia's names, but again, the only children listed are David and Brooke. But what if the child was stillborn? A tragedy, but how could I find out? Or what if the child was born before their marriage, and they used Claudia's maiden name to register the birth? I know it's harsh, but I could imagine

Claudia not being able to cope with a child who wouldn't live up to their expectations. A child that is a bit odd. Someone like Marek, perhaps.

As I think about Marek, my thoughts turn to Pavla. She was devoted to Robin, and sometimes I've wondered whether she has grieved more than Robin's own family. She has a quiet way about her, but those tears seemed genuine. Could it have been more than an employee's devotion? I know she's married to Thomas – at least, I assume she is, as Marek calls Thomas 'Dad'. But could Marek be her and Robin's son? Is that why Robin has kept her on all these years, given her that cottage to live in?

But if so, why didn't he leave his estate to her? Of course, Pavla has access to every nook and cranny of this house and the trust of everyone. She's the linchpin who holds this family together. Even Tamsin, who I assume wasn't used to staff, has come to rely on Pavla. It was Pavla who told the police that I was here at Stave House on the morning of Robin's death.

Perhaps her relationship with Robin wasn't as relaxed as I had assumed. Maybe she resented him, especially as he became grouchy after his stroke. Could he have been rude to her, and she just snapped? It seems unlikely, but assuming she had some motive to kill Robin, it would have been possible for her to somehow engineer for Robin to invite me over that day. Or did she just take advantage of the fact that I'd been creeping in and out of the house early that morning? I would have made her perfect fall guy. The fact that I had a criminal record must have been ideal for her; possibly she's known about it all along. There could be no one more suspicious than a person with a conviction for fraud.

She certainly had the means for setting all of this up, but what I can't work out is the why. Why would she want to kill Robin? If she was after Robin's money, then she should have killed Tamsin and Robin, only setting her sights on me after Robin's death when the contents of the will were made known. Or perhaps that's what she tried to do, but failed. I wonder if there was any provision for Pavla and Marek in Robin's original will. Perhaps Tamsin might know.

My violin forgotten, I leave it lying on its case and hurry back through the house.

'Tamsin?' I shout, but there is no answer. I suppose she might be in her greenhouse, where she spends most of her time. Then I hear the crunch of tyres on the gravel drive and see the hideous pink Mini pulling up in front of the house. Brooke is back.

'Come to see what the damage is!' Brooke shouts up the stairs. I walk to the top of the stairs.

'Oh, it's you,' she says. 'Where's the damage? Are my clothes okay?'

'The fire was in the hallway. Your rooms are untouched.'

'Phewee.'

'I've got a question for you, Brooke. Did you ever see your dad's original will, the one before he married Tamsin?'

'Not exactly, but Dad told us what he was doing, and you certainly weren't in it. Dad set up powers of attorney for me and David in case he or Mum lost their marbles.'

'Was Pavla provided for?'

'You mean did he leave her anything?'

I nod.

'Of course he did. I don't know how much, but Pavla's almost family. Unlike you.'

'Thank you,' I say, but Brooke has already turned away.

I'm not sure if the news makes me feel better or more unsure. One thing I know for certain is that I need to get away from Stave House. I'm not going to spend another night here, because I want to wake up and see tomorrow. Now I don't trust any of them: Tamsin, David or Pavla. I suppose I should throw Brooke and Claudia into that mix, too.

I hurry back to my room and telephone Timothy Carter, Robin's original solicitor. Surely he will know what the relationship was between Robin and Pavla, and whether Marek might be their son.

'Ms Benton, what may I do for you? Has my colleague Ian Dunworthy been able to help?'

'Um, yes, he's great. I've got a question about Robin Featherstone's earlier will, the one that he changed when he came to see you shortly before he died. Can you tell me what provision he made for Pavla and Marek?'

'No, I certainly cannot divulge such information. Firstly, that will is null and void, so quite irrelevant. Secondly, I wouldn't even share such confidential information with Mr Featherstone's next of kin.'

I swallow a sigh. It was worth asking the question, even if Timothy Carter sounds really annoyed at my cheek.

'If that's all, Ms Benton–'

'No, please don't hang up. Is Marek Robin's son?'

There's a long hesitation, longer than there should be if the answer was a straight no. Timothy Carter is a hopeless lawyer if he can't tell a lie on behalf of his clients. 'As I've already said, Ms Benton, I am not at liberty to give you any personal information about my clients. Goodbye.'

I smile as I let the phone plop onto the bed. *Thank you, Mr Carter. You've just proven my theory.*

25

I'm furious with David. Yes, I know it's illogical. I know that I gave him the cold shoulder, but during those long minutes when we thought he might be dead, I realised how broken I would be if another Featherstone had died. More specifically, another Featherstone who had held me in his arms. However infuriating David is, I'm finding it hard to accept Mia's theory. Yes, David had the means, but did he really have the motive? Is the man a killer? He looked a little bashful when he admitted that he slept with some woman in the village, but was that just a convenient cover story? Did he set the fire and then go and drink himself into oblivion? Could he be punishing me for rejecting his advances, hoping to get Mia and me out of the way in one fell swoop so he could get his hands on his father's estate?

Even my cacti aren't bringing me any solace. I take my thick gloves off and manage to knock over one of my cholla cacti. I try to pick it up carefully, but even so, I stab my index finger on one of the spiny thorns. I'm an idiot. I know the cholla have some of the spiniest stems around; they're collo- quially called jumping chollas because they stick so easily to animals and people. I suck my finger, but the thorn is dug in deeply, and I wonder if I'll have to go to the doctors to get it removed.

I stare at my plants and realise that I'm scared. I'm scared what will happen if I'm chucked out of here with no money. I'm scared that someone is trying to harm me. I still don't trust Mia; in fact, I don't trust anyone in Stave House. It was such a short time ago that I thought I was fixed for life, that all my dreams had come true. Yet I'm not the sort of person to sit back and wait for things to happen. I go after them. I went after Robin, and look how that ended up. A dream come true.

Still sucking my throbbing finger, I make a decision. I'm going for a drive.

I take Robin's car, partly because it's my only option, and partly because I feel safer in it. It's big and high off the ground, even if the Range Rover is over ten years old. I head straight into the local village. It's not much of a hub, just a village shop with a post office counter, a small independent pharmacy and a pub. Opposite is a large green that doubles as a playing field, adjacent to the village hall and a small primary school. It's one of those pubs that's open all day, somewhere for the bored locals to hang out. I open the door and walk into the low-ceilinged room, dark with heavy black-ened beams and a long shiny wood counter. There are a couple of elderly men seated on the bar stools, but they don't look up as I approach. A woman, probably mid-fifties, sporting a diamond on the side of her nose, is standing behind the bar, wiping glasses with a tea towel. She smiles at me as I approach.

'What can I get you, love?'

'Sorry, I'm not here to have a drink.'

She raises an eyebrow. 'Food, then?'

'No, thanks. I'm, uh, Tamsin Featherstone, Robin Featherstone's wife.'

'Well, goodness me, so you are. Robin used to pop in here from time to time when he was married to Claudia, but between you and me, I think it was to get away from her. Their arguments used to be so loud, you could hear them across the fields. My condolences to you. He was a good man, was Robin.'

'I hope you don't mind me asking, but was David in here last night?'

'He certainly was, with a tab as long as my arm.'

'So he was drinking a lot?'

'He likes his beer and his shots, does young David. He was totally hammered. Could barely stand by closing time. Poor Lisa had to almost carry him out of here.'

'Lisa?'

She leans closer to me and lowers her voice. 'Lisa Morrison. David and Lisa have been having a little on-off fling for years and years. They try to keep it quiet, but this is a small place. It's an open secret. Poor Lisa holds a flame for him, but I tell her that David will never be the sort to settle down. I assume you've got to know him and his cheeky ways!'

I smile tightly. 'Do you know where I can find Lisa?'

She looks at me askance. 'It's Lisa over in the chemist's. She's the pharmacist. A bright girl who should be off in the big city, but she's taken over her parents' business and making a fine job of it, too. You must have met our Lisa?'

'Yes, of course. Silly me,' I say, although of course I haven't, at least not knowingly. Why would I ever use a chemist in this little backwater, where everyone knows everyone else's business? I can just imagine popping in to pick up my contraceptive pills, and it would be all around the village that the new Mrs Featherstone is still on the pill. And the old biddies would say, *Just as well – that Robin, he's much too old to be a father a second time around.*

'You sure you don't want a drink?' the pub landlady says. 'On the house.'

'That's really kind of you, but I must get going.' And I hotfoot it out of there.

The chemist is two doors down, on the other side of the village store. There's an older lady with curly grey hair and pink glasses standing behind the counter.

'Good afternoon,' I say. 'Is it possible to have a word with Lisa?'

'Of course. Just a moment.' She disappears through an open door and hollers, 'Lisa, love, a lady to talk to you.'

About twenty seconds later, a young woman walks out into the shop. She's got shoulder-length strawberry blonde hair, wide eyes and an engaging smile. *Oh, Lisa*, I want to say, *he's really no good for you.*

'Hello, Lisa. I'm Tamsin Featherstone. May I have a private word?'

Lisa widens her eyes slightly and glances towards the older woman, who waddles into the back room.

'It's about David Featherstone. Was he with you last night?'

Lisa obviously wasn't expecting that question, because she blushes deeply. 'Yes. He was so drunk that I had to put him straight to bed and be at the ready with a bucket. I told him to slow down with the drinking, but he refused to listen. He was on quite a bender. I guess he's got a sore head this morning.'

Lisa looks sincere; her words tally with what the pub landlady said and the sorry state that David was in earlier.

'By the way,' Lisa says, 'I haven't had the chance to offer you my condolences. I was thinking about Robin only a couple of days ago, when I found one of his uncollected prescriptions.'

'Thank you,' I say as I turn to leave.

'Is David alright?' she asks.

I speak over my shoulder. 'Under the circumstances, I'm sure he'll be just fine.'

When I get back to the car, I just sit there for several long moments and try to think. If David was with Lisa all last night, then it wasn't David who started the fire – assuming, of course, it wasn't an accident. If it wasn't him, who was it? Brooke wasn't at Stave House, and I just can't see her creeping in in the middle of the night and holding a lit flame to the carpet. Claudia, on the other hand, might have, but what would she have got to gain? The same applies to Pavla. It would have been easy enough for her to start the fire, but why? What reason would she have for wanting to burn down Stave House and everyone in it? I shiver.

And then my phone pings with an incoming text. It's Mia.

Did Pavla benefit from Robin's original will?

Why is she asking me about Pavla?

And then it hits me. That afternoon when I found Robin dead at the bottom of the stairs, Pavla said she was going out to collect Robin's prescription. Was this the same prescription that wasn't picked up at the chemist? If so, what was Pavla doing instead? Where was she when she told us she was out? Could that have been a ruse? Could she have returned to the house and pushed Robin? But why? Why would Pavla want to kill Robin? I've seen the way her face softens when she talks about him. Was Pavla in love with my Robin?

Oh my goodness! I have to tell Mia. I start up the car and put my foot on the accelerator, driving much too fast towards home. Could this all be of Pavla's making? But why? Why on earth would Pavla want to kill Robin?

26

MIA

I need to find out more about Pavla. I've never been inside her cottage and have barely spoken to Thomas, but I saw him on the sit-upon mower a few moments ago, so he's safely occupied elsewhere. I tiptoe down to the kitchen and see that Pavla is busy making something for supper. She doesn't see me, so I slip out of the front door and walk briskly towards her home.

The cottage was probably a gatehouse once upon a time. Red brick, it is quaint with a crooked chimney and a front door set behind brick pillars. The property is overhung by lots of trees, giving the place a sense of foreboding and making the house dark. I have no plan; I just want to know more about Pavla and her family. If it means sneaking inside the cottage, so be it. I knock on the white back door and peer through the window into the kitchen. It's all dark inside and difficult to see in. I knock again, then try to turn the handle.

'What are you doing?'

I jump, my heart clattering in my chest.

'You gave me a fright, Marek,' I say. How can someone that big walk around so silently?

'Are you looking for Mum or Dad?'

'Your mum, actually.'

'She's at the big house. Cooking.'

He stands there and stares at me, unflinching. I get the feeling that we all underestimate Marek's intelligence.

'I must have missed her,' I say, turning around and walking away from the cottage. When I stop to look over my shoulder, I'm relieved to see Marek loping off in the opposite direction, across the lawns towards Tamsin's greenhouse, no doubt. I hide behind a large oak tree, hoping that I'm properly out of sight. Then I wait until I can't see Marek any longer, and the only noises are the blackbirds chirping overhead and the distant hum of the mower. I step out from behind the tree and, glancing around, walk back towards the cottage. At the back door, I place my hand on the handle and, with a thumping heart, press it down. To my surprise, the door is unlocked.

I hesitate for a moment, because what excuse do I have to be here? Although under the terms of Robin's will all of this might be mine, I feel as if I'm trespassing. Perhaps I should just return to talk to Pavla and ask her permission to look around. But no. I'm here now. I slip in through the back door, closing it quietly behind me.

'Hello!' I shout, just to be sure that the cottage is indeed empty. The kitchen is small, with clay tiles on the floor and melamine work surfaces. Unsurprisingly, although the appliances are old, the place is spotless. I tiptoe through the kitchen into the tiny hall. There's a decent-sized living room to the left, filled with a green sofa and two armchairs and an oval table, which I assume they use as their dining table. The staircase rises steeply upwards. I hesitate at the bottom step and then kick off my shoes, tiptoeing as I climb upwards. The steps creak and startle me. Upstairs there are four doors, all of which are closed. The first room must be Marek's. There is a crumpled navy-blue duvet on the single bed and clothes scattered on the floor. The walls are decorated in posters, mainly of Katy Perry and Ariana Grande. Underneath the window is a chest of drawers, but from an initial glance, nothing of interest.

I step out of the room and close the door. The next door opens onto a bathroom, with a white bath surrounded by an opaque shower curtain. There's another bedroom next to the bathroom, and although it looks lived in, there is only a single bed. That's strange. I wonder if Thomas snores and Pavla chucks him out to sleep in here.

The final door opens up onto the master bedroom. A queen-sized bed with a dusty pink velvet headboard sits in the middle of the long wall. The bed is neatly made with two bedside tables either side. One is bare except for a thin tall lamp. A clock, a packet of paracetamol and a photo of a young boy stand on the other bedside table. It's clear that the photo is of Marek when he was five or six. Opposite the bed is a wardrobe, and a chest of drawers stands underneath the window. There's a large cut-glass vase standing on top of the chest without any flowers in it.

I pull open the drawer in the bedside table, but it holds nothing of interest except a little box with a necklace inside, a thin gold chain with a small gold locket attached. I pick up the necklace, but my fingers are trembling, and it slithers through them to the floor. I drop to my knees to pick up it up, and as I do so, I glance under the bed. There's a silver box wedged right under the centre of the bed. I have to lever myself onto my stomach in order to reach the box, which is heavy. After some undignified pushing and pulling, I drag it out. It's a safe-deposit box, about the size of a standard box file. I swallow hard as I try to lift the lid up. My fingers are shaking, and my breathing is shallow. The box is locked. I sit there on the floor for a long moment, wondering where Pavla would keep the key. I really need to see inside this box because I'm sure I'm going to find proof that Pavla is behind all the evil happenings at Stave House.

After standing up, I put the necklace back into its little box and place it inside the bedside drawer. Walking across the room, I open the wardrobe. Skirts, trousers and dresses hang neatly, colour-coordinated, and several pairs of shoes are lined up on the floor of the cupboard. It's strange that there are only Pavla's clothes in here. I guess she and Thomas are no longer intimate. I suppose I could rifle through her clothes, but I don't have the stomach for that. Instead, I walk to the chest of drawers and pull them open. Pavla doesn't have many clothes, but the jumpers she owns are all neatly folded inside clear plastic bags. I am not going to lower myself to rifling through her underwear.

I stand in the middle of the room and think. If I wanted to hide a key, where would I put it? I recall my time in prison and what I did with anything that was of value to me. A bar of chocolate. A tea bag. I hid it in my pillow. Not an original place, but effective. I walk over to the bed and lift up the pillow, sliding my hand inside the pillowcase. Bingo. My fingers wrap around a small pouch. Pulling it out, I see that it's a small black velvet drawstring bag, the sort of pouch that jewellery might be sold in. I undo the bag and tip it up so the contents fall out onto the palm of my hand.

And there it is, a small key. I kneel back down on the floor and insert the key into the box. It slides in perfectly. Inhaling loudly, I lift the lid off the box. There are papers, passports, photographs and some small notebooks inside. I open the passports first. Pavla Whittaker has a British passport, but she was born in the Czech Republic; she stares at me unsmiling in the passport photo. I close the document and open the next one. The photograph is of Thomas, and his name is listed as Thomas Whittaker, so they *are* a married couple.

There is no passport for Marek. Picking up the pile of papers, I flick through them until I find a birth certificate, and I'm just scanning the page when ...

'What are you doing?'

I let out a little yelp, because I had no idea Pavla was standing there. How long has she been watching me? She must have crept up the stairs, avoiding all the steps that creak.

I stand up quickly, dropping the papers as I do so.

'What are you doing, Mia?' she asks, narrowing her eyes at me. There is something utterly menacing about her expression, even though she is talking so quietly. It feels as if my throat is closing up.

'I'm sorry. It's just. I know I shouldn't have.' I fumble around for some excuse, but really I have none. I've been caught red-handed.

She takes another step towards me. 'Where I come from, we used to cut off the fingers of thieves. Imagine how that would be for you, Mia.'

I inhale audibly. I'm sure she's talking absolute nonsense, as Czechoslovakia was one of the most advanced nations in Europe, nothing like somewhere such as Iran, where that really did happen. It's not the history lesson that I'm terrified of, but the intensity of Pavla's stare. I take a step sideways, but she mirrors me. Her eyes are fixed on mine, unblinking.

'I'm really sorry, Pavla. I was snooping, and I shouldn't have. I just wanted to see the cottage, especially as I'm likely to inherit it, and–'

'Really?' Pavla says, her look of disbelief making my stomach clench.

'Actually, I was after this.' I glance down at the birth certificate. 'Marek is Robin's son, and you killed Robin, didn't you?'

'No. No, you've got it all wrong.' Pavla shakes her head

rapidly and waves her hands around. 'Robin was Marek's father, but I didn't kill Robin. I loved him. Why would I kill Robin?'

'The money? The will? There were plenty of motives.'

As her jaw slackens and her eyes well up, her shoulders drop. Either she is a first-class actress, or I have got it wrong. Rather than stepping towards me, Pavla walks backwards so she's standing next to the bed.

'Did you set the fire? Did you tamper with my car brakes, Pavla?'

'I didn't do anything,' she murmurs. 'My only crime was loving Robin.'

'If you didn't, who did?' I feel emboldened now as I stare at Pavla.

Then we both freeze. A door groans downstairs, and there are slow, steady footsteps.

'You've got to get out of here now!' Pavla speaks quickly in a chilling whisper.

'Why?'

'It's Thomas. He'll kill you if he thinks you've been snooping.' She tries to push the chest of drawers to one side. 'Help me! Hurry!' She gestures to me to come towards her, and I wonder if she's just going to push me out of the window. I think of genial Thomas, who has only ever been warm towards me. Do I really believe her?

The steps are slow and steady, the staircase creaking heavily as he gets nearer and nearer.

'Come!' she says as I move hesitatingly towards the chest of drawers. I have a split second to make my decision, and as I see the terror in Pavla's eyes, I decide that I have to believe her. I grab the other side of the chest to help her move it away from the window, but we're not quick enough.

The bedroom door swings open, and Thomas is standing there. The big man who I thought was genial looks nothing of the sort now. His smile is a grimace, and as he steps towards me, I see that he is clutching a carving knife that glints as he holds it out in front of him. His left hand, the one with only three fingers, is stretched grotesquely out to one side.

Thomas looks at Pavla, then at the birth certificate, which has drifted to the floor, and then his deep-set eyes settle on mine.

'Don't move,' he says, his voice low and gravelly. The room seems to shrink in size, the walls falling in towards me as my heart pumps so wildly I think my chest might explode.

'You snoop. You die.' His smile is like a grimace. I shrink back towards the wall.

'No, Thomas,' Pavla says.

'It's all your fault,' he spits. Just one step and he will be on me. That knife is coming nearer and nearer, and Pavla is just standing there next to the bed, her eyes frozen open, her mouth contorted.

'If it's about the money, then I promise that you and Pavla can have whatever you want if I win the case. You'll be well provided for. We can forget all about this.'

Thomas laughs, but it's cold and sharp, just like the blade of that knife, which is mere centimetres from my neck, so close that I can feel Thomas's hot, damp breath on my cheek. I flinch, but there is nowhere for me to go, no way that I can dart out behind him, no possibility of me being strong and quick enough to haul myself onto the window ledge. This is it. This is my end. And for what? I didn't ask for any of this. Thomas lifts his arm high into the air. I turn my face towards Pavla, my eyes begging her to intervene, but she just stands there like a statue.

I kick out at Thomas and catch his knee, but he's too strong. The knife plunges into my side. There's a high-pitched scream. I assume it's me, as I wait for the searing pain, for the life to seep out of me. Will it take seconds, or will it be a drawn-out agony as Thomas and Pavla leave me here to bleed out? I scream again as he pulls the knife out, the blade gleaming with my red blood. He draws his arm back, and I know that this time he's going straight for my heart.

'No!' I try to scream, but I'm not sure if the word comes out.

But then Thomas crumples to the ground, and the knife flies out of his hand, skidding across the carpet. A black boot crashes into Thomas' back. With a loud grunt, he collapses next to me.

What just happened? Did Pavla attack her husband? But no, it's not Pavla's voice.

'We need to get out of here!' Tamsin says as she leans down and grabs my hand, but I'm so weak. The room is spinning around me, and as my hand clutches my side, it comes away sticky and wet. 'Get up, Mia. We've got to go.'

'What? I can't,' I mutter.

'You're bleeding, but you're going to be okay. Come on, Mia.' She leans down and puts her hands under my shoulders, levering me upwards.

'Where's Pavla?' I whisper.

'I'm here. I'm sorry. I didn't want any of this,' Pavla says, her voice so faint it's barely audible.

Tamsin slaps Pavla across the face, the sound reverberating around the room. Then Tamsin puts her arm around me, and I lean into her.

'Why?' Tamsin spits at Pavla, who is still standing frozen like a statue, the side of her face red from where Tamsin slapped her.

'I'm sorry,' Pavla murmurs.

'I think Thomas killed Robin,' I say to Tamsin. 'Robin is Marek's father.'

And then blackness descends.

W hen I got back to Stave House, I searched everywhere for Mia, but the house was empty. Then I saw Marek loitering near my greenhouse.

'Have you seen Mia?' I shouted across the lawn.

Marek sauntered towards me. 'Yes. She was knocking on the door.'

'What door?'

'My home. She was looking for Mum.'

'Did you tell your mum that Mia was looking for her?'

'Yes, of course. But Mia left the cottage, so she won't be there anymore.'

But a flicker of doubt crossed Marek's face, and I knew in that second that I had to race to the cottage. If neither Mia nor Pavla were in Stave House, it meant Pavla was already in the cottage or on her way to a possible confrontation with Mia. I have never run so fast, but when I looked over my shoulder, I saw that Marek was following me. 'Stay here, Marek!' I yelled. He stopped totally still. For one horrific moment, I wondered if he was going to charge at me. But I had no time to worry about Marek. I raced onto the drive and then down the short driveway to the cottage. When I glanced over my shoulder, I saw that Marek had walked off in the opposite direction. The back door to the cottage was slightly ajar. I pushed it open, trying to control my breathing, and that's when I heard them.

Thomas, Pavla and Mia. Thomas said, 'You snoop, you die,' and when I heard those words and his contemptuous tone of voice, I pushed the door further open. Then I heard Mia's voice and her scream. Here I am, having to make a split-second decision. Do I run up to confront them, or do I run away? I think of Robin and how I wish I could reverse time.

I tiptoe as quietly as I can up the stairs.

Thomas is standing over Mia, poised to plunge a knife into her heart. I don't hesitate, and I throw myself forwards, kicking him in the knees from behind with all the force I can muster, glad I'm wearing heavy boots. The shock makes him tumble, and the knife spins across the floor, but I know my kick isn't enough. I turn around and pick up a heavy glass vase that stands on top of the chest of drawers. Without thinking, I bring it down, crashing onto Thomas's head. He crumples onto the carpet, and I wonder if I've killed him. In that moment, I hope so. There's a gasp, and I realise that Pavla is standing on the other side of the bed, her eyes wide with shock. Is she dangerous, too? Has she been complicit in all of this? I grab the knife off the floor, just in case.

Glancing at Mia, I see blood seeping from her side. I've no idea how badly hurt she is, and although I want to run away from this scene of horror, I have to help Mia and get her away from Pavla.

'We need to get out of here,' I say as I put my arm around Mia, holding the knife with the other hand. Thomas lies motionless on the floor; Pavla just stares at us. I drag Mia out of the room and down the stairs, worried that I'm making her wound worse, but I know I just have to get us out of here. To begin with, she's leaden and lifeless, and I hope that it's just because she's fainted. Then she groans, but I'm not sure that she's fully conscious. Outside, I prop her up so that her back is leaning against the brick wall, her face almost grey-green in colour.

'Wake up, Mia,' I say, rubbing my hand across her cheek. Her eyes flicker open. I think she recognises me.

'You need to stay awake.' I pull my mobile out of my jacket pocket and dial 999. 'I need police and ambulances right now.'

When I am reassured that both the ambulance and police are on their way, I run back into the cottage, still holding the knife that is covered with Mia's blood, just in case either Pavla or Thomas reappear before the emergency services arrive. I find a tea towel in the kitchen, which I press into Mia's wound, hoping that's the right thing to do. Mia whimpers, her face ghostly.

'Help is coming,' I say, squeezing her hand. 'You're going to be okay.'

'Marek is Robin's son,' Mia gasps.

'Shush, no talking. Just concentrate on slow breathing until the ambulance arrives. You're going to be fine.' My stomach churns, as I have no idea if she really is going to be okay, or if Thomas or Pavla will come out of the house and try to attack us again. I just hold the tea towel hard against her side and wrap my arms around her shaking body.

Five minutes later, I hear sirens. Two ambulances and police cars come roaring up to the cottage. Time stands still as I watch Mia being attended to, and then Thomas is stretchered out of the cottage. Have I killed him? Will I be tried for manslaughter, or will they accept that it was self-defence? Then Pavla appears by my side, accompanied by two uniformed policemen.

'Why?' I snarl at her. 'Why?'

'Because Thomas wanted to leave here, and I didn't. I couldn't take Marek away from his real father.' Tears pour down her face.

'Did Thomas kill Robin?' I growl at her.

'I think so.' Her voice is barely a whisper. 'He's always known that Marek wasn't his child, and that our marriage was one of convenience – it was his dream to move out of London and live the quiet life. But I'd never told him that Robin was Marek's birth father.'

Then DS Chabra and DC Degreen stride towards us. I am so relieved to see them. I would also like to say, 'I told you so,' but then I realise I got it all wrong.

'You need to tell the police the truth,' I say. 'Everything.'

'What's happened?' DS Chabra asks.

'This story begins a long time ago,' Pavla says, wringing her hands in front of her. 'I had a love affair with Robin. I hadn't been working here for long. Claudia was never a good wife to Robin. When I discovered I was pregnant, Robin was torn. I met Thomas on the train. I'd dropped my bag, and he helped me. We got talking, and we clicked. It wasn't until a few weeks later that he explained he was in trouble with some London gang and needed to get out of the city. I suggested Robin might give him a job here as a handyman and gardener. And when Thomas asked me to marry him, it seemed like a good arrangement for us all. Thomas had a job and could live safely in the countryside. Marek had two fathers: One he knew about; the other he didn't. Robin ended our affair, but I never stopped loving him.

'After his stroke, Robin changed. He became angry and treated me with contempt. Thomas wanted to leave here and get work elsewhere. He didn't like how Robin treated us. I refused. The day that Robin died, Thomas told me that he had accepted a new job offer. The three of us would be moving to a manor house in Suffolk, working for a new family. I refused to go. We had a massive argument, and I told him that I would never leave here. I couldn't, because Robin was Marek's father and he was providing for us all in his will. But it wasn't so much the money, it was the thought of never seeing Robin again.

'Thomas was livid. There was fury coming out of every vein. He screamed at me, he slapped my face, and then he locked me in the bedroom. When he returned, he was so calm. Happy. He apologised and let me out. Then I discovered that Robin had fallen down the stairs.'

'But if you knew that Thomas had killed Robin, why didn't you say anything?' I ask. I'm so angry, I have to clasp my hands together to stop myself from punching Pavla.

'I didn't know for sure.'

I scoff. 'Of course you did. So that's why you didn't collect Robin's prescription.'

She nods. 'But then we couldn't leave, not until after Robin's funeral, not until we could collect the inheritance that Robin promised us.'

'And then you discovered everything was being left to Mia.'

Pavla nods again. 'Thomas was so angry. He wanted the will to revert back to how it was before. He needed to get rid of Mia and you, ideally.'

'So you knew that he set the fire, and you knew that he tampered with Mia's brakes?'

'No, no, of course I didn't know.'

'Yeah, right,' I say. I turn away from this woman and see Marek standing next to a police car. His mouth hangs open, and his eyes are wide. I feel sorry for him. This young man who has been the pawn in a game of horror played by his parents.

'Pavla Whittaker, we are arresting you on suspicion of

accessory to murder,' DS Chabra says. 'You do not have to say anything. But it may harm your defence if you do not mention when questioned something which you later rely on in court.' DS Chabra nods her head towards DS Degreen, who leads Pavla to a marked police car.

'How are you, Tamsin?' DS Chabra softens her voice as she looks at me.

'Shocked,' I say as tears well in my eyes. All I can think about is that my wonderful husband was murdered, and all this time I have been directing my suspicions to the wrong person.

'I'll get one of my officers to accompany you up to the house so you can have a cup of tea and warm up. I'll then pop up shortly to take a formal statement. Is that alright?'

I nod.

28

TAMSIN

A FEW DAYS LATER

I knock on the door of the hospital room and walk in, placing the big bouquet of pale pink roses on the windowsill.

'That's kind of you and absolutely not necessary,' Mia says. She still looks ghostly pale and winces with pain when she moves.

'How are you doing?' I ask, settling into the grey plastic chair next to her bed.

'Getting there. I should be discharged the day after tomorrow. How are you doing?'

'Honestly, it's hard. I'm finding it difficult to sleep.'

'I'm not surprised. Me too, and they're giving me strong painkillers that are meant to make me drowsy.'

I can't stop reliving those horrific moments, the lead-up to me rushing to Pavla's cottage.

'I still can't believe it,' Mia says. 'We both got it so wrong. Is Thomas going to survive?'

'Yes,' I say, pulling a face, although deep down, I'm glad I didn't inflict any long-lasting injury. I don't like the thought of killing someone, even if that person is a murderer himself. And what if the police hadn't accepted that I was acting in self-defence? I'm not as strong as Mia; I doubt I could survive a stint in prison. 'Marek is living in the house with me at the moment.'

'And Pavla?'

'She's being held in prison and will be up for bail at some point. It looks like she'll be charged as an accessory to murder.'

'Marek is a strange lad, but I'm sorry this has happened to him,' Mia says.

'Me too. I'm going to look after him until he can stand on his own two feet. After all, he is Robin's son, and I owe that to Robin. Oh,' I say as I rifle in my handbag. 'I nearly forgot. I've got a letter for you.' I hand her the envelope. She opens it and takes out the formal letter, reading it slowly. It takes a long moment for her to register what it says. Then she looks at me, her eyes wide.

'You're no longer contesting the will?'

'Yup. I've done some soul-searching, and I wasn't a good wife to Robin. After his stroke, I didn't support him in the way I should have done. If he wanted you to have everything, then I need to respect his wishes.'

'Really?' Mia whispers. There are tears in her eyes. 'But I still don't know why he chose me.'

'Perhaps we'll never know,' I suggest.

'I want you to keep Stave House,' Mia says.

'What?' I can't believe my ears. 'You're only saying that because of everything that's just happened. You don't owe me anything, Mia,' I say.

'I've had nothing else to think about whilst I've been lying here. I genuinely want you to have it. It's not my home and never will be. You should stay there. It belongs to the Feather-stones, and if you're going to look after Marek, it should remain his home, too.'

I am astonished. I freely admit that I got Mia totally wrong. 'Please don't make any promises right now; just think about it.'

'I already have, Tamsin. It's yours.'

'You could live there too if you wanted,' I say. 'It's big enough.'

Mia smiles and shakes her head. 'It's yours, Tamsin. So long as I have enough money to buy a small place for Dad and to be able to travel playing the violin, I'm happy. Thank goodness Thomas didn't stab my hands or arms.'

We're both silent for a long moment.

'David and Brooke are refusing to accept Marek as their half-brother,' I say. I decide not to tell Mia the full detail of that conversation.

Both David and Brooke were sitting in the living room, summoned by DS Chabra. When she showed them Marek's birth certificate and explained that Robin was Marek's father, Brooke burst into tears, and David said some truly horrible things, bigoted, deeply offensive words directed towards Marek's learning disabilities. I realised then that David was a bully, and he had none of his father's generosity of spirit. Both of them disgusted me. They said they would never recognise Marek as their brother. They were united in their view that they refused to set eyes on him ever again. I hope it was just the shock of the announcement and that their opin-ions will mellow with time.

'Are you going to give them anything?' I ask.

Mia shakes her head. 'If Robin didn't want his children to get any of his inheritance, then so be it. But I will give Claudia fifty percent of Robin's royalties, and no doubt that will eventually filter down to them. That seems fair, doesn't it?'

I nod. I think it sounds very fair.

'David might not have killed anyone, but he's not a very nice person, is he?' Mia says.

I try to contain my blush, because I really don't want to admit to Mia that I slept with him.

'I asked him why he lied about not being in the country when his father was killed, and why he didn't bother to turn up to the funeral,' I say.

'And?' Mia asks.

'He said he couldn't be bothered. What son couldn't be bothered to attend his own father's funeral? And then he only tipped up when Brooke told him about the will.'

'At which point he started following me,' Mia says. 'I still feel a bit bad about them getting nothing.'

'Don't.'

Mia shifts in bed and grimaces slightly. 'What are you going to do next, or haven't you decided yet?'

'Actually, I have. I want to set up a nursery specialising in succulents. I was going to apply for a business loan, but if I'm really going to be able to stay at Stave House, I won't need to do that.' I still can't believe that Mia is being so kind. 'There's enough space to expand the greenhouse at Stave House,' I say. 'I can employ Marek, too. I think he'd like that.'

'That's a lovely idea.' Mia smiles.

'And you, what is next for you?'

Mia briefly closes her eyes. 'I'm going to focus on my violin playing. The manager of the group I toured with has reached out, and it's possible there might be some gigs for me. But first I need to get out of here. I just wish I knew why Robin left everything to me.'

'I don't suppose we'll ever know. I expect it's just the

obvious – he didn't like his kids much, and he thought I was the grasping second wife.'

'I think he loved you, Tamsin. It was the way his voice softened when he talked about you, and how his eyes crinkled at the corners when he looked at you.'

I smile, but I don't say anything. Mia doesn't know how beastly I was towards Robin in his final weeks. I suppose I must forget about that and just focus on the Robin I loved before his stroke. 'Do you know, I think I can grieve for Robin properly now we know the truth. I really hate Thomas and Pavla.'

'You mustn't hate them, Tamsin. He is an evil money-grasping man, and she's just sad. Think how she spent all of those years yearning for a man who no longer had eyes for her. It must have been so galling for Pavla when you turned up as Robin's new wife. But hate won't bring Robin back, it won't change how Pavla or Thomas are, it'll just eat you up from the inside. Those first few weeks in prison, I thought I hated my sister, but actually all I was doing was poisoning myself. I think what Sara did was awful, but somehow I've come to a place of peace. Does that all sound a bit woo-woo?'

I shake my head slowly. 'No, not at all. But I still think I need to hate Thomas just for a short while, and then perhaps I can look back and feel gratitude for having a wonderful fifteen months with a man I loved and being thankful for having met you and what you've given me.' I stand up. 'You look exhausted, Mia. I need to leave you to sleep.'

'Thanks, Tamsin. And thank you for the flowers. Oh, and thank you for saving my life.'

I laugh. 'Don't forget you saved me from the fire, so I reckon we're even.'

She smiles briefly and then closes her eyes. As I walk out of the hospital, I wonder what my fierce solicitor Shayla

Chatterton will think of the agreement Mia and I have come to. Not a lot, I suppose.

29

TEN MONTHS LATER

I'm at Vienna International airport, waiting for my flight to Gatwick. My violin is in its case strapped over my shoulder. It's a new violin – well, new to me only, as it's nearly three hundred years old. I am in love with its deep, melodic tones and the way it makes my playing so much more heartfelt. Robin's probate came through a few weeks ago, and I was left a lot more money than I had anticipated. The biggest chunk has gone on this violin; the rest I will use to put towards a down payment for a house for Dad and me. Obviously we can't afford to live in Fulham, but I'll find somewhere out of London. Dad fancies being near the sea.

I've just completed a fortnight of performances travelling around Austria with my new trio: Zac, who plays the cello, and Gabriel, who plays the viola.

'Over here.' Zac beckons to me. 'Have you seen the newspapers?'

'My German isn't very good.' I stand on tiptoes to give Zac a kiss on the cheek. We hadn't meant to start a relationship, but sometimes these things just happen, and for now, I'm going with the flow. My new motto is to grab happiness whenever possible. Gabriel doesn't seem to mind, as he has a husband waiting for him back at home. There's a theory that the best artists in whatever genre need to be in pain to imbue their work with heartfelt emotion. I think being in a place of happiness is far stronger for making meaningful music, although perhaps all the horrors I've faced in the past allow me to express the full gamut of emotions.

Zac has *The Times* open on the second page and runs his finger along the headline.

Thomas Whittaker to Spend Rest of Life in Prison

'Oh,' I say as a ripple of fear runs through me. I'm working on deep-breathing techniques and meditation, but it's hard to forget the terror that Tamsin and I faced. From time to time it resurfaces and catches me unaware.

Zac puts his arm around my shoulders and pulls me towards him. 'Look. He's been convicted of murder and attempted murder. It's all over now.' Zac places a kiss on the top of my head. I nod, but deep down I wonder if it will ever be all over. Despite the money, my newfound freedom, the success I'm having with my music, and my wonderful boyfriend, dark thoughts swirl in the back of my mind. Particularly at night, when I lie in bed frozen with fear should there be an unexpected sound, or sniffing desperately to make sure that there's no smell of burning. And then there's the guilt. Why did Robin leave me everything?

I don't have time to think, because our flight is called. We hurry to the gate and onto the plane. Once we've taken off, Zac encourages me to drink a gin and tonic. I fall asleep with my head resting on his shoulder.

I dream that I am standing on the stage of the Albert

Hall in London, taking a bow in front of five thousand adoring fans, all of whom have risen to their feet to applaud me with a standing ovation. But then I catch the eye of someone standing in the front row, someone who isn't clapping, but staring at me with fury in his eyes. It's Robin Featherstone.

'Stop clapping!' he shouts. Extraordinarily, his voice halts the crowd. 'She's a fraudster. Mia Benton stole my work. She doesn't deserve your respect.' And then Robin steps forwards and leaps up onto the stage. The knife glints under the stage lights. There's a terrible scream ...

'Mia, wake up. We've started our descent.' Zac has his hand on my knee. 'Are you okay?'

I nod and rub my eyes.

'Another nightmare?' he asks.

'Yup.'

They're a frequent occurrence and normally feature Robin holding a knife. I've tried to work through why I have these dreams; I suppose it's the guilt. The guilt that he gave me so much, yet I will likely never know why. I wonder whether lottery winners feel the same way: *Why me? What should I do with all of this newfound luck?* I know I shouldn't compare myself to survivors of war atrocities, because I have experienced just an iota of what they go through, but they have survivor's guilt, don't they?

The passengers are disembarking the plane now. I stand up in the cramped aisle, and like everyone else, I turn my mobile phone back on. I've got a voicemail message from Tamsin. I suppose she wants to discuss Thomas's sentencing with me. I press play and hold it up to my ear.

'Mia, as soon as you're back in England, can you give me a call? I've found something, and I need you to come over. It's urgent. Tx'

I tap Zac on the arm.

'I know it's going the wrong way, but I need to go to Horsham before returning to London. Do you mind?'

'Really?' he asks, disappointment clouding his face. 'I wanted to take you out to dinner tonight to celebrate a great tour. Will you be back in time?'

I glance at my watch. It's already mid-afternoon. 'Rain check until tomorrow night? I'll stay with Dad this evening and come to you tomorrow. Is that alright?'

'Of course it is,' Zac says, placing a light kiss on my lips.

I send Tamsin a text message.

Collecting luggage now. Will hop on the train and see you in an hour or so. Is that convenient?

She messages back instantly.

Great. Let me know what train you're on, and I'll collect you from the station. Tx

As I'm sitting on the train, I remember when I first met Tamsin: How on the one hand, I felt we had nothing in common, but on the other, I wished we could have been friends. I honestly never thought that would happen, but look at us now. We have so many shared experiences, not just the horrors of what took place at Stave House, but also losing parents at a young age. I don't suppose we'll ever socialise together, but our bond runs so deep, the sort that you might have with a sibling perhaps, where you know that you will always have each other's backs, come what may. Or perhaps that is just an idealised notion, because that certainly didn't happen with my sister.

.   .   .

'HOW WAS THE TRIP?' Tamsin has to speak loudly over the noisy engine of her Defender.

'It was great. We sold out at every venue.'

'Did you know that your recording of Robin's song has over twenty million views on YouTube now?'

'No way!' I laugh.

It was the tune that Robin wrote for Marek. I rearranged it slightly and recorded all the string parts myself, putting the piece up on YouTube. It's created quite a buzz, probably due to the notoriety of Thomas and Pavla. Nevertheless, I'm confident it's a great showcase both of Robin's composition talent and my violin playing. I'm hopeful it could be the start of something big for me.

'Tell me, what is it that was so important for me to see?'

She taps the side of her nose and throws me a grin. 'Five minutes and we'll be home. I'll show you.'

It's strange driving up to Stave House. I suppose I thought I'd never visit the place again, because it holds too many confusing and unpleasant memories ... but that feeling of panic that I feared doesn't come. Tamsin pulls into the carport and hoots the horn. I barely have time to jump down from the car before a big figure appears in front of me.

'Mia! I'm happy to see you,' Marek says, surprising me with a warm smile.

'And I'm happy to see you, too.' And a little bit sad. Marek has been the true victim in all of this. The three of us walk up the steps into the house.

'I'm living in the big house now,' Marek says, grinning at me. 'And Tamsin is cooking for me, but she's not a very good cook.'

Tamsin chuckles. 'Too true.'

'I'm sorry for everything that has happened,' I say. Marek shrugs his shoulders.

We're standing in the hallway. 'Right, Marek. Can you

make Mia and me a cup of tea? There's something I need to show her in private,' Tamsin says.

'Oh.' Marek's face falls.

'Nothing to worry about.' Tamsin gives Marek a little reassuring squeeze of the arm.

As he lopes towards the kitchen, Tamsin leads me into the living room.

'I'm getting him counselling,' she says. I'm glad to hear it.

Tamsin sits down on the sofa and gestures for me to sit next to her. There's a box file on the coffee table, which she pulls towards her.

'What was your Mum's name?' Tamsin asks.

I frown. 'Charlotte Benton. Why?'

'Open the box.'

I lift the lid and see a pile of newspaper cuttings. The top one reads, *'Mum Of Two Killed In Car Crash Tragedy'*. I know that newspaper headline, and it sends a shiver down my spine. I then lift the next cutting up. It's covering the same story, but written by a different journalist from a different newspaper. As I flick through all the cuttings, which span a period of about a year, each one is about the death of my mother. Most of them are familiar, because Dad has a similar pile of cuttings kept in a cardboard folder at his flat.

'Where did you find these?'

'Hidden at the back of Robin's cupboard in his study. Why did Robin have newspaper cuttings about the death of your mother? The cuttings are fifteen years old.'

'Do you think he knew Mum?' I ask quietly.

'Don't tell me you're also his secret love child,' Tamsin says.

I let out a snort. 'No, I'm definitely not. You only have to look at me and Dad to know that we're related.'

'So what is it?'

I lean back against the sofa. Either Mum knew Robin, or

else Robin had something to do with the accident. Could that really be possible?

'Did they ever find the person whose car caused your mum's to leave the road?'

I shake my head. 'They knew another car was involved because of the witnesses and the tyre marks, but no one ever came forwards. The driver was never found.'

'So it could be–' Tamsin's voice fades away.

'Are we putting two and two together?' I ask.

'It would explain why he left everything to you. It might have eased his guilt if Robin was involved.'

'How will we ever find out what happened on the night my mum died? How can we know for sure why Robin kept those cuttings?'

'Claudia might have some answers,' Tamsin suggests.

I cringe. She's the last person I want to talk to, but it's true. We can't talk to Pavla, so it's only Claudia who is left.

'Do you think she'd talk to me?' I ask. 'I can't exactly be at the top of her list of people she likes.'

'No, but she's definitely warmer towards you than Brooke or David are. She was surprised you gave her fifty percent of Robin's royalties.'

'This isn't a conversation to be had over the phone,' I say. 'Do you think she'd talk to me face to face?'

'It's worth a try.'

CLAUDIA AGREES to meet us in the village pub; frankly, I'm surprised she's prepared to meet us at all. Perhaps she's hopeful that she'll get another handout from me.

She's already there when we arrive, a gin and tonic in hand – which, considering the amount of tonic left in the bottle, is mainly gin.

'What can I do for you two?' she asks, leaning back

against the banquette, her horsehair-covered gilet leaving fine white hairs on the dark red velvet fabric.

Tamsin takes the box file out of her canvas bag and places it on the table between us. She lifts the lid up.

'What do you know about the death of Charlotte Benton?'

Claudia goes so pale I wonder if she's going to pass out.

'I've no idea who she is,' Claudia says, but she's not a very convincing liar.

'She was my mother,' I say.

'I'm sorry for your loss.' Claudia speaks in a monotone.

'What did Robin have to do with Charlotte Benton? Were they having an affair?' Tamsin asks.

I open my mouth to object, because she's casting aspersions on my mother, but Claudia speaks first.

'Of course not,' she scoffs. 'He never met her.'

'So why did he keep a file full of cuttings about her death?' I ask.

'Bloody idiot,' Claudia mutters under her breath.

'Who? Me or your late husband?' Tamsin asks curtly.

Claudia's eyes dart around the pub as if she's desperately looking for a way out. Tamsin leans towards her. I'm so grateful that I have her on my side.

'You owe it to Mia to tell the truth, Claudia. Robin is dead, and there's nothing we can do about that, but this was Mia's mother. She has never found out the truth about her mother's death. Why did Robin keep these cuttings?'

It's as if the air has been squeezed out of the woman. Claudia's shoulders sink, and her chest collapses in on itself.

'Robin did it for me.'

'Did what for you?' I ask quietly.

'Hid it. Covered up for me. Made sure that no one knew the truth. It bound us together for all those years, but guilt eats you up. It gets to you in the end.'

Tamsin raps her hand on the table, making the tonic

bottle wobble. 'Claudia, we've been through hell, Mia and me. We nearly died twice over. You owe it to us to tell us the truth.'

'It was me,' Claudia whispers, shrinking back into the bench seat.

'What was you?' Tamsin asks.

My heart is pumping too hard. I can barely breathe as I wait for Claudia to reply.

'I caused the accident that killed Charlotte Benton. I didn't mean to, but I did. I'd been to pick up Robin from a rehearsal, but I'd been drinking. Our marriage was in trouble even back then, and alcohol became my best friend.' She glances at her gin and tonic, and I wonder whether it still is.

'It was dark, and I was driving too fast along that country lane. I edged into the middle of the road around a bend, but there was a car coming towards us. I saw it too late. I heard the screech of brakes, but I didn't stop. Robin screamed at me, and I pulled over about twenty seconds later. He grabbed my shoulders and asked what the hell I had done. It was then that he smelled the alcohol on my breath. We both knew what would happen if we turned around and went back to the scene of the accident. I was shaking much too much to drive, so Robin got out of the car, walked around to the driver's side whilst I shuffled into the passenger seat. We returned home in silence. He didn't speak to me for a whole month.'

'You could have saved my mother,' I whisper in horror.

Claudia can't meet my eyes. 'We found out on the news the next day that the driver had died. Reports said she'd died instantly, so there was nothing we could have done.'

'And you think that makes it okay?' I ask, my voice rising in pitch.

Tamsin places her hand over mine and gives it a gentle squeeze.

'So you and Robin covered up what you did for all of those years?' Tamsin asks, her voice full of disbelief.

Claudia nods. There are tears in her eyes, and her face has gone from white to flushed.

'When Timothy Carter read out Robin's will, you must have realised exactly what Robin had done,' Tamsin says.

'Yes. He wanted to make it up to Mia.'

'So why didn't you tell me the truth? Why didn't you tell your children the truth? If I'd known, I never would have contested the will!' Tamsin exclaims.

'How could I say anything?' Claudia whispers. 'It seemed right that Mia should have it. It was retribution for what we did.'

'What *you* did,' I say. 'Yet you were all for Tamsin contesting the will.' Just looking at her makes me feel sick.

We sit there in stunned silence for long seconds. 'How did Robin find me?' I ask eventually.

'He sought you out.'

'What does that mean?'

'When you started working for Robin, I didn't know your surname. There was no reason for Robin or Pavla to mention it, but when I discovered that a "Mia Benton" was getting the lot, I realised you must be Charlotte Benton's daughter. I asked Pavla why she had employed someone with a criminal record. She said that Robin had signed up to a scheme offering work to ex-convicts, particularly musicians. She wasn't best pleased, but she did what Robin wanted. He asked Pavla to interview you, and you seemed alright, as far as ex-prisoners go. According to Pavla, Robin found a friend of yours from prison who told you about the vacancy here.'

'You mean it was all a set-up? That Robin wanted me to come and work for him?'

'I suppose so.'

'Yet he pretended he knew nothing about me. He never

asked about my family or my past; we just talked about music,' I say.

'Safer territory, perhaps,' Tamsin adds. 'Did Pavla know the truth about your drink driving?'

'Good heavens, no!' Claudia says. 'Robin never told a soul. I know that for a fact. Don't forget he would have been implicated too, and he was never going to risk that.'

There is a long silence, which eventually Claudia breaks, her voice quivering. 'What are you going to do now, Mia? Will you tell the police?' Claudia takes a final swig of her gin, then clasps her hands together as if she's praying.

Tamsin and I look at each other. 'I don't know,' I say very quietly. 'It's not going to bring Mum back. It's not going to bring Robin back.'

'But it does explain everything,' Tamsin says.

'I gave you fifty percent of Robin's royalties,' I say. 'I want you to give those to charity. I'll find a music charity, and you can donate to them. It's what Robin would have wanted.'

Claudia nods. 'I agree.'

I get up from the table then, because I can't sit here any longer facing the woman who killed my mother. Tamsin hurries after me, putting her arm around my shoulders. When we get back into the Defender, I burst into tears. They're a strange mixture of shock, relief, sadness and understanding. Tamsin lets me cry until there are no more tears left. She then starts the engine, which splutters and coughs into life.

'I'm so sorry for your loss,' she says.

'And I'm sorry for yours.'

'But we have freedom now, don't we, Mia? We have answers to all our questions, and that means we can carry on with our lives and truly put the past behind us.'

I nod, because Tamsin is right. I have closure. It's the not knowing, the indecision that is so exhausting, but now I have all the answers. Even though I feel a well of sadness, I can move into the future unfettered.

'Do you mind taking me straight back to the station?' I ask. 'I need to go and see Dad, and then I want to spend the night with my boyfriend.'

'No problem,' Tamsin says as she swings the car around.

We hug each other goodbye at the station.

'You'll stay in touch, won't you?' she asks.

'Of course,' I say, gently squeezing her arm.

A LETTER FROM MIRANDA

Thank you very much for reading The Second Wife.

My dad was my most avid reader. He used to take great pleasure in discovering all the little personal details in my books: names that meant something to our family, places we might have visited, experiences that I drew upon. He knew all about my last psychological thriller, The New Neighbour, although he wasn't well enough to read it. This is the first book I've written since he passed away and it's tough. On the one hand, it's not easy to be creative when you're grieving, on the other, it's a welcome escape.

The working title for this book was The Inheritance. The idea came to me as I was spending so much time around elderly people, some with loving families, others heartbreakingly, with no visitors. This book was quite challenging having two protagonists. I hope you warmed to both Mia and Tamsin eventually.

Huge thanks to my amazing editor Jan Smith, who helps me untangle all the knots I inevitably tie myself in and listens to me when I hit that mid-write dip of confidence (you'd have thought I might have overcome that by now, considering this is my fourteenth psychological thriller – alas, not so!).

Thank you so much to the amazing team at Inkubator Books. In particular, thank you to Brian Lynch and Garret Ryan, Jan, Jodi, Claire, Stephen and the rest of the team. You have made my writing dreams come true.

I would also like to thank the book blogging community who so generously review my books, do cover reveals and share their thoughts with readers. A very big thank you to Carrie Shields (@carriereadsthem_all) and Zooloos Book Tours.

Lastly but most importantly, thank *you* for reading my books. I love to chat with readers via BookBub, Goodreads or Instagram so please reach out and say hello. Reviews on Amazon and Goodreads help other people discover my novels, so if you could spend a moment writing an honest review, no matter how short it is, I would be massively grateful.

My warmest wishes,

Miranda

www.mirandarijks.com

ALSO BY MIRANDA RIJKS

Psychological Thrillers

THE VISITORS

I WANT YOU GONE

DESERVE TO DIE

YOU ARE MINE

ROSES ARE RED

THE ARRANGEMENT

THE INFLUENCER

WHAT SHE KNEW

THE ONLY CHILD

THE NEW NEIGHBOUR

THE SECOND WIFE

THE INSOMNIAC

FORGET ME NOT

THE CONCIERGE

The Dr Pippa Durrant Mystery Series

FATAL FORTUNE

(Book 1)

FATAL FLOWERS

(Book 2)

FATAL FINALE

(Book 3)